CHOOSE
YOUR
CONSEQUENCES

A Chance and Choices Adventure
Book Two

Lisa Gay

Chance and Choices

This book is a work of fiction. The names, characters, places, and incidents either are the product of the author's imagination or used factitiously. Any resemblance to an actual person, living or dead, business establishment, or event is entirely coincidental.

ISBN-13: 978-1-945858-02-4
ISBN -10: 1-945858-02-8

Arkansas River Basin

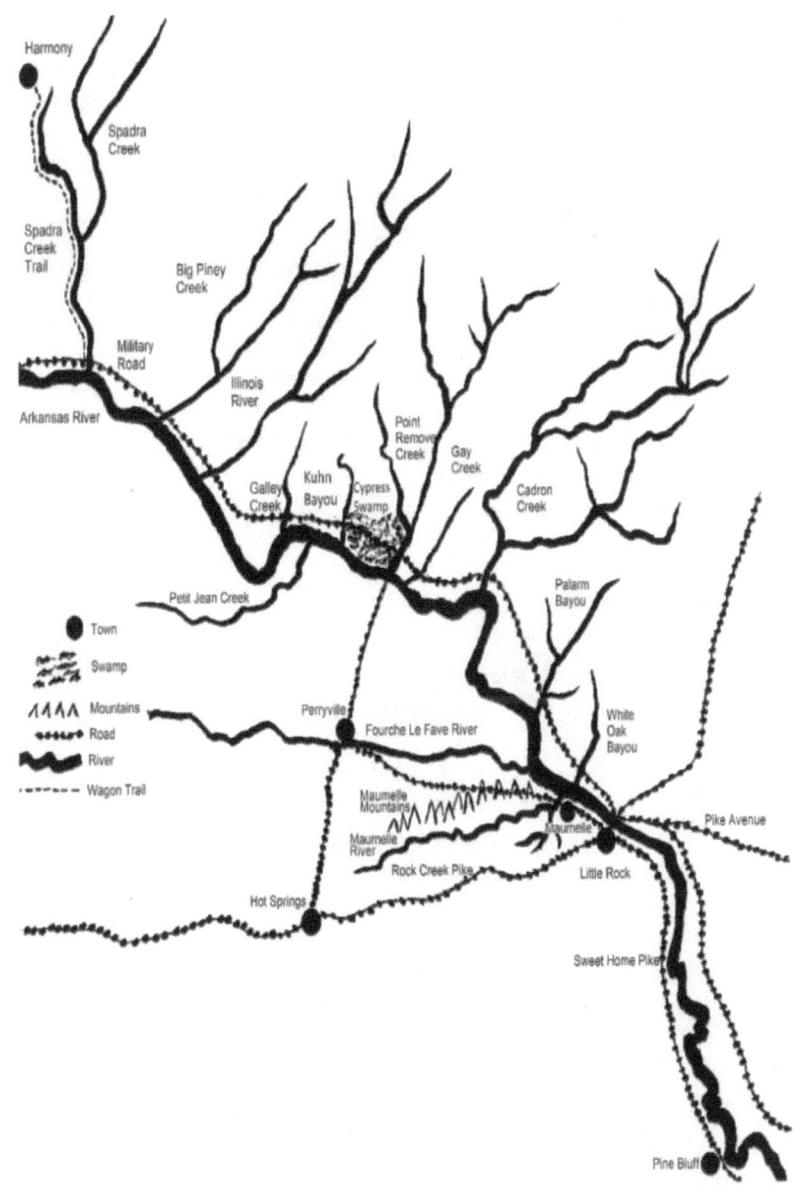

Those Involved in these incidents:

Place of Origin – Harmony

Ann Williams – oldest sister/owner of Williams Farm
Stephanie Williams – middle sister/owner of Williams Farm
Sally Williams – youngest sister/owner of Williams Farm
Eli Yates - farm hand at Williams Farm
Tom Yates - owner of Yates Mercantile / Eli's father
Zachariah Eggleston – deputy of Harmony
Smithfield Wyman – sheriff of Harmony (Smitty)
Mara Wyman – Smitty's wife
Horace Devine- owner of rented wagon
Betsy Devine- Horace's wife/Schoolmarm
Earl Carpenter - previous owner of Eyanosa
Bliss - Smitty's horse
Tequila - Zachariah's horse
Eyanosa – Noah's horse

Place of Origin – Indian Territory

Noah Swift Hawk- farm hand at Williams Farm
Arabella – Noah's horse
James Williams – Ann's, Stephanie's, & Sally's uncle

Place of Origin – Fort Smith

Richard Atwood – Judge of State of Arkansas
Warren Lampson – lieutenant – U.S. Army

Place of Origin – Various/Unknown

Hank Butterfield – dead leader of the Butterfield Gang
Roy Butterfield – Butterfield Gang member
Gus Hutchinson - Butterfield Gang member
Benjamin Rowe - Butterfield Gang member (Ben)
Alvin Ives – dead Butterfield Gang member (Al)
Charlie Cobb – dead Butterfield Gang member
Pete Drake – dead Butterfield Gang member

Place of Origin – Little Rock

Daniel Hall – Judge of State of Arkansas

Miles Cornish – captain– U.S. Army

Jeremiah Pratt– specialist- U.S. Army

Melvin Hatcher– private- U.S. Army

Henry Fenn – private- U.S. Army

John Jackson – private- U.S. Army

Justus Keen - private- U.S. Army

Thaddeus Pratt- preacher / Jeremiah's uncle

Rudolph Andrews – Rev. Pratt's neighbor (Rudy)

Flossie Andrews - Rev. Pratt's neighbor

Harold LeBarron- associate clerk of Little Rock court

Laura LeBarron- Harold's wife

John Peabody- Peabody Inn owner

William – clerk of Little Rock court

Sheriff Taylor – sheriff of Little Rock

Chester – U.S. Army horse

Storm – U.S. Army horse

Peppermint – U.S. Army cow

Place of Origin – Kuhn Bayou

Harry Pitts- clerk of Kuhn Bayou court /
Key holder of the gate lock on the Kuhn Bayou Bridge

Minnie Pitts- Harry's wife

Place of Origin – Cadron Creek

Israel Cotton – ferry operator

Place of Origin – Perryville

Hazel – shopkeeper

Adeline - innkeeper

ONE

The sheriff of Harmony, Arkansas had a job to do: take the outlaws Roy Butterfield, Benjamin Rowe, and Gus Hutchinson to trial. He couldn't take them to the closest judge. There was no way the victims would get justice from Judge Atwood at Fort Smith. After all, if Judge Atwood had not let the men go free that spring, they would not have been able to burn down the Williams Farm two nights past. The outlaws could have gotten away, but Gus didn't have a burn-and-run mentality. He'd wanted to verify his success. When the outlaws realized their intended victims had escaped, they had chosen to go into Harmony to complete the task of killing the five people they irrationally hated. That plan hadn't worked for them either. The intended victims: Noah, only two years over twenty, Ann, just twenty, Stephanie and Eli, eighteen, and Sally, barely fourteen, had outsmarted and caught the culprits the night after the farm went down in a hundred-acre conflagration.

Any of the folks of Harmony could legally have shot the outlaws. Judge Atwood had ordered all three men to stay at least fifteen miles away from Harmony and Gus and Ben to also keep away from the Williams Farm. Those court orders might as well have dropped lifeless to the ground, and then been stomped into oblivion as to have gone into the ears of the outlaws. The people of Harmony weren't killers. Therefore, they also did not follow Judge Atwood's orders to shoot the men on sight if caught on the farm or in town. They didn't want to send anybody to Hell, and there was no doubt in their minds that Hell waited for the last three living members of the Butterfield Gang. Even though the trip was going to be long, the townsfolk decided not to have an execution in Harmony but would let the blood of the outlaws stain the hands of the Little Rock judge over a hundred miles away.

The sheriff, Smithfield Wyman, who went by the name Smitty, needed supplies to transport the prisoners. The man's blond hair gleamed in the morning sun as he walked to Yates Mercantile to buy provisions. Smitty explained the procedure to the owner of the store. "Write up an invoice. I'll draw the money from the state treasurer in Little Rock and pay you when I get back." Tom Yates, the owner of the store, knew Smitty was a man of his word. He readily agreed. Smitty also needed to haul the provisions, so he crossed the dirt street that ran down the center of the small town and stepped up onto the wooden boardwalk in front of the saloon across from the store. The townsfolk heard the clomping of the boots of the big man and knew Smitty was getting everything ready. The whole town hoped the outlaws would be gone for good. Smitty knocked on the door of the fourth house. "Horace, I need to rent a wagon."

"Since I won't be able to do anything for at least a

few more months, I might as well rent you my wagon and put it to good use."

Smitty knew Horace would agree without even hearing the terms, but he went ahead and explained the same thing that he had to Tom. Several minutes later, Smitty pulled the rented wagon to the front of Yates Mercantile. To load all the requisitioned provisions, Tom and his son Eli made trip after trip across the boardwalk in front of their store. Stephanie Williams watched them and thought that Tom was a very handsome man. That was good because she was in love with Eli. They looked so much alike that she thought she saw what Eli would look like twenty years in the future when he was thirty-eight years old. Their faces had the same strong chins. Both had dark brown hair and eyes, and both had well-developed muscles from carrying the heavy sacks and barrels that they sold. They were exceedingly strong and completely capable of loading all the supplies.

However, three of the five people pressing charges against the still living members of the Butterfield Gang, were Ann, Stephanie, and Sally Williams. Therefore, they were going on the trip. As farm girls, who had worked every day of their lives as far back as they could remember, they were accustomed to hard work and saw no reason to sit around when there was work to do. Therefore, to keep it out of their way, Ann tied back her long, wavy, raven hair, and Stephanie tied back her long, straight as an arrow, blonde hair. Then, they both helped carry provisions to the wagon. Sally, the youngest sister, was also a hard-working farm girl. On this day, she only flipped her chestnut hair away from her face and notated each item on the invoice as it went out the door.

The sisters were glad the sheriff had rented the wagon from Horace. Horace had been shot as one of the posse that had captured the Butterfield Gang after their first attack on the Williams Farm that spring. For that reason, the girls felt partially responsible for the hole shot through his stomach. As a result, of that injury, Horace had not been able to work. Now, at the end of August in the year of 1839, he needed to pay for everything Tom Yates had let him charge that summer.

Noah Swift Hawk felt most responsible. He believed that he had caused all the bad things that had happened in Harmony that year. If he hadn't ridden into town that March day, and then sat in a white man's saloon wearing Indian clothing, the Butterfield Gang leader would not have known he was part Indian. Noah's oak-bark-colored hair and blue eyes displayed the white half of him. If his hair had been cut short, and if he had worn wool trousers and a wool shirt as he currently did, he would not have offended the man. If he had gotten up, walked out of the saloon, and then ridden out of town, maybe the fight could have been avoided. Noah had not chosen either. He had elected to sit silently and continue to eat the meal on the bar in front of him. Consequently, Noah had almost died from a cracked skull and massive bleeding. He was alive only because Ann Williams had saved him. Not only had he and Horace come near death, another man of Harmony, Earl, had a crushed leg. In addition, Noah, Ann, Stephanie, Sally, and Eli had almost been burned alive, the Williams sisters had lost everything, and four members of the Butterfield Gang had died.

The original leader of the gang, Hank Butterfield, had made the worst choice of all the people involved when he chose to draw his gun on that fateful day of March 12th. He had died with six bullet holes bored through him by the guns of the men of Harmony.

The people of Harmony had also made a horrible mistake. They had chosen to run Hank's gang and one of their horses out of town. Because it carried their guns, the men followed the horse that had been innocently sold to the Butterfield Gang by Ann Williams the previous winter. The horse knew that it was close to home and hoped to escape the horrible treatment it had been receiving from the Butterfield Gang. The horse was going back to the people who had loved it. It had led the men in the gang straight to the Williams Farm.

This morning, as Smitty prepared for the journey, one of the Butterfield Gang members sat up in his cot. Gus felt no remorse for what he had done. Instead, he felt pain where Noah had removed part of his scalp. Everybody thought that Noah hadn't kept the patch of black hair cut from Gus's head. As an Indian who would have to tell the story of his journey in his village back home, Noah had secretly gone back out into the night and retrieved it. Gus also swore that Ann's spit still clung to his round face. As he waited for the start of the voyage to Little Rock, he paced in the small cell with rage and a strong desire for retaliation in his heart. The scowl on his face deepened the crease that thirty years of unhappiness and anger had etched between his eyes.

While the others packed the last items into the rented wagon, Smitty went to get the wagon he had altered the night before. He had welded the shackle grommets to long thick chains. Then, to make the chains non-removable, he had welded the nuts to the bolts that went through the wagon boards. The prisoners could get out of the wagon, lie on the ground, and move several feet away.

Smitty knew when it rained that they would have to sleep inside the wagon. Since the wagon was only ten feet long, and they had to have room for some of the provisions, he was glad that none of the prisoners, Zachariah, nor himself was extremely tall. He and Roy were the tallest at six feet. It was also a good thing, even though Smitty was bulky with muscles, that none of them was overweight. On top of that, the wagon was only six feet wide, so only four would be able to lie down at the same time, and that was going to be a tight fit. When they did have to sleep in the wagon, he or Zachariah would have to remain awake on guard duty. Therefore, he believed that the wagon would work and drove it to the jail. Since Smitty was also the town's blacksmith and the strongest man in Harmony, he hoped that the outlaws would remain passive, knowing that they couldn't win a fight against him.

Choose Your Consequences

Smitty entered the small jail. "We'll be leaving soon. A word of warning; if you want to get there alive, come along peacefully." He passed plates of eggs and ham, and cups of black coffee into the cell through the slot. Fifteen minutes later, Smitty and his newly deputized fellow townsman, Zachariah, escorted the accused to the wagon. Smitty locked a cuff around each prisoner as Zachariah kept his rifle trained on the men they hoped to permanently remove from Harmony. Gus looked at Zachariah. He thought Zachariah's brown, mouse-colored hair matched his personality and figured he could easily intimidate Smitty's new deputy. As he got into the wagon, Gus contemplated on how he could work that to his advantage.

That same morning, Earl decided to help the man who had saved his life when they'd captured the outlaws the first time. Noah's beloved horse, Arabella, had been one of the victims that did not survive the destruction of the Williams Farm. As Noah stood in the wagon, packing food to take up as little room as possible, Earl led over a saddled and bridled horse. To take the weight off his leg, crushed when he had avoided a Butterfield Gang bullet, Earl leaned against the wagon. "He's a good one, and he's yours now."

Noah declined, "Earl, I can't take your horse."

"You keep him. It's the least I can do."

Noah felt all-overish. "I can't take your horse."

"If you don't ride out on him, I'm going to have to take him to you, and I don't want to walk home with my leg like this."

Noah uncomfortably consented, "Well then, I'm

much obliged. I'll take good care of him. What's his name?"

"Eyanosa was his name when I got him. His name means 'big both ways'. He was overweight. I've been feeding him right. He's normal now, but he's still seventeen hands. You can change his name if you want."

Noah stepped over onto Eyanosa. "I'll keep this name."

Smitty's quarter horse, Bliss, pulled the prisoner wagon carrying Zachariah, Gus, Roy, and Ben. Smitty himself sat in the driver's box. The wagon driven by Eli carried the provisions, Ann, Stephanie, and Sally. Zachariah's draft horse, Tequila, hired for service by Smitty, towed it. An hour after sunrise, the good, the confused, and the evil rode out of Harmony. Together under the post oak, gum, ash, and shagbark hickory trees, on the overgrown wagon track beside Spadra Creek, they headed towards the consequences of their past choices.

As she walked beside the wagon, Ann scooped up a handful of roundish, four-lobed nuts that looked like tiny green pumpkins. "I love hickory nuts." She tossed them into the wagon. Except for the prisoners, who rode glumly, the others joined her. The pile of nuts grew large during the fifteen-mile trip beside Spadra Creek.

At the end of the day's ride, Zachariah sat in the wagon and looked at the creek. "Do you want to cross today?"

Smitty had thought about water crossings before

leaving home. "We should wait until morning, in case we have any problems."

Sally wished she didn't have to be any place but home. Now without a home, she might as well have been in any location as another, but she hated to leave farther and farther behind what had been her home. "I've seen enough new country for the day. Let's make camp."

Ann loved the adventure. "I've never been more than ten miles from home. I think traveling is exciting."

Zachariah had felt stagnated in Harmony. He looked into Ann's green eyes. He admired her long, dark hair and shapely, well-toned body. He was glad that he had something in common with her. "I feel the same way; like something is finally happening. I'm happy to be going somewhere."

In the few remaining hours of daylight, the men built a fire, and the women prepared the evening meal. As the fire roared under the cooking pots, Eli got out his father's Bible to read silently. Just a few days before, he had made a deal with God; if God would help them escape the well, where they had become trapped while trying to survive the fire that burned away everything around them, then Eli would talk to God every day and believe in Him. Now, Eli wanted to learn who God is. He decided the best way to do that would be to read the Bible.

Ann knew she had to try to get God back into her heart. She asked Eli for a favor. "Our Bible was destroyed in the fire. Would you read aloud, so I can hear?"

Gus ordered Smitty, "I don't wanna hear. Tell him he can't."

Sally didn't want Gus to have any say-so about anything. She looked him in his eyes; eyes possessed by something evil. "It's your fault that we don't have ours, and we all want to hear, so if you don't like it, too bad. And I want our music box back." Sally stood defiantly in front of Gus with her hands on her hips.

Gus wanted to smack her off her feet. Sally was close enough, but men with guns watched. He only returned the glare.

Smitty settled the dispute. "Go ahead and read aloud."

Gus walked as far away as he could and talked to himself loudly while Eli read. Roy stuck with Gus, but Ben stayed close to the fire and listened until the sun went down. When Eli could no longer see to read, he closed the book. The seven transporting the prisoners put their bedrolls far out of reach of the three prisoners, but they all slept under the same stars. Chained to the opposite side of the wagon from Gus and Roy, Ben slept at the very end of his chain out of reach of his captors because they kept themselves away and away from his fellow outlaws because he didn't want to be close or have anything more to do with them. He was on his way to his execution because of their choices. Unknown to Roy and Gus, Ben planned to testify against them.

After breakfast, Noah rode Eyanosa into the water at the ford. At the deepest point, the water skimmed across the underside of the horse's belly but didn't push him at all. He rode back across. "No problem. It's not fast, and it's shallow enough that the horses won't even have to swim."

"Let's head out." Smitty signaled Bliss to go. His horse pulled Smitty, Roy, Gus, Ben, half the supplies, and the wagon into the water. Tequila had never pulled a wagon across a large creek. Since Zachariah knew his horse best, he sat in the driver's box of the other wagon. Eli sat beside Zachariah as Tequila pulled the second wagon, the girls, and the rest of the supplies. Noah rode his new horse back across Spadra Creek beside the second wagon. Over gently rolling land, surrounded by the same forest that filled most of the state, they traveled the road going southeast towards the Arkansas River. At mid-day, they sat beside the river's crystal waters and ate a cold meal.

After only a brief stop, they traveled the remainder of the second fifteen-mile leg of their journey along the north side of the Arkansas River. Big Piney Creek looked too wide and deep to ford, but there was a ferry. Smitty wanted to keep up their progress and cross immediately. Eli and Zachariah got off the wagons. Smitty stopped his deputy. "Watch the prisoners." Zachariah sat beside the women with his loaded and cocked rifle pointed towards the men of the Butterfield Gang, just in case they got an idea to try to get away or do anything else equally stupid.

Noah and Eli went with Smitty. Smitty handled the negotiations. "We're taking prisoners to Little Rock. I'll leave a script for the fare. You can go to the county seat to collect, or I'll pay you on my way home."

The ferryman thought it over. The travelers were under duress to transport prisoners. He decided to accept the script. However, since it was an official expense, and because he was taking the risk that he might not collect, he asked top dollar rates. "Only one wagon will fit on the ferry at a time. Five dollars each trip. The extra horse with rider will be one dollar more. Everybody crosses in two trips."

Noah hadn't paid that much when he had traveled to Harmony that spring. "That's highway robbery."

"Pay it or stay on this side."

"I'll write you the script." Smitty did the same as he had done in Harmony. He wrote out the payee, the provided service, the agreed amount, and the date of service, signed it, and handed it to the ferryman. He wrote a duplicate and held it out. "Sign this copy." The man scribbled something he said was his name. Smitty printed the man's name under the signature before he told everybody how he wanted to proceed. "We'll take the prisoner wagon first. Most of us men will go with the prisoners. One man needs to stay over here with the second wagon and the girls."

Zachariah offered, "I'll bring the women."

Noah preferred to be the one to remain. "I can stay. That wagon is narrower. Eyanosa will fit better."

"Tequila will feel calmer if I'm with him."

Smitty needed information to make the best choice. "Has Tequila ridden on a ferry before?"

"No. That's why I want to be with him."

Smitty was in charge of the prisoner transportation trip. He settled the dispute. "Noah and Eli, you ride with me. Zachariah, you come in the second wagon with Tequila and Eyanosa."

Noah saw the look of victory in Zachariah's hazel eyes. He had also noticed how much Zachariah stayed around Ann.

Both trips across Big Piney Creek went smoothly. They traveled only a short distance further before they found a clearing and stopped for the night. Since they couldn't escape, Gus, Roy, and Ben behaved peacefully, except that Gus again tried, by making noise, not to listen to the Bible reading. Later that night, when the others slept, Gus woke Roy. "You seen the way that Indian acts 'round Ann?"

"Yeah, he wants ta have a taste a her."

"I have an idea," Gus whispered his thoughts, "... Remember, don't say anything ta anybody."

The next day, the prisoners walked Military Road through the soaring oak and hickory trees. Out of hearing of their captors, Gus hissed his disdain to Ben and Roy, "I hate these people. I can't stand that heathen or Ann. It's cause a them we got this problem."

Ben refuted the statement, "They didn't make us do the things we did, so keep your cogitations to yourself."

Gus pointed to his head. "You forgettin' he tried ta scalp me, an she spit in my face?"

Roy agreed with Gus, "Eli said he was gonna blow my brains inta the floor, Smitty an Zachariah shot Hank, an it's all that Indian's fault cause he come ta Arkansas. Ann woulda shot me if the others hadn't shown up. I hate all of 'em."

Ben warned them, "Hate 'em if ya want, but don't make no more problems."

As he walked with Ann on the other side of the road, Zachariah noticed a tree not far off their path. "Ann, you want some persimmons?"

"If they're ripe, that'd be great."

Zachariah bushwhacked to the tree. The fruit was nowhere close to ripe. He left them on the tree. "Sorry. They aren't ripe."

"I sure don't want to eat any that aren't. I tried one when I was little. That was some pucker power."

Zachariah confessed, "I did too." They laughed together, told each other about their awful green persimmon experiences, and enjoyed the beautiful day as they walked and talked.

Later, Zachariah saw pawpaws. He hoped he could still get something good for Ann. She was so beautiful, and he wanted her to like him. He slipped away without saying anything. When they arrived at Illinois Bayou, Smitty again decided not to try to ford the creek at the end of the day. As they set up camp, Zachariah revealed his surprise. He held out the bag of fruit to Ann. "I found pawpaws."

A smile lit up Ann's face as she took the bag. "This is wonderful. I'll make pawpaw pie." She carried them to the back of the wagon where her sisters had already started to prepare the evening meal. "Look what Zachariah got for us. With this many, we should be able to make two pies."

The large moon rose, and the stars twinkled.

Everybody ate standard rations along with a big slice of delicious pawpaw pie. After the meal, they lay around the fire or at least as close as their chains would let them. It wasn't long before they were all asleep, except Ben. He lay awake trying to understand why they had given him pawpaw pie. Sure, they had to feed him, but they didn't have to give him pie. He thought they were so curious.

TWO

The morning of their fourth day on the trail, they crossed the Illinois Bayou. The wagon rolled along the dirt path called Military Road. Eyanosa carried his new owner who saw something out of the corner of his eye. Noah focused on the flashing black tail of a two-foot-long jackrabbit and quickly asked for permission to take the life of the rabbit. Then, in the blink of an eye, he swung his bow around from his back, nocked his only arrow, let it fly, and cleanly skewered the animal. As he cleaned what was to be supper, he silently thanked the animal's spirit for giving its life to feed them. Noah hung the carcass on the wagon. He watched the dead creature paint a red triangle of blood as it swung back and forth. Noah was glad that he hadn't broken the only arrow he had been able to make before the outlaws had tried to burn him alive. The rest of the arrows he had been making, and a sack of turkey feathers had been some of the few things they had saved when they had escaped the fire. He decided he would work on the rest of the arrows in the evenings.

Halfway between Illinois Bayou and Gally Creek, they stopped a few miles inland from the Arkansas River at a clearing created by the builders of the road. Noah skinned the rabbit, set their iron spit over the fire, and roasted it. Sally served the hot, savory rabbit meat along with their daily serving of rice and beans.

Even with the tasty rabbit in his stomach, hatred filled Gus. He hated that his perverse plans to catch the girls and force himself on them had been thwarted. He hated that his life would soon be over. Really, he hated life altogether.

As Gus walked behind Ann, to get another helping of beans, he felt intense hatred for two of the people with him. He dropped his plate, swung his chain around Ann's neck, and pulled tight.

Noah bolted to his feet. His arrow was gone in a blink, but Smitty's fist had already made contact with Gus's head. The arrow shot through the edge of Smitty's sleeve out into the night behind the place Gus had stood only a second before. Gus crashed to the ground. The chain jerked Ann down from between Sally and Stephanie. With knife in hand, Noah jumped across the fire to put an end to the Gus problem.

At the same time that Gus attacked, Roy charged. He screamed, "You killed my brother."

Smitty tumbled backward under the impact. Zachariah jumped up. There was no way he was letting Roy take out Smitty. He came at Roy from behind just as Roy started his chain into a swing to send Smitty to join Hank in the afterworld. Before the chain came up to velocity, it ceased its forward motion against Zachariah's skull. Zachariah dropped into the dirt.

Gus squeezed the chain. He clamped Ann down on top of him on her back. She tried to breathe, but not a smidgen of air could get through her choked throat. Eli and Stephanie both tried to get control of the chain, but couldn't get their fingers under it.

Sally whacked Gus in the face with her plate. Hot beans, rice, and rabbit slopped into his face. "Let her go!" She saw Roy's chain headed for Smitty and sailed the plate into the chain. The chain veered off course as Sally jammed her thumb into Gus's eye.

Smitty tried to snatch Roy's chain before he could use it as a weapon again. He missed but dodged the swirling mass of deadly metal links.

Ben had not known about the plan to attack. He felt highly ticked off. Roy and Gus just kept on creating problems for him. He sat paralyzed and afraid to face the retaliation of the two men he had previously felt were his friends. When he saw the chain around Roy's foot, he decided to act. He reached over, jerked as hard as he could, and toppled Roy. Roy assumed he had tripped himself and quickly untangled from the chain.

Noah saw a part of Gus he could reach. He swiped his knife across the exposed skin. Gus screamed in pain. As blood spurted from the back of his hand, he lost his grip. "Get the chain," Noah ordered.

Eli grabbed and pulled. The chain rose slightly from Ann's neck. She sucked in a deep breath and thrust her arm under the chain.

Stephanie also slid her hand under the chain and pulled. The chain, securely wedged under Gus, did not budge. "How can Gus be so strong?"

Roy jumped back to his feet and lashed his chain. Smitty dashed away and managed to stay clear.

Gus recovered his grip. He attempted to tighten the chain again, but something prevented him. He changed his plan and whipped his arms up. The chain ripped away from Eli and Stephanie. As it flew up, it knocked the knife out of Noah's hand and then dropped around him.

Eli immediately seized Ann's hand, pulled her away, and passed her to Stephanie. With Ann safe, Eli changed his focus. He let the swirling chain pass and then darted at Roy from the rear. He jerked Roy's arm up behind his back as the two of them slammed face first into the ground. "Get my piggin' string."

Ben knew where Eli kept the long strip of rawhide. He picked up Eli's hat, jerked off the leather strip, and whipped it over.

Noah and Gus wrestled on the ground. Sally ran for her plate. Twice she tried to hit Gus but instead whacked Noah. Noah knew she was trying to help, but she wasn't succeeding. "Sally, stop."

Eli had Roy trussed up, so Smitty grabbed Gus's foot. Gus told himself, *I don't deserve to die.* He kicked and rolled as a man possessed.

Smitty barely held on. "Help me."

Sally dropped the plate and grabbed Gus's other leg. Gus focused on the two holding his feet. Noah took advantage of the distraction and slipped out of the chain that had him around his waist. He saw that Stephanie and Sally held Ann as she gasped for breath then turned back to Gus, snatched the chain, and wound it around Gus's throat. Noah aimed to give Gus the fate he had tried to inflict on Ann.

Smitty ordered Noah, "Don't do it." Noah

continued to squeeze. "It's not your place to be his judge and executioner."

"He's going to kill one of us if we let him live."

Gus tried to punch Noah's side. *I don't deserve this.*

Smitty picked up his rifle and pointed it at Noah. "I mean it. Everybody gets a fair trial. If you kill him, I'll have to arrest you. I don't want to do that."

"Smitty, you wouldn't shoot me or arrest me. You know Gus deserves to die, and Judge Atwood gave us permission to kill him if he came on Ann's Farm." Noah constricted the chain around Gus's neck.

Gus' windpipe started to crush. He tried to pull the chain. *I'm done for.*

"There was a fire, and you were in a panic. You could have been mistaken when you thought you saw Gus."

"It was Gus. Besides, you just saw him try to kill Ann."

Smitty cocked his rifle. "It's the law. Gus gets a trial." *If I drop my gun and charge Noah, Gus will get loose again.* "Eli, stop him before he makes me shoot him."

"Don't drag Eli into this." Noah glared at Smitty. "Why are you protecting this evil man?"

Gus's arms dropped. His unconscious body slumped. Smitty drew a bead. Ann was afraid. *Smitty might pull the trigger. He'd probably shoot Noah in the arm, but Gus isn't worth Noah getting injured.* She had recovered enough to speak, "Noah, let Gus loose."

Noah looked at Ann then Smitty. "$^&@ you, Smitty. Gus deserves to die." Noah let the chain go. He stood up and kicked Gus as hard as he could before he joined Stephanie and Sally as they held Ann.

Smitty put down his rifle and got his pigging strings. As Smitty hogtied him, Sally glared at Gus with a swollen, bloody eye where she had jabbed her finger, rabbit and a knot on his head because she had hit him with her plate, a swollen ear where Smitty had slugged him, and a bleeding hand that Noah had cut. "Too bad I didn't gouge his eye completely out."

Stephanie whispered to Noah, "You should have scalped him when you had the chance."

"I know." Noah focused on Ann. "Let me check you." As softly as he could, he felt Ann's throat to determine the amount of damage then gently examined the arm she had jammed under the chain. Both were badly bruised and swollen. Noah held Ann not only covered in cuts and bruises from their painful escape from the well after Gus had burned down the farm but now also with a severely injured arm and neck after Gus had almost choked her to death. Noah felt furious. He could barely keep himself from throwing his knife into the man's heart.

Eli and Smitty looked at each other. They both knew that Ben had helped. They both shook their heads in the negative. Neither of them was willing to let him loose.

Stephanie marched over to Smitty. "What are you going to do about them?"

Ben thought about the question. There only one logical course of action. He saw no reason he would not suffer the same fate as his fellow gang members. Once again, it was their actions, but he would pay.

"Let them eat the dust for now." Smitty knelt over Zachariah and attempted to revive him.

Zachariah came to. "My head hurts something terrible. What happened?"

Stephanie explained, "You were hit with a chain."

"I was?"

Sally thought it strange that he didn't recall the incident. "Don't you remember what happened?"

"Last thing I remember is starting the campfire."

Stephanie had read about this, and she remembered almost everything she had ever read. "The blow made him forget."

Ann's voice came from behind Zachariah. "Smitty, you saw Gus try to kill me. Roy tried to kill you, and he almost killed Zachariah. How long are you going to make us go through this?" Zachariah turned towards the voice. Ann stood wrapped in Noah's arms.

"We're not executioners. Everybody gets a trial." Smitty had believed that before the posse had gone to Clarksville to capture the outlaws in March, he had believed it when they had destroyed the Williams Farm a week ago, and he believed it now.

"At least get them out of my sight." Ann turned away from them into Noah's embrace.

"I'll move them." Zachariah wanted to get Noah away from Ann. "Noah, come help." Zachariah thought it was unfair. Noah had spent the whole summer with Ann at the farm. He felt he was just as good and just as handsome as Noah was, and he believed that he deserved a fair chance. *How can I get Ann to notice me?*

The men dragged Roy across the ground to the wagon then picked him up and dropped him still hogtied into the wagon. Noah slammed Gus in as hard as he could. Gus looked up at him with a genuinely wild look in his eyes. Noah looked twice before he walked away.

Ann hated Gus passionately. She bellowed to be sure that Gus heard, "I can't stand it that Gus still walks the earth. Smitty should have let you kill him."

Even though they had Roy and Gus hogtied, Smitty moved the wagon where they wouldn't be able to reach any of them. Ben really, really didn't want to be near Gus or Roy either. Like every previous night, he stayed at the end of his chain out of reach of both groups.

Not willing to take a chance that anything would hurt her again, Noah lay close to Ann. Late in the night, he felt Ann against him. His arm encircled her. He wanted her to be there all the time. He wanted to kiss her and love her. He gently hugged her closer. She woke. The stars reflected in her beautiful green eyes. He told her what had been in his heart for quite a while, "I love you."

"I love you too." Her lips joined his. He kissed her deeply. Their passion grew.

Noah wondered if anybody else was awake, but then Ann winced with pain from her injured neck. He couldn't do anything that would hurt her or the future they might share. He wanted them to be together full of love and joy. He chose to protect their future love. "I want you very much but not like this."

Ann snuggled tight. "I feel safe. Can I sleep here the rest of the night?"

Noah held her to his heart. "Tonight."

The next morning, Ann was the first awake. She had found no way to lie that her neck didn't hurt and had hardly slept a wink, so she got up to cook breakfast. Without turning her head, Ann stoked the fire, added wood, started the coffee brewing and the oats cooking. She cut pieces of bacon that sizzled in the hot frying pan. When Noah joined her at the fire, she turned her head towards him. Pain shot up her neck. The knife dropped from her hand. "I can't turn my head."

"I'll cook. You be still." Noah drew the Arkansas Toothpick he always carried at his side. He held the knife in the flames for a few seconds and then used it to stir the thick porridge.

Smitty woke. He couldn't keep his prisoners hogtied the rest of the trip, so he went to the wagon to untie them. Gus lay in a pool of blood draining from his slit throat. "Who killed him?"

Roy made sure Smitty knew he was innocent. "Weren't me. I'm all tied up like I'm a hog or somethin'. It ain't right."

They all gathered around the wagon. Gus was definitely dead. Smitty knew from Ben right down to Sally that any one of them might have done it. He questioned them all. Nobody saw anything, heard anything, or knew anything. The only two he knew didn't do it were himself and Roy.

Sally didn't feel the least bit sorry for the man. "He was as guilty and as evil as they come. You shouldn't even be worrying about it, but look around as long as you want."

Smitty contemplated the cooking knife. Ann had used the butcher knife to cut bacon before Smitty had known about Gus. Ann could have cut Gus's neck as easily as she had the bacon, and she had more than enough motive. They all had access to the cooking knife, except for Ben and Roy.

Noah had the knife that he always wore on his belt. He was the only person who had access to that weapon. Everybody knew Indians were well-trained hunters and warriors. Smitty knew Noah was an expert with his knife. He doubted Noah would have any problem killing a man, especially one who had tried to hurt Ann. He had already tried to kill Gus during the fight the previous night and would have done it if Smitty hadn't stopped him.

Ben interrupted Smitty's contemplations. "What ya gonna do with Gus's boots?"

"You want them?"

"I wouldn't mind having 'em."

"Take them."

Ben casually ambled over to the wagon. He took Gus's boots off his corpse.

Roy didn't like it. "Gus ain't hardly cold, an you're taking his boots. It ain't right."

"He ain't gonna use 'em." Ben shined the boots with his shirtsleeve as he walked away. Smitty remembered how Ben had helped them the day before, and he knew that Ben was planning to spill the beans about Gus. Ben obviously no longer liked Gus, or Roy for that matter. He blamed them for his current state of captivity and probable execution. Smitty believed Ben also was afraid of them. He didn't want to be near either of them. Now, he knew that Ben coveted Gus's boots, but he doubted that Ben would have killed Gus for his boots. Smitty wondered if Ben was the one then discarded the idea. Ben wouldn't have been able to get a knife.

Smitty watched Sally get out the tin plates and cups and lay them out on a blanket just like a picnic. She poured coffee for everybody as if she was celebrating. "May I use the knife to cut some maple sugar for the coffee?" she asked. Smitty noticed how expertly and precisely Sally cut up the hard block of sugar. There were as many reasons for Sally to want Gus dead as the rest of her family. When they had been at the farm, the morning after it had burned down, she had told the whole town that she would execute him, and she had just said Gus deserved to be dead. She easily could have gotten to the butcher knife. However, Smitty found it hard to believe that the young slip of a girl was a killer.

He turned his attention to Stephanie. She had just as much motive to want Gus dead as her sisters, and Stephanie was very strong. He remembered how they had chopped the wood at his livery when he had first met them. He had no doubt that she could have sliced Gus's throat as deep as the gash. She wasn't boisterous like her sisters, but he knew from experience that the quiet ones were usually the ones to watch, and she could have accessed the cooking knife easily.

Then there was Eli. Many times Smitty had seen him expertly skin and cut up an animal at Yates Mercantile. That boy possessed an extraordinary talent for cutting up meat. He would know the best place to cut a man to kill him quickly and silently.

The five of them were a very close group. Smitty had no doubt that they would cover for each other. After everything that had happened, none of them would consider killing Gus murder. They would think they were executing justice, but slitting the throat of a tied up man was murder.

Smitty turned his thoughts to Zachariah. He had said he felt like the farm burning was an attack also against him and had wanted to come with them even though there wasn't any real reason to do so. Lately, he frequently acted out of sorts. Smitty could tell Zachariah was interested in Ann. He sensed the competition between him and Noah. *If he thinks he can win Ann by ridding the world of the man who has done so much to hurt her, Zachariah might have killed Gus.*

Smitty mulled everything over. He looked for footprints, blood drops, or anything that might help him solve the mystery. The only thing he found was the place where somebody had wiped blood off a thin blade onto Gus's clothes under his arm.

After he had eaten his breakfast, Smitty took food

to Roy. He laid down the plate and untied him. "You sure you didn't see anything? You were right beside him."

"Not a thing. I wish I did know. I might be next."

Smitty saw no reason for Roy to cover for any of them. Smitty decided Roy didn't know anything and left him to eat his breakfast. He took Eli his piggin strings.

Eli wound the long strips of leather around his hat, tucked in the end, fed it through the loop, and then pulled it tight. He left one long end hanging, so he could jerk it off in a second. "Should we bury him, or feed the coyotes?"

Smitty answered, "Everybody should have a proper burial."

Noah didn't feel that way. "Gus doesn't deserve a grave."

Roy, however, said, "Gus didn't even have a chance ta defend himself being all tied up when a coward killed him. He was my friend. I want Gus ta have a decent burial. I'll help bury him."

Smitty informed Roy, "Help isn't the word; you'll bury him," then he helped Zachariah carry Gus away from the wagon before he unlocked Roy. "Dig and don't try to run, or you'll be under the sod with him."

"Why ain't Ben helpin'?" Roy picked up one of the shovels lying beside the body.

Zachariah cocked his rifle and clicked back the set trigger. If Roy tried anything, he only had to pull the firing trigger. Roy watched Zachariah holding a gun on him. Zachariah swore Roy looked at him like a cougar eyeing its prey, the same look that had always been in Gus's eyes; possessed.

"Ben, get over here and help." Smitty handed Ben the key to their locks. "Unlock yourself and dig." The last two of the Butterfield Gang dug until Smitty decided the hole was deep enough for the next gang member going into the ground. "Both of you throw your shovels over there." Smitty looked towards Eli, Noah, and Zachariah. "Keep your guns on them." Smitty relocked Roy and Ben to their chains. They left Gus behind under several feet of dirt and rocks.

THREE

Zachariah rode on the wagon seat beside Ann with a painful throbbing in his head. Every bump jarred Ann and sent a shooting pain up her neck. Even though they both hurt, Zachariah tried to have a conversation. "It's beautiful land."

She barely replied, "Yes, it is."

"Gus deserved what he got."

"He got off easy. He deserved more torture."

Zachariah perceived Ann as gentle, not as a person who would want to torture a man. He pushed the idea away.

Noah repeatedly rode Eyanosa over to ask Ann if she was all right and if he could do anything for her. Ann finally told him to stop asking but assured him that she would let him know if anything changed. However, she did appreciate how much he cared about her well-being, and it touched her deeply.

Zachariah could see Ann was in pain and that it was hard for her to talk. He felt like he was bothering her. When she asked Noah to leave her alone, he stopped talking and imagined that they were together, riding in their own wagon.

Before long, Ann touched Zachariah's arm. "Excuse me. I have to lie in the wagon."

Zachariah stopped. "Let me help you." He helped her get to the back then laid out all the bedrolls for her to lie on.

"I appreciate your help. I hurt so much." Ann lay in the wagon and thought about the previous night. She had wanted to share her love with Noah and had been disappointed when he'd said that he thought it was the wrong time. Today, Ann was glad he had refused. Even though she was mad at God, and had not felt Him with her since she had let hatred of Gus fill her heart, she still wanted to follow God's plan. She knew that Noah had made the right choice. As Ann thought about what had happened, it became clear to her that Noah made her well-being his priority. She turned her heart and trust over to him completely. She lay in the wagon and tried to think about Noah. Every bump made her think about Gus.

After too much jarring, Ann decided it was better to walk. "Please, stop." Zachariah reined Tequila to a halt and then helped Ann get out.

As they traveled the river valley, Sally watched her sister hurting. "I'm glad Gus is dead. I only wish he suffered more for what he did to you and us. I think he got off too easy."

Stephanie walked with her sisters. "I want to go back and kick him as hard as I can, repeatedly."

Ann tried to keep her neck still. "I do too, except it would hurt too much to do it."

Noah rode away from the group. He came back a few hours later, put a pouch full of something in the wagon, then went over and walked with Eli. As they walked, Noah resumed the lessons he had been giving Eli about how to shoot with a bow and arrow.

Stephanie watched Noah and Eli walking side by side. "I'm glad Noah and Eli are such good friends. I hope they'll be our family just like Sally dreamed."

Ann had been watching them as well, mostly because she had been watching Noah. "I do too. Between the two of them, what would we ever lack?"

"I know they love you two. I hope someday I'll find somebody." Sally did know how Eli and Noah felt about her sisters. She loved her sisters, but she also loved Noah and Eli, and she wanted them to be her brothers, so she had asked them straight out if they loved her sisters. Sally was euphoric when they both said they did. Also, she believed the two men thought of each other as brothers. She felt surrounded by a family again, and she wanted it to stay that way.

Eli and Noah stopped practicing. Eli changed the topic to what they would do in Little Rock. He waited for Noah to reply. "Noah. Noah? Are you there?" Eli attempted to get Noah's attention. Noah looked at him. Eli asked, "What's wrong? You've been distracted all morning."

"I'm so mad that Gus was able to hurt Ann. Gus being dead doesn't make me less furious."

"I feel the same."

"No, you don't. I love Ann."

"I saw you last night. You need to stop kissing and holding her. You're going to go too far."

"You don't understand. Keep out of it."

"No, I won't stay out of it. You say you're mad because Gus hurt her. Well, I'm protecting her as well but from you. Why do you think I don't kiss Stephanie? Do you think I don't ever think about it? You're making it hard. If you love her, why don't you want to marry her?"

"I do want to marry her."

"Then ask her and get married."

"You don't need to protect her from me. Stay out of this." Irritated that Eli had said he was hurting Ann, Noah stalked away and joined the girls.

Sally wanted a close sisterly relationship with Noah and Eli. "Will you teach me how to use a bow?"

"I'll be happy to teach you."

Stephanie said, "I like that it's a stealthy way to hunt."

"I can also teach you if you want."

"I do."

Ann knew she couldn't practice immediately, but she wanted to be included. "When I can do something again, I'd like to learn how to shoot and how to make a bow."

"Since you're teaching everybody, will you also show me?" Zachariah wanted to be part of the group, he wanted to be close to Ann, and he actually did want to learn.

Noah was happy that everybody thought he possessed a valuable skill. He was more than willing to train them all. He saw a stand of the appropriate type of trees ahead and heard running water not far away. "I will. We're going to need more bows and arrows. Group lessons start now. Lesson one. Gather materials. Smitty, can we make camp over there?" He pointed to a stand of cedar trees covered in small, blue, berry-like cones.

Noah walked among the trees until he found a perfect example of what they needed to make a bow. "Cut a branch about this big around and at least this long." He chopped off the branch then handed the hatchet to Eli. While they took turns with the hatchet, Noah gathered cedar boughs to make a pallet. He had slept on a bed of cedar boughs when he was home with his parents. Noah knew it was soft, calming, refreshing, relaxing, and would help Ann feel better. A short distance away from the fire, he laid down the cedar boughs and covered them with Ann's bedroll. Sally and Stephanie ordered Ann to go over, lie down, rest, and heal. She lay on the cedar bed while the others gathered fallen cedar branches.

Zachariah and Eli started the fire. Noah filled the big pot with blue cedar cones, the very tips of cedar branches, and water. While Noah cooked the cedar tips and cone-berries, the pleasing aroma of the burning cedar filled the camp. In the other pot, Noah heated plain water until it boiled then removed the pot from the heat and put in pinkish wood fibers from the pouch he'd filled earlier in the day. He left the pot close enough to the fire to keep it warm but not cook it. While the water boiled whatever it was that Noah was making with cedar cones and branch tips, he explained how to shape a cedar branch into a bow. Ten minutes later, Noah took the pot of deep, pinkish-red-liquid away from the heat to cool. When it was cool enough, he poured it through a clean handkerchief into Ann's and his tin cup then made a request. "I need more cups, anybody willing to let me use theirs?"

"Take mine. What is it?" Sally handed Noah her cup.

Smitty put his with the others. "Looks like blood."

Including Ben, the others passed Noah their cups, except Roy, who silently retained his cup. "It's a painkiller made from willow trees. I'm making it for Ann." After he had poured all the medicine through the cloth into their cups, he gave the pot to Stephanie. "I appreciate you letting me delay supper."

Zachariah sat cross-legged by the fire. "I'm glad you made something to help Ann. She's been in a lot of pain today. I wanted to help. All I could do was sit there and watch her suffer."

Eli looked at the mash in the other pot. "What will the cedar cones and branch tips do?"

"It makes the swelling go down, helps with pain and stiffness, and makes a wound heal without infection. And Zachariah, you did do something for her. You made her the place to lay down in the wagon and helped her get to it." Noah handed him a cup of the red liquid. "You drink some of this too. Everybody probably hurts. Drink what's in your cups."

Each of them retrieved his or her cup of warm,

willow tea. Ben had offered his cup. Noah decided he should have a share. Since Ben sat chained and out of reach, Noah carried him his cup of tea. "Here's yours."

"Much obliged." Ben took the cup with surprise.

Roy sulked. They had left him hogtied all night. He wished they would give him some. He whined to Ben, "I need some. It's not right that they didn't give any to me."

Ben decided he would do what he had been watching his captors do: be kind and generous. "'Cept you tried to kill 'em, an you didn't offer to let 'em use your cup, but I'm sure you hurt, an' I don't. You can have mine."

Noah carried a cup full to Ann. "This is a warm tea, but mainly it's a painkiller. I made it for you."

"That is very thoughtful and so is sharing it with everybody." Ann sipped the tea.

Noah went back to the fire. He removed the other pot from the fire and mashed the cooked cedar concoction into a poultice. He spread some of the mixture onto two of his handkerchiefs. "Stephanie and Eli, use some. Zachariah, you should do the same. Put it on your injuries. I made plenty. Anybody who needs some may use it." He took the two handkerchiefs full of cedar poultice to Ann. "This will help your neck feel better and heal better. May I put it on you?"

Ann motioned for Noah to go ahead. He draped one across her neck, gently tucked it under, and then tied it. He put the other around her arm before he stretched out on the ground beside her. The warm poultice started soothing her injuries. Noah knew for sure what he wanted, and he felt that the proper time had arrived. "I meant what I told you last night. You are an incredible woman. You're kind, generous, thoughtful, and loving. You always do what you need to do without complaining. I want to protect you, and I'm so mad that I didn't. I love you so very much. I want to share every bit of my life with you. I'll do everything I can to make you happy if you'll let me. I want you to marry me. Will you spend your life with me?"

Ann's heart leaped with joy. "Last night, my heart hurt because I wanted us to be together, but I would have been upset about it today. This morning, I realized that you care more about me than sharing passion. I couldn't love you more. I trust you completely. The most wonderful life I can imagine is a life with you. I want to love you, and I'll do everything I can to bring you happiness every day of our lives, and I'll do what you ask and not be so stubborn. If you forgive me for being hard-headed, then yes, I'll marry you."

"We'll be happy. I promise." He leaned over and gently kissed her. "Until we're married, I'm not going to kiss you again. It's too hard to resist my desire to share love with you. I don't want to damage our future. I want you to understand that I don't feel anything less when I don't kiss you or hold you until then."

"Let's not wait a long time."

"Maybe we can get married when we get to Little Rock."

"Perfect. I love you, Noah."

"And I love you, very much." Noah set up his cedar bed beside Ann's but not as close as the night before. He still wanted to be close enough to protect her and all the rest of them as well.

Nobody made Roy or Ben a cedar bed, but the scent of the cedar from all the other soft and fragrant beds wafted over them all. Everybody slept peacefully. They felt so nice in the morning that Smitty and Eli cut more cedar boughs to take for Ben and Roy.

Zachariah's headache was mostly gone. "That willow tea really helped. How do you make it?"

Noah explained how to gather the willow bark and showed them how to make the tea and poultice.

Ben again gave his to Roy and asked for some of the cedar treatment. "Noah, Roy's wrists an ankles are raw. Please let 'em use some o' your poultice."

Noah glared at Roy. "Pull up your sleeves." Roy complied. His skin was abraded, red, and swollen. "You'll have to use your own clothes to hold the poultice in place." Noah gave him two handfuls of the cedar.

Ann tied one handkerchief of poultice around her almost-strangled neck. She tied the other around her chain-bruised arm after squeezing some of the liquid onto the injuries she'd acquired when they had pulled her unconscious body across one razor-sharp rock after another when getting her out of the well. Stephanie used it on the knot on her head that she'd received when she had fallen partway back down into the well.

The knot was almost gone, but the gash was not. Eli treated his arm, rope-burned when trying to get Stephanie out of the well, and Zachariah tied poultice around his chain-whacked head. With their injuries treated, they drank willow tea and finished breakfast.

Afterward, they packed up all the cedar branches, a big pile of the blue cones, and fallen cedar for fires. In water only halfway up the wheels, the horses pulled the wagons across the gravelly ford of Gally Creek.

They practiced with the bow, kept their eyes open for game, and made their way east in the calming cedar forest. Stephanie did not spot an animal. It was something much more spectacular. She noticed a large clearing back from the road filled with bright yellow flowers hanging their seed-laden heads towards the ground from the tops of six-foot-high green stalks. "Look at that! Let's stop here to eat."

Ann had never seen a flower bigger than herself before. "How beautiful! How could something like this exist?"

Once again, Stephanie remembered what she had read in one of the books that her mother had used to teach them. "I think they're called sunflowers. We can eat the ripe seeds. Let's get some. Come on, men, I need your help." Stephanie led them into the field of flowers.

Ben watched them disappear into the yellow and green wonderland then looked at Roy. "You been watching 'em?"

"I'm trying not to."

"They remind me o' home where people liked an'

cared 'bout each other. That's the way it oughta be, not like us."

"They're making you soft. Act like a man." Roy walked as far away from Ben as his chain let him.

Looking for heads with mature seeds, Eli walked with Stephanie beneath the giant, bright-yellow flowers as miniaturized beings. "I've never seen anything like this."

Sally cut a flower off its stalk. "It seems unreal."

Zachariah followed close behind. "Who would think of making something so magnificent?"

Stephanie offered her opinion, "A God who loves us."

Ann had frequently felt that way when she looked at the incredible wonders of nature. After losing so much, she wondered about that. "Maybe so." Eli also pondered that thought as he gathered sunflower heads. Ann wanted Sally to see that it wasn't bad to explore. "I told you the world is full of wonderful things just waiting for us to find them."

"Well, I am very happy that I got to see these flowers. This one is so tall that I can't even reach the head." Noah drew his knife from its sheath, reached up, and sliced it off for her. They wandered through the field of towering flowers and collected as many heads as the seven of them could carry before they went back to the wagon.

"These are heavier than you'd think," Sally put her flower heads into the wagon with the hickory nuts, willow bark, cedar cones, and cedar branches.

After dinner, when back on their way, Ben pointed out to Roy another difference that he had noticed, "When we traveled we never found things like this."

"Who cares?" Roy sulked.

Ben replied, "I do. Now that I'm gonna hang, I see what I've been missing. I've been so stupid."

Not far from his prisoners, Smitty heard the conversation. "Then enjoy the time you have left." He listened and watched constantly. Knowing one of the people traveling with him was the murderer of Gus, in his heart Smitty held himself away from everybody. The problem he had was that he just couldn't see how any of them could be a killer. How could the people who had just walked in a field of giant sunflowers like innocent children have killed somebody? Ben or Roy surely could kill a man without a shred of remorse, but Roy had been tied up, and Ben didn't have access to a knife. The thing Smitty noticed most was that the only one who acted differently from when they had walked out of Harmony was Ben. His change in behavior was consistent with a man in flux. Smitty wondered if Ben had managed to murder Gus then felt guilty about killing a friend, but it just wasn't possible. There was no way Ben could have gotten access to a weapon.

Near to Kuhn Bayou, Eli spotted another jackrabbit and easily shot it with his rifle. That night, they again ate roasted rabbit. This time with rice mixed with cedar berries and sunflower seeds, and with cornbread. They passed the delicious meal to Roy. He tried his best not to enjoy it. He certainly didn't appreciate it.

Ben, however, drew as near as his chain allowed, savored his meal, and listened to Eli read Matthew 10: 26-31. "So do not be afraid of them, for there is nothing concealed that will not be disclosed, or hidden that will not be made known. What I tell you in the dark, speak in the daylight; what is whispered in your ear, proclaim from the roofs. Do not be afraid of those who kill the body but cannot kill the soul. Rather, be afraid of the One who can destroy both soul and body in Hell. Are not two sparrows sold for a penny? Yet not one of them will fall to the ground outside your Father's care. And even the very hairs on your head are all numbered. So don't be afraid; you are worth more than many sparrows."

Ben wondered, *what will happen to my soul when my dead body is swinging from a rope?*

Stephanie poured willow tea into Ben and Roy's cups. After she gave the others their share, she let the prisoners have the last of the cedar poultice.

As Stephanie and Sally prepared the morning food and medications, Ann read Romans 8:38-39. "For I am certain that nothing can separate us from his love: neither death nor life, neither angels nor other heavenly rulers or powers, neither the present nor the future, neither the world above or the world below- there is nothing in all creation that will ever be able to separate us from the love of God which is ours through Christ Jesus our Lord."

The words reverberated in Ben's mind. *Is there a way God could love me?*

As the others prepared to move on, Smitty walked to the bridge to buy their passage. He found a locked gate. He turned and saw a cabin nestled in the woods, so he walked over. He was surprised when a lone woman, who was approaching thirty, opened the door. The woman had a straight figure, narrow hips, and a rather flat chest. She wasn't what most men would think of as beautiful, but she wasn't ugly either. Her brown hair gleamed nicely. Her face was pleasant and welcoming, and her attractive hazel eyes looked directly at him as she asked as a statement, "I guess you want to cross the bridge."

"I do."

"How many?"

"Nine people, two wagons, and another horse."

"You'll have to wait for Harry. He has the key."

"When will that be?"

"Don't know. Harry's been gone for a week now."

"We can't wait. You're supposed to allow transport promptly. That's the law."

"Harry has the key, so pocket the disappointment."

Smitty went back to the camp and passed on the bad news. Zachariah offered a solution to the problem, "If he doesn't come home soon, we can use the hatchet and chop open the gate."

Ben felt it was a gift to have more days added to his life. It was fine with him if it took months for Harry to get there. "We shouldn't damage somebody else's property." As if his mind came out of a fog, it occurred to him that he should not have let Gus set the fire that had burned down the Williams Farm.

Sally stood beside the wagon as she listened to the statement of the problem. She decided they might as well make good use of the time. Mainly, she wanted to proceed with her plan to draw Noah and Eli into her family. "Since we're stuck, let's practice shooting and work on our bows."

Everybody agreed that was as good an idea as any other idea. Ben didn't look Noah in the eyes. He sheepishly looked at the ground. "Can I watch you show the others how to use the bow?"

Noah decided to include him if Smitty allowed it. He asked for permission. Smitty agreed conditionally. "You can watch, but you can't have a bow." Ben agreed. Beside Kuhn Bayou, the victims and one of those who had wreaked so much destruction practiced archery and waited for Harry, the key holder, to return.

The next morning, Eli walked to the river for no particular reason. All of a sudden, he ran back to the camp. "Come look!" Those not chained followed Eli as he sneaked up to the river's edge. There in the shallows, a huge sturgeon dug for freshwater mollusks with its big shovel-shaped head.

"I'll get the fishing gear." Zachariah dashed away.

Noah shadowed him. "You can't catch it with a fishing pole. We don't have the right bait. Besides, a pole will snap. We have to spear it." Noah grabbed the spear he had made while the others had worked on their bows.

They hurried back to the river. Barely in range, the sturgeon still dug for its breakfast. Eli pushed Noah forward. "We'll only get one try. You better do it."

Ann watched Noah take two steps back, raise the spear above his head, quickly step forward, and then hurl the spear through the sturgeon into the rocks. Ann thought Noah was magnificent.

All other eyes watched the fish thrash, quickly free itself, and then try to swim away still impaled. Zachariah jumped in and chased the pole up the river. The huge fish pulled him into deeper water. Ann turned her attention to the river. She feared Zachariah would soon be in trouble. "Let it go!" she screamed.

Zachariah heard Ann. *There's no way I'm letting this fish get away with Ann watching, but I am in waist-deep water. I better get back to the shore.*

At Ann's scream, Roy hurried over. *I hope I get to watch Zachariah drown.* Noah moved Ann away from Roy. He signaled to Eli to bring Stephanie and Sally.

Instead of trying to hold the fish, Zachariah shoved it towards the bank. In a few minutes, the sturgeon thrashed in the shallow water beside the bank.

Ben jumped into the river. He felt like part of a group of decent men as he helped get the fish onto the bank. "Must be more an a hundred pounds."

Smitty and Eli pulled up as Zachariah and Ben pushed the wiggling fish from below.

"Well done!" Ann praised Zachariah. Feeling happy that Ann appreciated his efforts, Zachariah climbed the bank and triumphantly pulled the spear out of the sturgeon. All nine of them feasted on grilled sturgeon, caught with the group effort of Noah, Zachariah, Smitty, Eli, and Ben.

FOUR

Ann hoped that a woman could convince another woman to open the gate, so on the third day of waiting, she decided to try her hand at the task. The gatekeeper, without the key to the gate, opened the cabin door. "Hello. I'm Ann Williams. May I speak to you?"

"Of course, come in. I'm Minnie Pitts."

Ann walked past tables and goods for sale. On the wall in front of her, she saw a sign that read: *land deeds, notary, certificates of trade, deputations, livestock brand recording, civil actions, marriages, divorces, wills.* Ann was surprised. She very much wanted to know if the sign stated the truth. "Do you perform all those functions here?"

"We sure do. Officially, Harry does, but I do them, then Harry has it recorded in Dover."

Ann was interested in only one of them. "What's the fee to perform a marriage, and what is the procedure?"

"Five dollars if you want to use a dress and the room in the cabin for one night. You can make a meal for a celebration if you want to have one, and you can serve it in this room. You and your man fill out the application. I'll do the ceremony. Harry will file the papers."

Ann didn't have money, so there wasn't any sense in asking. She did anyway. "How much so it's legal?"

"Four dollars."

"I might be back." Ann started to leave but then remembered why she had come. "Oh. Is there any way we can get across the bridge right after the wedding?"

"Sure."

"Really?" Her success surprised Ann.

"If you get married after Harry gets home."

"I understand." Ann hurried back to camp. She didn't see Noah. "Where's Noah?"

Eli replied, "Down in the river."

Ann enjoyed the sound of the moving water as she searched from one end of the loop towards the other. She found Noah at the bottom of the steepest part of the bank. She carefully started down the muddy bank but immediately slipped, slid down on her rear, and hit the water. *Oh, foot! Now I'm going to have to talk to Noah about getting married covered in mud.* "I'm coming in to help." Ann waded through the cool water towards Noah.

When she joined Noah, the mud had washed away, but Noah had seen her mode of arrival into the river. "I saw you get down here the same way I did."

"You noticed that? Well, knowing that you also got to the river on your bottom, I don't feel so clumsy."

Noah informed Ann about what he was doing with the clearly visible abundance of mussels clinging to the rocks. "Tonight, we'll eat mussels."

"I've never eaten one. Have you?" Ann watched him detach then toss a few mollusks onto the pile on the bank.

"Many times, and I know how to cook them. You have to steam them to get them to open."

"I'm glad you know how. I have no idea." Ann picked up a rock to remove the creatures. "I went to talk to the gatekeeper this morning. They have a little resupply station, but they also provide legal services, one of which is marriages."

Noah stood up straight and focused on what Ann was saying. "What did you find out?"

"We would go fill out the application. Minnie would perform the ceremony when we're ready. We can use the front room to have the ceremony. It has tables and benches. If we want, we can rent a wedding dress and a room inside the cabin for one night." Ann blushed as she thought of the night together.

Noah imagined what she was thinking when Ann's cheeks turned a lovely shade of pink at the mention of the room. He decided it wouldn't be wise for him to follow that thought for long. He pushed it away. "How much will she charge?"

"She said for everything she charges five dollars. If we only have a ceremony and they register the marriage, it's four dollars. But we don't have any money or anything to trade, so I don't know why I'm even talking about it."

"I have the bow and arrows, and the spear I made."

"I don't want you to trade the bow or arrows. That's all we have left of the cedars from home."

Noah picked up the pouch he had previously emptied of willow bark. "Maybe she'll trade for the spear." They loaded up their harvest of mussels and scrambled through the mud back up the bank. Ann and Noah entered the gatehouse carrying the bag full of mussels, the bow, the quiver of arrows, and the spear.

"Minnie, this is Noah."

Minnie looked at the dirty man with short brown hair and blue eyes and the equally muddy woman with long almost black hair and green eyes. They looked acceptable. "Fill out this form."

Noah negotiated, "We don't have any money. Would you trade for this spear?"

"I'll take the bow and arrows."

Ann picked up the paper. "I told him I wouldn't let him. That's all that's left of my home. Those men we are taking to Little Rock burned down my farm, my home, the crops, our animals, and the woods."

"From the looks and the smell of you two, I guess you have mussels in the bag. If there are enough, they're fresh, and the spear is any good, I'll trade the whole wedding package for the spear and the mussels."

Noah accepted before the woman could change her mind. "Where do you want us to put the mussels?"

Minnie retrieved a ten-gallon tub. "I'll get them right into this tub. They need to have plenty of time to breathe out all the sand inside of 'em." Noah poured in the large batch of mussels and carried in several buckets of water from the pump. Minnie picked up the spear and looked it over. "These designs are beautiful, intricate, and unusual. This is very nice." While Ann and Noah filled out the application, Minnie stepped outside, hurled the spear, walked over, picked it up, and went back inside. "It'll do." Ann handed Minnie the application. Minnie looked it over. "I don't see Noah's last name."

"I don't have one." Swift Hawk was not Noah's last name. It was the meaning of his Indian name, and he thought it would be better if his heritage was not known.

"Without a last name, I can't fill out the form." Minnie contemplated. The spear hadn't even wobbled as it had soared through the air. She was a woman alone in a remote location. She wanted the spear.

"Noah, what do you think of the name Williams?"

"It would be perfect. It's your name and also the name of my friend, your Uncle James."

"Can we do that?" Ann hoped it would be acceptable.

"I think we can do that." Minnie completed the form. "Now, let's get you cleaned up, so you can look at the dresses."

Noah gently squeezed Ann's hand, picked up the empty pouch, his bow, and the arrows. "I'm going to get more mussels."

"Don't tell anybody." Ann went with Minnie.

FIVE

Minnie laid four dresses on the bed. Ann was very disappointed. "They're all much too large."

"I'll make the dress fit. Just pick the one you like. Clean up good before you put it on." Minnie brought a ten-gallon tub into the bedroom.

They carried in several buckets of cold water, but Minnie brought only one of hot. Ann bathed in the barely warm water then threw in her dirty clothes and slipped on the dress she liked best. It hung on her hundred-pound body like a tent for five. "I'm ready."

"That one's my favorite. I married Harry in that dress." Minnie slid the excess dress material to the back of the dress along the ivory ribbon woven at the waist. "What happened to your neck and face, sweetie?"

The dress covered all the rest of Ann. Minnie didn't even know about the majority of the injuries Ann had received when they'd pulled her out of the well.

"Gus tried to strangle me with a chain."

"Is he one of the prisoners?" Minnie pleated the extra dress material at the back.

Ann looked in the mirror. The pleats enhanced the rather plain dress. "He's dead, and the world's a better place. It'd be wonderful if we could cover the bruises on my neck."

"I think I have just the thing." Minnie pulled a large lace handkerchief from a drawer, wrapped it around Ann's neck, tucked it into the neckline of the dress, and then pinned it with a green brooch that matched Ann's eyes.

Ann liked it not only because it covered her neck but also because it beautifully accented the dress. "Perfect."

Minnie drew the long sleeves up to Ann's wrists using ribbons sewn inside that came out a slit at the top over the shoulders. She tied the ribbons in a bow. The long ends flowed down over Ann's upper arms with the extra bloused-down material. They each drew up six of the ribbons attached halfway down the shirt of the dress. The ribbons came out from the inside of the dress at the waist. With the ribbons pulled up, the top layer of the skirt became scalloped and the bottom drawn up to the correct length. Minnie tied the ribbons to each other at Ann's waist. She opened a basket and removed an emerald-green sash to cover the knots. The ribbons' ends floated down the outside of the dress from under the sash.

Minnie looked at her handy work. "Noah is blind if he doesn't think you are the most gorgeous woman in the world."

Ann looked at herself in the mirror. It wasn't practical, but she felt beautiful. She hugged Minnie. "I would never have thought this dress could be so lovely."

"A person's wedding day should be as perfect as it can be. I try to give that to the people I marry."

"You're a very thoughtful woman. It was so unlikely to have found you here at this exact time."

Minnie stated, "God knows what we need and arranges things so that they'll be there when we need them."

"You're right. I've been so angry about everything that's happened that I haven't believed that God cares. I'm glad He didn't forget about me." Gratitude filled Ann's heart; gratitude for the woman God had placed in her path to allow her to marry Noah, and even more for putting Minnie there to turn her heart back to the One she truly needed. Ann got out of the dress. She quickly scrubbed her clothes sitting in the tub of tepid water, wrung them out, and put them back on. She walked back into the front room. "I'll let you know when we'll want to have the ceremony. We need to tell everybody. They have no idea." She went out the door.

Minnie doubted that their friends had no idea. It would take a blind person not to see how much Noah and Ann loved each other. She could tell in just a few minutes.

Just as Ann returned, Noah walked into the camp with another sack full of mussels. "Did you find what you wanted?"

"I think you'll like it." Ann looked at Noah with a smile that was sweet, beautiful, and full of anticipation.

Stephanie chastised them, "Where have you two been? You missed dinner. I'll see if any of it is still worth eating."

Noah showed Stephanie the bag full of black shells.

"I got mussels for later." He looked around. Roy sat in the wagon. Since Smitty had given Ben permission to make a bow, as long as he never got a bowstring, Ben sat beside the wagon with the shackle around his waist and tried to shape his branch with a small, but sharp, piece of chert. Everybody else practiced archery in the clearing. Noah turned towards Ann with his back towards Stephanie. He whispered, "Should we tell Stephanie first?"

"Maybe we should tell everybody at the same time. I don't want Sally to feel that she was left out."

Sally came up behind Ann. "Tell me what?"

Ann jumped. "Goodness, girl; you about scared me out of my skin."

Stephanie saw Noah's grin. "What's going on?"

Noah looked at Ann. She nodded her approval. "Your sister and I are getting married."

Sally was disappointed. "That's not news. I've known you two were going to marry before you did."

Ann filled in the missing but pertinent detail. "But not that Minnie is going to marry us now. I went over there to see if I could get her to let us cross the bridge. I saw a sign that said they perform marriages, so I talked with Noah."

"You asked Noah to marry you? I can't believe you did that. He's supposed to ask you." Stephanie felt irritated because she wanted Eli to ask her, but he hadn't.

Noah corrected Stephanie's assumption. "Ann didn't ask me. I asked Ann a few days ago. Today, Ann just told me that Minnie could perform a marriage, so we went to talk with her. We traded my spear and a sack of mussels for her wedding services. We just need to tell everybody, but I'm glad we were able to let you know first."

Sally hugged Noah. "I can't tell you how happy it makes me that I'm going to have you as my brother."

"Me too." Stephanie joined Sally as they wrapped their arms around Noah. She drew Ann over, so they could all hug Noah together. He reveled in the love.

Eli saw the hug and wondered what was happening. He walked over. Stephanie updated him, "Eli, guess what. Noah and Ann are getting married."

"Congratulations." Eli was glad they had made the right choice. Noah had done what he'd suggested and had also been keeping his distance from Ann.

Sally added, "And they're going to get married now!"

Eli looked at Noah. "How are you going to do that?" Noah stood with his arm on Ann's shoulder while Sally explained. Noah and Ann were glad to let her. Eli asked about the timing, "Is it going to be today?"

Noah confessed what he wanted, "Harry could get home at any time, and then we'll have to go. I don't want to take a chance. I want to get married today, even right now."

Stephanie stated her thoughts, "We have to tell the others, and we have to prepare for the celebration. This is my sister's wedding, and I want to make it as wonderful as possible, so not before tonight."

"Well, I guess that settles it." Noah smiled then gave Ann a big loud kiss on the cheek.

Smitty saw the meeting and thought, *maybe all of them killed Gus together, and they're still conspiring.* He walked over. "What're you cooking up?"

The rest of the men joined them. Noah told the whole group straight out, "I asked Ann to marry me, she agreed, and since Minnie can perform marriages, we're going to get married today."

Smitty knew everything they had gone through and felt that they deserved the happiness. He hoped that neither of them would be spending the first years of their marriage in jail when he figured out who had killed Gus. "Congratulations."

Zachariah echoed, "Congratulations," but he walked away upset. *Now there's nobody for me.*

Ben came as close as his chain allowed. "Wish I could give ya the gift o' undoing what Gus did."

Roy commanded him sharply, "Shut up, Ben."

Stephanie shooed them away. "You men go do something. You too, Noah. We're going to plan."

The sisters went to look at the room where they would have the wedding. Ann introduced her sisters and told Minnie, "We want to marry later today. I would like you to celebrate with us."

The few people Minnie had married had not included her beyond the ceremony. She looked forward to relief from the loneliness of her life. She offered to make a cake, and if they would bring her another large batch of mussels, to cook them for the celebration. The four women got everything planned before Ann left to tell Noah that Minnie would cook mussels for everybody, but they had to bring her more.

Noah and Ann carried the second batch of mussels to the cabin. Minnie dropped the mollusks into the water with the previous batch and then explained the ceremony. The three of them talked and laughed as they practiced. Minnie enjoyed Noah and Ann. She offered to prepare a bath for Noah in the kitchen and one for Ann in the bedroom. After Ann and Noah got back to camp, Stephanie and Sally went over and decorated the room with cedar boughs laden with their small blue cones. Then, so it would be close when it was time to serve the meal, they took the food they'd prepared to the cabin's kitchen.

Late that afternoon, Ann again went to the cabin. She bathed in the lavender-scented bath that Minnie had prepared for her. Noah found his tub of warm water waiting for him in the kitchen. Minnie had put the bottle of lavender toilet water beside the tub, so he could use it or not as he chose.

Noah didn't want to leave even one speck of dirt that might spoil the upcoming events. He thoroughly washed before he picked up the Sunday-go-to-meeting clothes that Ann had given him when he'd first gone to their farm. Blessedly, Noah had all the clothes that had belonged to Ann's father in his dresser in the bunkroom. In the few minutes that they'd had to gather what they could, he had gotten all the clothes. Noah put his arm into a shirtsleeve and wondered if Ann's father had married Ann's mother in the same outfit.

Smitty unchained Roy and Ben from the wagon but then chained them together. With Eli and Zachariah, he marched them to the cabin at the end of their rifle barrels. Smitty ordered the prisoners, "Sit." They sat on the bench close to the back of the room but in front of Smitty. Smitty pulled the chain to the ring he'd bolted through the floor earlier in the day.

Roy yanked at the chain. "There ain't enough chain here for me ta stand up."

"Exactly, so sit, and don't make any problems."

Minnie arranged Ann's dress again. "Perfect and beautiful, come when you hear the bell."

Through the kitchen door, Minnie asked, "Are you ready, Noah?"

"Never more so."

"Then come to your place." The scent of lavender followed Noah into the room where everybody else, except the bride, sat on benches. At the tinkling of the small brass bell, Ann entered the room. She glided across the room wearing the ivory dress with ivory satin ribbons, a green sash around her waist, and lace pinned in place around her neck with a green brooch that glittered like her green eyes. Like black feathers of a raven, her hair flowed loosely over her shoulders.

Noah knew Ann had to be the most beautiful woman on the planet. She stopped beside him and looked into his eyes. They believed they were the most blessed couple ever. He took her hands in his.

Minnie started the ceremony. "We are gathered together to unite Noah and Ann in holy matrimony. If anybody here knows of any reason why Ann and Noah should not be married, speak now, or forever hold your peace." Zachariah thought about it, but the fact that he also wanted to marry her was not a reason any of them would accept. He remained silent. "Since there are no objections we will continue. At this time, Stephanie will read a passage from the Bible."

Stephanie walked to the front of the room and stood beside Noah and Ann. "First Corinthians 13:1-13. 'Though I speak with the tongues of men and of angels but have not love, I am as sounding brass or a tinkling cymbal. And though I have the gift of prophecy, and understand all mysteries, and have all knowledge; and I could remove mountains but have not love, I am nothing. And though I bestow all my goods to feed the poor, and though I give my body to be burned but have not love, it profits me not. Love suffers long, and is kind; love envies not, is not proud, is not puffed up. Love does not behave unseemly, seeks not its own, is not easily provoked, thinks no evil; rejoices not in iniquity but rejoices in the truth; bears all things, believes all things, hopes all things and endures all things. Love never fails, but as for prophecies, they will pass; as to tongues, they will cease; as for knowledge, it will vanish away. For now, we know in part, and we prophesy in part. But when that which is perfect comes then that which is in part shall be done away. When I was a child, I spoke as a child, I understood as a child, I thought as a child; when I became a man, I put away childish things. For now we see through a glass, darkly;

but then face to face: now I know in part; but then I shall know even as also I am known. And now abides faith, hope, and love, these three; but the greatest of these is love.'" Before walking back to her seat, Stephanie turned. "Ann and Noah, may you always have each other's love."

Minnie continued the ceremony. "Noah and Ann will now take their vows. Will you, Ann, take Noah to be your wedded husband, to live together under God's ordinance in the holy state of matrimony? Will you obey and serve him, love, honor, and keep him, in sickness and in health; and, forsaking all others, keep yourself to him only, so long as you both shall live?"

Ann happily repeated the words Minnie had taught them. "I, Ann, take you, Noah, to be my wedded husband, to have and to hold from this day forward, for better or for worse, for richer or for poorer, in sickness and in health, to love, to cherish, and to obey, till death us do part, according to God's holy ordinance."

"And Noah, will you have Ann to be your wedded wife, to live together under God's ordinance in the holy state of Matrimony? Will you love her, comfort her, honor, and keep her, in sickness and in health; and, forsaking all others, keep yourself to her only, so long as you both shall live?"

"I, Noah, take you, Ann, to be my wedded wife, to have and to hold, from this day forward, for better or for worse, for richer or for poorer, in sickness and in health, to love and to cherish, till death us do part, according to God's holy ordinance."

"Then, under God's eyes and by the power vested in Harry by the state of Arkansas, I pronounce you man and wife. You may kiss your bride."

Noah kissed Ann with a respectful brief kiss. They turned towards the others in the room.

Sally got up from the bench. "Let's celebrate." Minnie, Stephanie, and Sally brought in all the food, along with the mussels steamed in wine and smothered in canned butter.

Noah praised Minnie. "It's a good thing you're the cook. These are much better than if I had cooked them."

After the food, Minnie brought out a rum-soaked wedding cake made with candied fruit. Smitty smelled the rum as Minnie cut slices. He handed Roy and Ben their pieces of cake. "Don't think you're going to eat a lot of this cake." Ben sat at the table, joked, and ate with the others. Roy didn't completely hate everything.

Zachariah stared at his cake. *Why couldn't it have been me? I'm not going to sit here and watch Noah take Ann into the bedroom.* He forcefully put his fork on the table then stood up and left the cabin. At the bridge, he kicked the gate then pressed his forehead into his arm that he had draped over the gate. He kicked the gate again then got his bedroll and walked into the woods with his rifle.

Eli, Smitty, Zachariah, and Noah had planned to have Stephanie and Sally safely out of the path of Roy and Ben when they escorted the prisoners back to camp. It was long after Zachariah left before Eli told Stephanie and Sally, "It's time to go." He walked over to the newly wedded couple. "Congratulations again, I wish you a wonderful life. Stephanie, Sally, and I are going back to camp."

"The wedding was some pumpkins." Ann hugged her sisters.

Stephanie whispered in Ann's ear, "Have a fantastic night."

"Love you both to the moon and back. See you tomorrow." Sally hugged her oldest sister then Noah.

Since Zachariah wasn't there, Noah needed to take his place. "I'm going to help Smitty get Roy and Ben back to camp and locked to the wagon then I'll be back.

Ann hugged her husband. "I'll be waiting for you. Don't take too long."

Noah whispered, "You can be sure that I'll be back as fast as I can."

"I'll clean up in the kitchen." Minnie set up a cot in the room farthest from the bedroom.

Noah returned fifteen minutes later, took Ann's hand, raised it to his lips, and kissed it. "This way my love." He walked backward towards the bedroom while looking at Ann whose cheeks were rosy as she thought about the love they would soon share. "You are so beautiful. When you came through the door in your wedding dress, my heart filled to overflowing with joy. I thought to myself, 'How did I ever win such a treasure?'"

"I'm the blessed one. God couldn't have brought me a better husband." They stepped into the room. She raised her lips to his. He closed the door.

SIX

After what seemed like a very short night, Minnie stood on the other side of the door. "Your night is over."

"We'll be out in a minute." Noah wished he didn't have to leave the embrace of his wife.

Ann placed more kisses on him. "So I guess we can't make love all day."

"I wish we could. Unfortunately, we have to go." After the first experience of love either of them had known, Noah hated that Ann had to stop showering him with her kisses. They dressed, shared one last, long, kiss wrapped in each other's arms, and then left.

Ann and Noah walked towards camp. Sally hurried towards them. She gave Ann a big hug. "Good morning, sister." She hugged Noah even longer. "Good morning, brother."

Noah hugged her back. "Good morning, sister." Sally felt overjoyed to have Noah in her family. She put her arm around Noah's waist as they walked into camp.

When the newlyweds rejoined the group, Eli echoed Sally's greeting, "Good morning."

Since he was in an excellent mood, Noah replied with an emphatically happy tone, "The same back to everybody."

Stephanie teased them, "Good morning. Hope your night wasn't too horrible."

Noah joked, "Completely awful!"

Ann joined in jest, "Horrendous." When alone with her sisters, preparing hot porridge with sunflower seeds and maple sugar, Ann whispered, "Actually, last night was wonderful."

Zachariah sat with the men and worked on his bow. "Would you stop doing that?" he exclaimed.

"Doing what?" Noah had no clue what he was doing that was bothering Zachariah.

Zachariah enlightened him of his offense, "Looking at Ann with that expression on your face."

Noah straightened out Zachariah definitively, "She's my wife. I'll look at her whatever way I want." Zachariah threw his bow down and stalked away. Noah looked at Eli and Smitty. "I didn't realize I was looking at Ann any particular way. I know Zachariah has feelings for Ann, and I'm not trying to be mean, but he's not going to tell me anything about what we can or can't do."

Due to their short tethers, Ben and Roy sat within hearing. Ben stopped sanding his bow. "It ain't fair ta us who ain't got a woman."

"I'm just sitting here. What am I doing?"

Smitty explained, "You look at her then get this smile, and you're obviously thinking about last night's loving."

"I can't help it. Wouldn't you?"

Ben offered his history, "I forgot 'em before I left the bed." He thought, *'cept Ruby.*

"First of all, I don't want to know about it, and second of all, Ann is not a woman you forget."

After having been almost entirely silent the whole trip, Roy spoke up, "I 'spect not."

Noah warned Roy with death in his eyes, "You better not even start thinking about her."

Eli extended the warning, "Any of them."

Noah stopped the conversation. "Here they come. Drop it. I'll try not to be obvious, but there's no way I won't be thinking about her."

Sally sat next to Noah. "I've got this knot in my bow. What should I do?"

"You can't cut it off because if you pull it out and leave a hole, it'll break as soon as you try to use it. You have to sand it down. Let's go find a rough rock." He stood up and held his hand out to Sally. They went looking for the perfect tool. Noah felt doubly blessed. Actually, he felt quadruply blessed with Ann as a wife, two sisters, and soon he figured, Eli as a brother.

Smitty got the fishing gear and found Zachariah. "Help me catch some supper."

"All right." Zachariah slid down the bank after Smitty.

Zachariah related his frustration, "I don't have a life. I want my life to begin, but there's no way to make it happen."

Smitty said, "Your life is happening. It's always happening." He then let Zachariah vent his feelings as they fished. Late in the afternoon, they returned to camp with several catfish, stripers, and bass.

"Fish for everybody." Zachariah plopped the fish on the rock they had set up as a table. The girls cleaned the whole mess of fish and fried them up. Zachariah passed them out. Stephanie gave everybody a serving of boiled rice again mixed with cedar berries but this time without the beans.

Stephanie ate the last bite of striper on her plate. "You sure caught a lot of good fish."

Sally put a second fish on her plate. "Yes, I sure love bass. I'm much obliged to both of you."

Ben hadn't fished for years. After eating the fish, and seeing the change in Zachariah's attitude, Ben asked Smitty for a special privilege, "I wonder if you would put the wagon close enough to the river for me to fish."

Smitty agreed. The men pulled the prisoner wagon to the riverbank. Smitty took Ben's bow. Noah handed Ben a long braided sinew string with a hook attached and a strong, but crooked, cedar branch that could not be formed into a bow. "You'll have to dig up your bait."

"Caught some hoppers today." Ben pulled four dead insects from his vest pocket.

"Good luck." Noah walked away.

That night, while the others slept, Noah woke Ann and told her about Zachariah.

"I never did anything to make him think I would be interested in a relationship with him."

"I know, but that doesn't mean a man wouldn't want you anyway. You're a very lovable woman."

Ann wanted to be sure she understood, so she asked, "You're saying we have to behave like friends because we need his horse?"

"I think so. We don't need to make matters worse by flaunting our love in front of him."

"I don't like it, but I'll do it because you asked." Ann kissed him well before they went back to sleep.

"Got one! I got one! A big one!"

Stephanie woke. "What's all that hollering?" She saw Ben come up from the river with a smile spread across his face and a glittering in his gold-colored eyes. He held an enormous black crappie over his head. *He's good-looking when he smiles like that.*

"I forgot how much fun fishing can be. It's asking a lot, 'specially after everything we done ta ya, but I sure would like ta eat this fish. Only problem is, I can't get ta the fire ta cook it."

"I'll cook it." Stephanie took the fish.

Roy whispered, "Say one more word 'bout being responsible for anythin', an you'll be joining Gus."

Stephanie handed Eli the plate with Ben's fish fried up crispy. "Would you give this to Ben?"

Now that Ben thought his life would end in a few weeks he savored and appreciated things that had been lost to him while living a wicked life. He thought the fish was the best he had ever eaten. When Eli came over to get the empty plate, Ben asked, "There ain't no reason for Stephanie ta cook this fish for me, an she cooked it perfectly; why'd she do it?"

"She's a fantastic and forgiving woman."

"You're a lucky man ta have a girl like her."

"I know." Eli took the plate and turned away.

"Make sure you always let her know how special

she is." Ben knew they had no doubt that he and Roy had been part of the group that had done everything to them. He was amazed that they didn't treat him or Roy meanly. They had something he didn't have. They reminded him of home. He wondered why he had left home where he'd had parents and a sister who'd loved him. As he tried to reason out how he'd come to the place where he was about to lose his life, a drop of rain hit his face. He looked up. Dark clouds were rolling in.

"Get everything in the wagon." Ann ran with her hands full of cedar boughs and her bedroll.

Smitty hurried to the other wagon. "Pull the canvas over the wagons." He kept his eyes and gun on the prisoners as Zachariah, Roy, and Ben pulled the oiled canvas cover over the wagon. Noah, Eli, and the girls covered the other wagon.

The sky dropped everything it had. Ann pulled the pucker strings closed. "One good thing about the rain is that I can cuddle with my husband." Ann cozied up to Noah and turned her face up for a kiss.

"Very true." Noah sat Ann in his lap and gladly complied.

Sally asked, "What does that mean? Why can't you cuddle?" Noah explained about Zachariah. "That's ridiculous. I think you should do what you want."

Smitty and Zachariah sat in the other wagon with their rifles pointing at Roy and Ben, in case they again got the idea to attack.

Shortly before nightfall, Stephanie took cold food to the prisoner wagon. Smitty reached out for the food. "If it's still raining at the end of the day tomorrow, send Noah or Eli to the cabin to see if Harry is back."

"I'll tell them." She turned to leave.

Ben called out, "Wait! I wonder if there's a way a person like me can ever fix what he's done wrong."

Roy ordered Ben, "Shut up!"

"Leave me alone, Roy. This ain't your business."

Stephanie stopped. "It depends on what you mean."

Roy jerked Ben's chain and pulled him over. "You shouldn't be saying nothin'."

No longer afraid of a man, Ben got off the wagon floor and slugged Roy in the jaw. Smitty fully cocked his rifle. "Stop it, or I'll shoot you both!"

Ben pulled back the second punch he was about to land on Roy. "You're an idiot. You're gonna be dying soon. When you meet God, what you think He's gonna do? Don't know 'bout you, but I want to choose my consequences."

Eli went to the prisoner wagon because Stephanie hadn't returned. "What's going on? Is everything all right?"

"Everything is fine." Stephanie turned to Ben. "You can't fix our farm. Charlie, Al, Pete, Hank, and Gus are still going to be dead just like our animals, but God can fix your heart."

After listening to the Bible readings day after day, Ben had come to believe that God was the one to fear. He wanted to fix the real problem. "How can I get Him ta fix my heart?"

Stephanie enlightened him, "Since you asked that question, He's already working on your heart. First, you have to admit that you have sinned and are a sinner."

Ben sighed. "Guess there's no doubt 'bout that."

Stephanie explained as she stood in the rain beside Eli, "You have to understand that the outcome of sin is death. Not physical death, although that can happen, but spiritual death and eternity separated from God. You can't save yourself from the Hell that you deserve; the rest of us can't either. No one can. That's where Jesus comes in. He's the only one who can pay the penalty owed due to sin. The good news is that Jesus did. The debt is already completely paid. Anybody can claim forgiveness by believing that Jesus is the Son of God and accepting Him as his or her Lord. That means that you obey Him. People still do things wrong sometimes, but we try to follow His teaching. Not only because He tells us to obey Him but also because we believe that His ways are right. Then you have to repent."

"What's that mean? How do I repent?"

"That means that you agree with God that what you've done is wrong, you turn away from those things, and you don't do them anymore. Then ask Him to come into your heart and life, and to live there. He will. Do you want to ask Him?"

"I'm not good 'nough. I don't deserve ta be forgiven. I don't think He'd do it."

"I'm not good enough. Poor you, what a baby," Roy belittled Ben.

Ben ignored him. He no longer cared the least little bit about Roy's opinion.

"Let me tell you about an adulterer, liar, and murderer who God called His friend and a man after His own heart." Stephanie told a true story, "King David saw the wife of his good friend, Uriah, bathing on the roof of her house. The woman's name was Bathsheba. King David desired her, so he told his men to bring her to him. He lay with her, and she became pregnant. Then, so Uriah wouldn't know that the child wasn't his, David tried to trick Uriah into going home and being with his wife.

"Uriah wouldn't go to his wife when all his men weren't able to do the same, so David devised a plan to have Uriah killed. He told Abner, his general, to station Uriah where he knew the fighting was the fiercest and then to leave him and his men. Abner did what King David told him, and Uriah lost his life.

"Later, the prophet Nathan caused the King to confess and acknowledge what he had done. David admitted that he had sinned against Uriah, Bathsheba, and most of all, against God. He asked God to forgive him and to create a clean heart in him again. God did just that and even promised someday that his descendant would rule eternally. That descendant is Jesus. If God forgave David and created a clean heart in him, then He can do the same for you."

Ben wanted forgiveness, and he wanted to have a clean heart. "How do I do it?"

Stephanie revealed the mystery of salvation, "Do

the same thing David did. Acknowledge that you're a sinner and need to have a clean heart created in you. Ask Him to come into your heart, make it clean, and rule in your life. Then turn away from your sinful life."

Ben believed he would soon be swinging from a rope. He did what his heart and mind told him to do. "God, I'm a horrible sinner. I done so many things wrong I can't even remember 'em all. I don't deserve forgiveness, but these people say you'll forgive me, so take away this rotten heart o' mine, an give me a new clean one before I'm hanged."

"Amen. Lord, let it be." Even though Ben had destroyed her home, Stephanie felt it was up to God to decide whom He would forgive.

God had put it into Eli's mind to check on Stephanie so that he would hear the conversation. Eli heard God call him into the next step of their relationship. He prayed silently. *I told You I would believe and pray. I don't want just to believe and pray. I want You in my heart. Please come in and rule.*

Smitty and Zachariah listened but didn't hear the love of God reaching out. They didn't feel the sin in their lives and allowed the blessing to pass by. Roy's heart was too hard. The walls of bitterness he had built let nothing in and nothing out.

Stephanie stood with Eli at the back of the wagon in the pouring rain. "I'll talk more with you about this later on."

Ben felt incredibly grateful. "Much obliged, Stephanie. Go on an' get outta the rain."

Ann moved their bedding away as Stephanie and Eli climbed into the wagon. "Where have you two been?"

"Ben asked about salvation. Stephanie told him all about King David killing Uriah. Ben asked Jesus into his heart and life. Stephanie, you are some pumpkins!"

SEVEN

When Noah went to see if Harry was back, he could barely tell it was day. Dark clouds filled the sky, and the rain still fell in torrents. Minnie sat alone in the cabin. "I was hoping we would be able to move on. We don't have much space in the wagons, and we're all crammed in there staying out of the rain."

Minnie felt bad that Harry wasn't back and was preventing the group from moving on. "You can sleep on the floor in here in the front room."

"That would be wonderful. We'll try to figure out how to get our blankets and some clothes over here in a dry condition."

"I have plenty you can use, but you'll have to leave them when you go."

"What about our horses?"

"Put them in the shed."

"I appreciate that. Harry's a lucky man to have such a nice woman as his wife."

"I don't know why he's gone so much. He does have to turn in the records, but every time he goes, it takes longer for him to get home."

"I hope he gets here soon. Not just for us, but for you as well."

Noah went back to the camp and told everybody

that Minnie offered the front room, dry blankets, and dry clothes for the night. They readily accepted the offer and hurried to the cabin with the horses.

Ann went directly into the cabin. "We're so grateful that you let us come in out of the storm."

Each expressed their gratitude as they ran into the cabin. Smitty locked Ben and Roy to the ring bolted to the floor. Minnie brought out blankets, pillows, and a big pile of clothes. She put more wood on the fire to warm up the wet, cold people. Each picked through the clothes to find something that would fit and took turns changing in the bedroom. The girls went to the kitchen when the prisoners redressed under the guard of the men. In dry clothes and a warm room, they sat and enjoyed the fire. Minnie surprised them with hot stew, bread, and coffee.

Smitty accepted the hot meal, "I'll give you a court script for this food and the lodging, or I'll pay you when I come back."

"I'll take the script, but I'd like you to redeem it when you come back through."

It was lonely by herself beside the bridge. Minnie sat and savored the company. The travelers also enjoyed the fellowship as well as spending the rest of the day in Minnie's house dry and warm.

That night, everybody slept on the floor except Minnie and Zachariah. They felt a familiar despair and loneliness in each other that she knew in her mostly solitary existence, and he endured in Harmony with nobody to love. They stayed up late into the night talking. He told her that he was waiting for his life to begin, but there was no way to make it happen. She told him that Harry had taken hers when he had brought her out to the bridge. When she retired to her room, she took Zachariah with her.

Smitty was the first awake. He no longer heard the sound of falling rain, so he got up to look out the window. He noticed that Zachariah wasn't in the room. After verifying that the rain had indeed stopped, he walked across the room and added more logs to the fire then lay back in his blanket. Zachariah crept into the room and covered up with the blanket that had lain empty all night. Smitty didn't say a word.

The sun rose, found its way into the windows, and woke the people inside the cabin. Minnie came through the room on her way to the kitchen to fry salt-cured ham. She returned and served the morning meal of ham along with eggs, flapjacks, canned butter, maple syrup, and hot English tea. Minnie hummed as she served them, gave plenty to Zachariah, and smiled at him sweetly.

When Minnie went back into the kitchen, Sally whispered in Ann's ear, "Minnie's different."

"She is, isn't she?" Ann remembered how she'd felt the morning after her wedding night. While they sat at the table enjoying the meal, Ann secretly observed the men. Roy and Ben had spent the night chained, and Noah's arms were around Ann all night. Eli was too much in love with Stephanie, and she doubted that Smitty would cheat on Mara. Zachariah, however, was in just the right state to be susceptible.

Harry walked in the door. Zachariah dropped his fork on the floor and choked on the ham he was chewing. Minnie stopped short in the kitchen doorway when she saw her husband in the room.

"Harry, you're home!" She glanced at Zachariah practically under the table retrieving his fork.

"Yes, I am. Is that a problem?" Harry didn't like the unusual reaction from his wife.

"Of course not, I'm so glad you're home." Minnie walked across the floor and kissed Harry on the cheek.

"I'm Sheriff Smithfield Wyman transporting prisoners to Little Rock. This is the fifth day we've waited here. Unlock the bridge immediately!"

"Get ready to cross. The bridge will be open when you get there."

Smitty issued marching orders to his group, "Come on. Let's pack up." They all followed him out the door, except Roy and Ben, who were under the gun in front.

Zachariah spoke to Minnie as he left the cabin, "Much obliged for all your hospitality, ma'am."

"Anytime." Minnie shut the door.

Harry wanted information, "What's going on?"

"Just as the Sheriff said. They've been waiting for you to get here. It's been pouring rain, so they stayed in this room."

Harry counted nine slept in blankets. That matched the number of people eating. He sat at the table. "Bring me some of that breakfast."

"Right away." Minnie hurried out of the room.

Smitty fussed as he hitched Bliss to the wagon. "I'm

going to give him a piece of my mind about providing immediate passage."

Noah went to him. "I want him to file our marriage paper. Please don't."

"Then I won't but only for that reason and maybe I'll file a complaint against him after he's had your marriage recorded."

The travelers changed back into their own clothes inside the wagons. They left the oiled wagon covers up not only to give them privacy to change but also to allow the canvas to dry.

When they got back to the bridge, Harry had unlocked the gate and had swung it wide open. Ann handed Minnie the bundle of clothes that she and her sisters had borrowed. "Thank you for a beautiful wedding and for taking us in out of the rain. I won't ever forget you."

Minnie eyes brimmed with tears. Maybe it was because they had been there for so many days instead of only minutes, but somehow Minnie felt attached to these people. Maybe she was supposed to care about them. Zachariah handed Minnie his clothes and touched her hand underneath. Tears rolled down Minnie's face. She hurried back into the house and watched through the window as they rode out of sight.

EIGHT

The land on the east side of the Bayou was low. Bald Cypress trees, with their knees out of the water, made resting places for frogs and turtles. The knees filled the swamp that surrounded them. The Black-and-yellow-bellied turtles jumped into the water as they passed along the wooden causeway made of logs laid parallel to their direction of travel with wooden planks nailed perpendicularly. The posts at the sides kept the whole thing together and provided landing pads for dragonflies. Snakes, along with alligators showing only their eyes above the surface of the water dark with tannin, swam through the swamp. The smell of rotting vegetation was stifling.

Ann stopped. "I know it smells bad, but let's stop and look around. I've never seen a place like this."

Smitty kept walking. "We need to move on."

Ann begged, "Only for a little while." Exploring was her favorite thing. She couldn't just pass through such a wonderfully different environment without taking it all in. Not caring whether the others liked it or not, Ann stood where she was and looked at a large mat of floating vegetation with small trees growing on it. A turtle, like a big craggy rock, crawled up onto the floating island with a fish in its sharp beak-shaped mouth. It clamped down. The fish snapped in half.

Sally stood beside Ann. "Did you see that?"

"I did. I sure wouldn't want that thing getting ahold of me."

The group stood on the causeway. The sounds of the swamp filled the air. A "wit, wit, wit" sound came from the trees. They had looked for several minutes before Zachariah saw the mottled gray body and bright green back of a frog puffing its throat in and out, as it called for a mate. It looked so much like a piece of bark with a leaf on its back that it was a wonder Zachariah saw it.

"Look at all these mudbugs," Noah called them over to the place where he lay on his belly on the causeway and peered into the water. It was hard to see anything in the dim light of the swamp. Finally, they identified, hidden in the rocks and mud, little creatures with big pincers at the front and a long segmented body that ended in a flat tail. Noah always hunted and looked for things they could add to their usual boring beans and rice. "I think we can eat these."

Eli did not like the look of the brown water. "There are a lot of them down there, but I wouldn't put my hand in there."

Noah decided to attempt the harvesting. "I don't see any alligators. I think it's safe. Get the pouch."

Ann handed Noah the bag that had previously held willow bark, then mussels, and was now about to contain crayfish. With a pot, Noah scooped several out of the murky water. Water, mud, and crayfish splashed onto the causeway. The others grabbed for the crayfish before they could scuttle away. One snapped on tight to Zachariah's finger. He hopped around and tried to shake it off before he finally pulled it loose. After he got his finger free, Zachariah informed them of the proper crayfish gathering procedure he had just learned. "You better grab them right behind the pincers."

Stephanie, Eli, Sally, and Ann scrambled after the crustaceans while Smitty and Ben laughed big belly laughs. Even Roy couldn't keep from laughing at the hysterical scene. Most of the crayfish darted away, but they got a few into the bag. Zachariah thought they had the most efficient and safest procedure figured out. "Scoop out some more. Now that we know what to do, we should be able to catch more of 'em."

Ben asked Smitty, "Can I help?"

"Just remember, I've got my rifle on you."

Noah scooped out another potful of the creatures. The chase commenced again. After many rounds, they had filled the pouch. Ben found more fun in the few minutes of the simple pleasure than he had for many years. Noah dipped the pot into the swamp and poured the water into the bag with the crayfish. Then, since he felt that the work was over, he reached down for another pot full without looking. He felt a sharp sting, dropped the pot, and quickly stood up. A snake's long slender body with dark brown and light brown hourglass-shaped bands writhed as it hung in the air with its mouth clamped onto the side of his hand.

Ann filled with fear. "It's a cottonmouth!"

All three girls clutched their hands to their chests and hysterically repeated, "Oh no!"

Smitty ordered the women, "Stop yelling!"

Noah seized the snake behind the head. Its head was not a diamond and was almost the same diameter as its neck. Noah pushed at the back of its jawbones to force them to open and let go. He looked at its eyes as he detached the snake. "It's all right. It's not a cottonmouth." He looked then showed Ann the inside of its mouth.

Ann was scared out of her mind. "Are you sure?"

"Look, its mouth is not white inside, and its pupils are round. It's not a cottonmouth." He held the snake securely behind its head while she looked.

"I believe you. Get rid of it."

Noah tossed the fanged culprit into the water.

Ann had thought her husband of only a few days was going to die. Not caring if Zachariah didn't like it, she threw herself into his arms. Suddenly, she was mad that he had been so careless. She stepped back and slapped him on the chest. "Don't you ever do that to me again!" She ran away down the causeway.

"Ouch." Noah rubbed his chest.

Eli laughed. "So which is worse, a snake bite or an upset wife?"

Stephanie snapped at Eli, "It's not funny." She and Sally went after their sister.

Ben stood there with his mouth open. "I've never seen a woman go through such a swing of emotions in less than a minute."

Noah had seen it before when they had experienced relief and gratitude that they were all alive and out of the well, and anger and grief that everything was gone. He wished he had paid more attention, not just because of the throbbing pain in his hand, but also because he'd upset Ann. Noah stood on the boardwalk and watched the three sisters with their arms around each other.

Smitty said, "Reach in there again and get the pot but be careful. You may not be so lucky the next time."

Ann prayed as Stephanie and Sally hugged her, "God, please help me. I can't take more of this. Things have to stop going wrong, and I can't even hug my husband. Help me."

Sally offered Ann her advice, "Forget Zachariah. Hug Noah and kiss him, right in front of everybody."

Noah stopped looking at his wife. This time, he looked carefully into the water before he got the pot. He poured water into the pouch that Zachariah held open. "Listen, Zachariah. I don't want to upset anybody, but I am not going to upset Ann so that I don't upset you. Do you understand?"

Zachariah understood. "I was just out of sorts. Love Ann like a husband should love his wife." Zachariah shut the pouch and hung it on the wagon.

Noah walked to Ann. They stood at the edge of the wooden causeway and looked at shiny, light gray frogs with dark spots that sat on big, green, water lily leaves and called out, "ribbit."

"I'm sorry I scared you." Noah put his arm around Ann's waist and looked at the beauty of the swamp with her.

"And I'm sorry that I got mad. If you had died, I couldn't stand it. I don't want to have all these problems. I'm worn out." Ann stood with her shoulders slumped over. She looked and felt completely beaten.

"We can make it. Everything will work out."

Ann turned to Noah. "Promise me."

Noah wrapped his arms around Ann. "I promise. I won't let anything happen."

Ann could barely put one foot in front of the other nor could she enjoy the mysteries of the world waiting for discovery. She just wanted Noah to be all right. "Get in the wagon, and let me look at your hand. Will this cedar poultice on my neck, help your hand?"

Noah did not want to take the medicine away from Ann's injured neck. "I want you to have it."

Ann removed the handkerchief whether Noah wanted her to do it or not. She wrapped it around the snakebite then put a kiss on the back of his hand. "Come over here." Ann patted the wagon bed. He leaned back into the corner of the wagon. Ann put his injured hand in her lap and his other arm around her shoulder. She leaned against him. He let her stay there as they traveled the remaining four miles through the swamp to Point Remove Creek where there was both a bridge across the creek and a ferry across the Arkansas.

Smitty got down from his wagon to make the arrangements. The prisoners sat inside the wagon out of view. Zachariah sat in the driver's seat, clearly visible. Eli and the three girls sat inside the other wagon also out of view. Noah sat on Eyanosa beside the wagon in plain view. The operator glanced into the wagons to count people then walked back to Smitty. Smitty again left a court script for the top dollar rates that everybody charged him, but he was happy that they were able to cross immediately. Smitty updated the group, "He said it's around six more miles to Gay Creek. Do you want to keep going or camp here?"

Stephanie didn't want to stop. "Let's keep going, at least until we get to fresh air."

"I agree." Ann felt much better after letting the emotions that were upsetting her drain away in the embrace of her husband.

Ben didn't want to hurry, but he didn't want to smell the swamp either. "Let's move on. This air is infecting my lungs."

Roy harassed Ben, "You're pathetic. They're gonna hang you in a few days. Why care?"

Ben glared at him but remained silent.

Smitty agreed to keep going. "We'll see how far we can get."

Ben knew Eli was the one he had to ask for permission for what he felt he needed. "Can I talk to Stephanie?"

Eli wanted to say, absolutely not, but instead said, "Only if she stays out of your reach, and only if she wants to."

Ann made sure Ben understood the consequences, "If you even try to do anything, I will kill you." She, Sally, Noah, and Eli set their rifles to the cocked position and sat in the wagon with the guns pointed directly at Ben.

Ben asked, "What should I do now that I asked God ta fix my heart?"

Stephanie answered as best as she could, "You

probably won't have time to do any of this before they hang you, but read the Bible, make friends with people who also have God in their hearts, and stay away from people who do not. If you can find a church, go there as much as you can."

Ann added something else that she knew was critical, "And talk to God about everything, all the time."

Noah told Ben, "Most recently, God showed me how to escape the fire and the well. God will help you when you are in a difficult situation, even when you see absolutely no way out."

Sally gave her advice as well, "And when you don't think God is there, choose to believe He is anyway. Even if you don't get the answer you want, He is always helping you get through everything."

Ben wondered if that was what had brought the ravens. "You pray ta God ta help ya when your house got shot up?"

Stephanie told him her opinion, "I assure you that we did, and it was God who sent the birds to save us."

Even though he didn't admit to being there, or having anything to do with it, he remembered what had happened. It had been such a strange event. Now that he knew these people, he believed that God had sent the birds to protect His servants.

After Ben stopped asking questions, Noah asked Ann, "Do you want to ride ahead with me to see what's coming up?"

"Sure."

Noah climbed out of the wagon onto his horse. He helped Ann onto Eyanosa in front of him. As they galloped ahead, Roy tried his best to agitate everybody, "Hey, Zachariah, the only thing he's planning on seeing up ahead is Ann."

Eli pointed his rifle at Roy. "Shut your mouth."

Sally laid down her gun, plunked her hands onto her hips, and leaned forward towards Roy. She sassed him, "Good for him. I hope so."

Zachariah had not thought about Ann or Noah since they had left Kuhn Bayou. His mind was much too busy thinking about Minnie. "She's his wife."

NINE

When the rest of the group arrived at Gay Creek, a fire already burned in the fire pit. After the fourteen-mile trip of the day, nobody wanted to struggle with high water. Therefore, to the serenade of crashing water, they ate crayfish at the campsite a hundred yards west of the creek. Stephanie nonchalantly asked, "What kind of guns did you use to shoot up our house? I didn't know there were guns that powerful or could shoot so many bullets so quickly."

Ben looked at her and then looked at Roy giving him a seriously menacing stare. It would be fun to tell them, but he was sitting with a lawman. Even though they had already been found innocent of shooting up the Williams House, he decided it would be wiser to deny than confess. "Got no idea 'bout fast or powerful guns cause we weren't there."

In the morning, they didn't hear the water roaring as they had the night before, so they ate, packed up, mounted up, and then rode the short distance over to the creek. Noah sat on his horse beside the creek that was still quite full with fast moving but much quieter muddy water. "I don't think we can cross."

Not wanting to lose yet another day, Smitty contemplated the options. "You can't see anything through the muddy water. It may not be very deep."

Sally objected, "It doesn't matter. It's too fast."

Smitty commanded Noah, "Try to ride Eyanosa across."

Noah refused, "I'm not going into that creek."

"Then, I'll try it." Smitty urged Bliss into the water.

"Don't do it." Ann tried to stop him.

Roy tried to reason with Smitty. "It's not fair to make us go against our wills."

Roy's opinion meant nothing to Smitty. He kept right on into the water. Ben and Roy rode inside the wagon and complained loudly. Halfway across, the rear of the wagon swung into the current. Bliss slipped. Smitty was sure they were washing away, and he was a fool, but then Bliss regained her footing, struggled against the current, and got them to the far side. Smitty called out from the other side. "I told you we could make it."

Zachariah refused to do the same, "You were lucky. I'm not going into that creek."

Noah looked at Zachariah. "Good man."

Eli joined the rebellion. "And I'm not letting these girls go into that creek either."

"You'll be safe. Tequila is stronger than Bliss, and your wagon is heavier than mine; the current won't move it."

"No." Noah unsaddled Eyanosa.

Smitty unhitched Bliss. *Don't they realize that I'm the boss?*

Zachariah knew he didn't do it. "Which one of you killed Gus? Smitty's over there, so somebody acknowledge the corn."

Noah answered, "I could have, and I sure wanted to, but I didn't."

Ann said, "I would have waited until I could have tortured him." Zachariah couldn't believe that Ann again said that she'd wanted to torture the man. He just couldn't perceive Ann as anything but sweet and kind.

"It wasn't me," Sally stated what her whole family thought, "but he deserved it, and I'm glad he's dead."

Stephanie didn't like being accused. "None of us needs to answer to you, and how do we know you didn't do it?"

Eli echoed, "Exactly, maybe you killed Gus."

"If I did it, why would I ask? I'd know it was me."

Ann stated the logical reason, "It could be a trick to make us think you didn't do it."

"Just forget it." Zachariah dropped the subject but thought he had it figured out. He decided it must have been Stephanie or Eli or probably they did it together.

Smitty, Ben, and Roy had a hungry day and night while those with all the food stayed on the west side of Gay Creek and enjoyed a relaxed dinner and supper. Then, protected by the fast-flowing creek taking the recent rain to the Arkansas River, they enjoyed a worry-free night safely separated from Roy and Ben. Smitty, however, spent the night awake worrying.

In the morning, those on the west side of the creek ate a hearty breakfast. While the girls cleaned up, the men went to look over the crossing. The water looked quite a bit lower. Smitty hollered across the water and again tried to get them to cross.

Noah agreed to test the waters. He went back to camp and saddled up. Eyanosa waded into the edge of the water. It didn't seem too bad. He continued in. The water pushed them where it was the deepest. Although they were several feet downstream, they arrived at the other side of the creek without any problem. Noah rode up the east side of the creek on the dry land. He joined Smitty and the prisoners. "I think we can get across." He told the people on the other side of the creek, "You can do it."

Eli and Zachariah knew Noah wouldn't let the girls cross if he didn't think it was safe, so they hitched up Tequila and packed everything, including the extra breakfast. The girls rode in the wagon as Zachariah returned to the creek. Tequila did not like it at all, but he did as Zachariah signaled and stepped into the water. The heavy wagon had no problem staying on the bottom as Tequila pulled it across the ford. Roy tried to provoke them as they pulled out of the water, "Cowards."

Noah expressed his priorities. "I'm not risking the safety of my family even to take you to your execution."

Sally had had more than enough irritation due to Roy. She held up the pan full of eggs and bacon, and the pot of hot coffee. "If you're going to be like that, I'll pour this on the ground."

Ben's stomach growled. "Apologize, Roy."

Smitty contemplated. If Sally was willing to pour their food out just because Roy called them cowards, maybe she was capable of killing a man. Smitty thought for sure Roy would never apologize. He wondered if Sally would do it. She turned the pot to the side. Coffee poured out the spout.

Roy was ravenous. "I'm sorry I called you a coward. You were smart."

"Exactly." Sally put down the coffee, bacon, and eggs, and climbed out of the wagon before she divided breakfast into their plates and cups. Smitty saw the expression of triumph on Sally's face as he took his share.

TEN

The next eight miles they barely spoke. Smitty rankled because he hadn't gotten what he wanted the day before and because Sally had almost destroyed his breakfast over something petty. Everybody else felt irritated that Smitty hadn't cared about safety. Roy, however, smiled happily because his captors were upset with each other.

Smitty stood beside Cadron Creek still irked over Gay Creek. A tall man with light brown hair graying at the temples joined them. Now, also highly agitated by the absence of the ferry, Smitty barked, "Where is it?"

The ferryman offered his opinion, "The water was running high and fast, the ropes snapped, and the ferry floated away. It's probably on the Arkansas River."

Smitty, filled with frustration over a third delay, encouraged them to cross immediately, "You were able to cross Gay Creek. We can ford this one, too."

The ferryman looked Smitty in the eyes. "Cadron Creek is much bigger. You won't make it."

Agitated and tired from the lack of sleep, Smitty begged, "Come on. We'll never get there. We're days behind, and we still have days to go." Nobody moved towards compliance. "I'll prove we can do it." He flicked the reins and ordered Bliss forward. She walked to the edge but then stopped. Smitty flicked the reins again. The horse tried to back away.

The ferryman warned, "Your horse knows not to go into the water. You should wait."

Smitty whipped Bliss hard on her rump. The horse stepped in. They were barely into the creek when the wheels lost contact with the ground. The current grabbed the wagon. Bliss tried to recover control, but her feet lost contact. She tried to swim, but along with the wagon, she ended up completely under the power of the swift waters. They rapidly floated away. Zachariah, the girls, and Eli ran alongside the creek screaming, "Cut loose!"

Bliss thrashed in a panic. Roy begged, "Don't do it! We'll drown!"

Ben realized his end was upon him. He decided to meet God with a clean heart. He screamed, "I killed Gus. Do you hear me? I killed him with this." He pulled a long thin blade out of the inside seam of the boots he had taken from Gus. Roy charged him. The shiv flew out of Ben's hand and skidded to the far end of the wagon. Roy lunged for the knife. Ben blocked. Roy attempted to shove Ben overboard.

Noah galloped beside the creek. "Get Bliss out of the harness!"

Smitty decided he'd let Roy and Ben kill each other. He climbed out and fumbled with the harness buckle but couldn't work it under the pressure of the fast water against his fingers. He started to cut the leather strap as the water carried them away faster than Noah could ride Eyanosa through the trees.

The ferryman made sure those who came back to the crossing knew he wasn't responsible, "I told him he wouldn't make it."

They all knew Smitty was responsible for his fate, but only Eli replied, "We know."

The man pointed. "You can camp over there while you wait for the water to go down. By the way, I'm Israel Cotton."

They introduced themselves then drove to the field where instructed to camp. Zachariah unhooked Tequila. "Now we know who killed Gus."

Stephanie handed the dutch oven to Sally. "I never would have guessed that he had a knife in his boot. It's a good thing everybody stayed out of reach."

Zachariah tethered his horse where it could feast on grass all night. "To tell you the truth, I thought you did it."

Stephanie couldn't believe anybody thought she had killed the man. "Why would you think I did it?"

"Because you didn't tell me you didn't, and you shifted to saying I did, which I know I didn't."

"That's ridiculous. Stephanie wouldn't hurt anybody," Eli defended Stephanie.

Zachariah rejoined the group at the wagon. "And I thought you helped her."

"Then why weren't you afraid of them?" Ann reached for the food Sally held out to her.

"I didn't shoot up your house, burn down your farm, or try to strangle any of you."

"True." Ann carried the food to the fire pit.

"Anyway, now we know it was Ben. I wonder if he's drowned." Sally climbed out of the wagon with the rest of the food she planned to prepare for supper.

Stephanie spread out a tablecloth on the ground. "If he did, at least he accepted Jesus first."

Ann laid the food on the cloth. "Let's pray that they didn't drown and don't drown, especially Smitty." They joined hands and knelt on the tablecloth as Ann prayed, "Smitty, Ben, Roy, and Bliss need your help, God. Even though Smitty stupidly drove the wagon into Cadron Creek, and it's his fault, save them from drowning. If You are going to allow them to die, put it into Smitty's heart to accept You first. I know he may only have minutes to decide, but please help him to do it." Then, as they prepared for the coming night, they individually silently prayed.

Even after he lost sight of the wagon, Noah continued to ride along the creek. When he arrived at the junction of Cadron Creek and the Arkansas River, he saw the wagon in the river channel. It was too far away to see what had happened to Bliss, Smitty, Ben, or Roy. Since there was nothing he could do to help, he rode back towards Military Road. Two hours later, Noah rode into camp.

Ann asked, "What happened?"

"Last I saw before they were out of view, Smitty was trying to get Bliss out of the harness. Roy and Ben were fighting each other in the wagon. I rode all the way to the Arkansas River. The wagon was floating way out in the river, but I couldn't tell if there was anybody in it or if Smitty was able to get Bliss free."

"We've been praying." Zachariah handed Noah a cup of hot coffee then took Eyanosa to the same spot where Tequila enjoyed the grass.

"I've been praying as well. We need to go to Little Rock and report what happened. There's nothing else we can do but pray while we wait to cross the creek."

Stephanie fretted, "How can we tell Mara?" She didn't actually want an answer because it would be too awful.

Noah tried to alleviate her concerns, "Smitty probably got to shore somewhere," but they went ahead, and each took a turn to add words in a prayer for them. Then they ate, and then they worried all night.

The following morning, the water was down significantly. Zachariah looked at the creek with the lanky middle-aged man who ran the ferry. "What do you think, Israel?"

"There's still a strong current. The problem with trying to take a wagon across is that the current grabs it, and it's too much for the horse. You might be able to cross without one."

Noah volunteered, "I can try it on Eyanosa."

Ann was not letting Noah go into the creek even if she had to drag him off his horse, "Don't you dare!"

Noah figured if the water swept him away, and he didn't drown, that Ann would kill him for trying. "All right, I won't."

Zachariah offered, "Tequila is much heavier. Maybe I can cross on my horse."

Ann pleaded, "We don't have to hurry. Just wait. Please. I do not want to lose anybody else. We just don't have to try right this very instant."

Sally backed her sister, "Ann's right. She always knows what we should do. Just like back home."

Ann snapped back, "Don't put it on me, Sally. I don't want to be responsible for any decisions."

Sally ran away to the wagon. Stephanie chastised Ann, "You already made the decision, Ann, and you didn't need to bark at Sally, she was on your side." Stephanie went to the wagon after Sally. As Sally cried, Stephanie held her.

Ann walked to the wagon with her head hung down. She climbed in with her sisters. "I'm sorry, Sally. I was wrong to snap at you. Remember when we were in the field in the rain with the lightning all around? You said you weren't afraid. Remember I told you that I was?"

"I remember." Sally sniffled.

"I didn't want you to get hurt. I was afraid I couldn't protect you. It's the same now. I'm afraid. I can't keep anything from happening, and God isn't keeping us safe. I feel helpless. I pray for God to protect us but these things just keep happening. I can't take it, but I shouldn't have taken out my frustration and fear on you."

Stephanie corrected Ann's thinking, "It's not your job to control the world. Stop trying to do God's job, and trust Him. Besides, He has gotten us safely through it all. We may have lost the farm, but we haven't lost each other, and we have Noah and Eli now. I think God has blessed us."

Sally pointed out that Ann was doing an excellent job of protecting them, "Besides, you have kept us safe. Smitty's the one who went into the creek when we all told him not to do it."

"Still, it's hard to feel like it's all on me. Both of you, please forgive me."

"I forgive you." Sally hugged Ann.

"Of course, I forgive you." Stephanie wrapped her arms around both her sisters. They drew strength from each other, then got out of the wagon, and rejoined the men.

Zachariah didn't want to upset the girls. "I won't try to go across yet."

Ann turned to Israel. "If Israel thinks it's safe, do what you want."

Everybody looked at the ferryman. "I can't guarantee it's safe, but if you don't try to take a wagon, start from here, and head straight over to that tree, I think you can make it." He pointed across the creek to a large tree with a board nailed to it.

"I'm going to try."

"Take these ropes across for me, and I'll consider the passage paid for all of you." Israel demonstrated how to thread the rope through the pulleys and how to tie the knots he needed by doing so with one end of the lines.

As Zachariah practiced, Noah watched carefully and examined the pulley system. Eli saddled Tequila and tied the other end of the ropes to the saddle horn. Zachariah mounted up and rode into the fast-moving water towards the target tree. Each time Tequila picked up his foot he struggled to put it down in front of the place it left. He then securely planted his foot before he picked up the next one. Zachariah redirected Tequila into an angle almost directly upstream so that there was less horse-body for the water to push. They moved barely towards the far bank. The rest of them watched anxiously and prayed that they would make it safely.

God answered their prayers. Zachariah and Tequila climbed out of the floodwaters across the ford. Everybody let out a cheer. Israel hollered over the roaring waters. "Tie the rope around the tree just above the board then put the feed line through the little pulley. Don't forget to tie it with the knot I showed you."

Feeling good about being the hero, Zachariah hitched the ropes using the proper knots. "It's tied on good, tight, and right."

"What now?" Noah asked Israel.

"Pack up."

On the west side of the creek, they got the wagon ready, and Noah hitched Eyanosa into the harness while Zachariah threaded the ropes through the primary pulley tied to the tree.

At the ford, Israel had attached a traveling board that would slide across the main support rope hooked on with "C" clamps. Around the front and the back end of the wagon, they ran the two thick straps bolted to the traveling board. They also tied the leads fastened at the front end of the moving board, to the side of Eyanosa's harness.

Noah and Eli sat in the driver's box with the girls in the wagon bed. The wagon, secured to the rope high above the creek, remained upright with no downstream pull. Eyanosa, also attached to the support line, safely pulled them across. They unhitched the wagon and waved to Israel who pulled the harness back to his side of the creek with the smaller feeder rope.

ELEVEN

Across Cadron Creek, under oaks and hickories, they started on the next leg of their journey without Smitty, Roy, or Ben. The land rose and fell in gentle slopes. They crossed the low areas full of the previous week's rainwater on short wooden causeways built to prevent travelers from sinking into the mire and becoming stuck until the land dried out. Happily, Military Road stayed close to the Arkansas River. If Smitty had made it to shore, they should find him and not miss him along the way.

They set up camp in a clearing close to the next stream. Unfortunately, previous travelers had used almost every piece of burnable wood in the immediate area, and they had already used all the cedar logs they had brought. All they had that was easily burnable were the cedar boughs on which they slept. They used them to get the fire started with the small amount of still damp wood they found reasonably close to camp.

While Stephanie cooked the rice and beans in the two cast iron pots, Ann made willow tea in the coffee pot and started the cedar poultice in the dutch oven. With so little wood to keep the fire going, it barely burned long enough to cook the rice. When the fire burned out, the beans were still hard in the middle. The tea had steeped correctly, but the cedar poultice was not thoroughly cooked.

Stephanie's head and Eli's rope-burned arm were healing well and didn't hurt at all. They declined the use of the tea but thought it best to go ahead and use the poultice to prevent infection from setting in. Before Ann tied her handkerchiefs of undercooked cedar to her neck and arm, she dabbed it onto all her cuts from her removal from the well. Noah put one around his snake-bit hand, and Zachariah tied one around his head. Ann, Noah, and Zachariah each drank a cup of willow tea.

Eli took a bite of food. "Crunchy beans. I love 'em."

"It's not my fault the fire burned out." Stephanie hit Noah's plate violently with the spoon as she put his share of beans on it. Noah's plate flew into the dirt.

Eli replied, "I know. I'm joking with you."

"We sure are a sorry bunch." Zachariah tried to change the subject.

Stephanie recovered Noah's plate. As she washed it, she looked at the group wrapped in bandages eating hard beans. She laughed. "I guess we do make quite a picture." She gave Noah his cleaned plate back full of beans he could barely eat.

Later, Noah took Eli to check the horses. "I think the girls are at their edge of tolerance. We should be careful about what we say."

"You're right. I knew Ann was upset, but I didn't realize Stephanie was too. Truthfully, I'm right there with them."

"I am too. After everything in Harmony, then people trying to get every penny out of us, but mostly Smitty being washed away, it just gets hard to take."

They walked back to camp in the twilight. Since the fire was out, they went ahead and put their bedrolls down over their cedar boughs. Noah lay beside Ann. She didn't understand. "What are you doing? I thought we needed to keep apart."

"I talked to Zachariah. I told him I wasn't going to hurt you to not hurt him."

"Thank you. It means so much to me that you care more about me than anybody else."

"Bring those lips over here." Noah kissed her then pulled her close and tried to sleep. Nobody slept well. They all fretted over the fate of Smitty and even about the fate of Ben and Roy.

Late in the night, Sally whispered, "I'm cold."

Ann offered her body heat, "Get your blankets, and come lay beside me."

"I've already got them." Sally put her blanket beside her sister. She lay right behind Ann and stretched her arm across Ann and Noah. "Love you to the moon and back."

Noah raised his head. "Good night, little sister."

"Good night, brother. I love you to the moon and back as well." Sally did love Noah, and she loved him being her brother. Her family had one more of the right people, and that made her happy.

In the morning, they scoured the area for usable wood. When they knew they had enough for a good long fire, they built one. The girls roasted the hickory nuts around the fire they used to make willow tea, cedar poultice, bran porridge with cedar cones and sunflower seeds, bacon, and coffee. While the food cooked, the men went on a second wood-gathering expedition. They brought the small additional amount of wood they found back to the fire before they filled their bellies.

Since they didn't know what they would find at their next stop, beside the fire, they left the hickory nuts to roast and the wet wood to dry. Again, they collected fallen branches even if the wood was rotten. After several hours, they had all returned. The girls moved the nuts away from the fire and put the new batch of wet branches beside it.

Zachariah, Eli, and Noah took turns chopping down a close-by dying tree. Meanwhile the girls opened the nuts, saved the shells to use as kindling, and put the nutmeat into empty pots. Except for the three rotten sticks Zachariah used to make an arrow pointing to the tree they had cut down and left, they departed with all the wood.

TWELVE

At Kuhn Bayou, Harry ate breakfast the third day after he had returned then put down his fork. "I'd better go report this marriage and collect this money. I'm going to leave the key with you. Let people cross and collect the money. I'll be back to get it and bring more supplies." He packed Smitty's scripts, which he'd billed at top rates for passage, boarding, meals, and against Minnie's protestations had even charged for the mussels that Noah had harvested from the river. Harry looked over the marriage document before he put it in his saddlebag then rode away leaving Minnie again alone in the woods beside the bridge.

THIRTEEN

Zachariah stood in the wagon. "I think I see something." He looked with the spyglass he had carried ever since Smitty had been ripped from them. "I do."

"Let's find out if it's Smitty." Noah hurried in the direction of what might be the remains of his friend.

"There it is." Eli pointed to a mass of wooden planks beside the river.

They left their wagon in the dirt road, and walked through the trees. Stephanie pointed out the scratches at the rear of the wagon. "I recognize these marks."

"Smitty got this side of the harness cut." Noah held up the end of the leather strap.

Zachariah examined the wagon bed. "The boards holding the chains are broken off. I think Roy and Ben are loose."

Noah knew he should, but right then, he didn't care about them. He and Smitty had been mad at each other. Noah felt horrible. He wanted to know what had become of his friend and looked for clues about Smitty and Bliss. "The wagon tongue is broken. I think Smitty freed Bliss."

Ann breathed a sigh of relief. "Since the wagon is here, they must have gotten to shore."

Sally worked the kingpin from the wagon tongue. In a cheerful voice she stated, "This is good news."

Eli unhitched the remains of the leather riggings. "Except, Ben and Roy are free again."

Stephanie stood beside Eli. "I don't know about Roy, but Ben's heart has changed. He won't come after us again."

Zachariah examined the wheels. Every one of them was cracked. He urged the others to go back to the road. "There's nothing else here to salvage."

Eli started back towards the working wagon. "We need to maintain a sharp lookout, in case Smitty needs our help or the others are waiting to attack us."

They had spent a long time in camp that morning and had traveled slowly looking for survivors, so they arrived at Palarm Bayou long after the sun had set. Without eating, they set up and immediately retired for the night.

In the morning, Noah explained to the bridge attendant, "We need to cross the Bayou to report the possible death of Sheriff Smithfield Wyman and the prisoners we were taking to Little Rock. We don't have money. We can write you a script just like Sheriff Wyman did at all the previous crossings."

"If you aren't the Sheriff, that script wouldn't be worth the paper it's written on. What you got to trade?"

"Nothing." Noah believed that to be the truth.

"Let me look through what you have. Maybe I'll take something in trade." Noah looked to see how the others felt about letting the man search their wagon. They nodded that it was acceptable. The attendant saw something he wanted safely tucked away but easily accessible. "I'll trade for the bow and arrows."

"No," together they emphatically refused.

"So, then, not the bow." He climbed into the wagon bed and left everything scrambled and strewn about as he dug around.

"I'll take the dutch oven and this big cast iron pot."

"We won't be able to cook if you take the big pot and the dutch oven." Stephanie looked at Ann and Sally.

Sally suggested a possibility, "We should only have a few more days. If you'll take the dutch oven and the little pot, we can get by with the skillets and the big pot. Will you trade for the dutch oven and the smaller pot?"

"Done." The man jumped out of the wagon then reached up for his pot and dutch oven. "Go on across."

FOURTEEN

They traveled seven miles through broken countryside filled with cedar, oaks, hickories, and pines looking for signs of those swept into the Arkansas River. When the sound of flowing water grew loud, and they had not found any more clues about Smitty's fate, they felt highly dejected. If Smitty had made it to shore, he should have done so much closer to the wagon's remains and surely before White Oak Bayou.

Sally cocked her head. "Do you hear somebody yelling?"

Zachariah pulled out the spyglass. "It's Smitty and Bliss! Jump in." Eli and the girls quickly climbed into the wagon. Zachariah urged Tequila into a run.

Noah ran his horse straight through the creek. He swung down beside Smitty and affectionately slapped him on the back. "Thank God you're safe."

"I almost didn't make it. I'll tell you what happened when everybody gets here."

"What about Ben and Roy?"

"They're gone. I think they're alive."

Zachariah knew how Ann felt about crossing through the water. He pulled Tequila to a halt just short of the ford, tested the water then navigated slowly to make sure it was safe. Ann, Stephanie, Sally, and Eli jumped out of the wagon before Zachariah completely stopped on the other side. The girls ran to Smitty and hugged him tightly. "I'm so glad you're safe. Thank God you're alive." Stephanie felt a huge relief. Not only was Smitty alive, but also she wouldn't have to tell Mara that her husband was gone.

"Come to the fire. I'll tell you what happened."

The men got Eyanosa and Tequila settled in beside Bliss. The girls brought out the one remaining pot and the two skillets to start cooking. Smitty had had no food since he had washed away. He'd hoped they would prepare a big meal. "What happened to the other pot and the dutch oven?"

Ann told him their plight, "We traded them to get across Palarm Bayou. Now that we have you with us again, we'll be able to cross the Arkansas River with your script. We didn't know how we'd get across."

Noah joined them at the fire. "We decided we should still go to Little Rock and report what happened. We thought we'd figure out how to cross the river when we got there."

"Tell us what happened." So she could hear every word, Sally sat close beside Smitty.

FIFTEEN

***

The outlaws and their captor went down the creek fast. Every splash flung muddy water into Smitty's face. The odor was strong and the flavor of the dirt filled his mouth. He could barely get a breath. Smitty thought, *we're all dead.* Through the water spray, he saw Noah racing beside the creek.

"Get Bliss loose." Noah ducked to avoid a low branch. In the deafening roar of water, Roy and Ben slugged it out in the wagon. Noah thought, *maybe those lowlifes will kill each other.*

As Smitty made his way out to Bliss, the wagon went out of view. He tried to work the buckle of the harness, but the water forced his fingers away. Since he couldn't do it, Smitty drew his knife and sawed at the leather. One strap cut through. *Finally!* He started toward the other and looked back to see what was happening in the wagon.

Roy had the shiv. He lunged, stabbed at Ben, and screamed, "You're not getting away with killing Gus."

Ben jumped back to slowly. Blood ran from his gut. "Maybe not but now Gus didn't get away with killing Pete either."

Roy charged again. Ben sidestepped. Roy went

over. The tension of Roy on the end of the chain pulled the wagon up on its side and Bliss part way out of the water. Smitty tried to get to his horse dangling on the tipped-up tongue of the wagon.

Ben looked at the tight chain. *Roy won't be able to get above the water. Maybe saving him will help make up for all the bad things I've done.* He kicked and kicked at the board holding Roy's chain. One end broke loose. He ran to the other end.

Roy went around one side of a huge rock. The wagon rolled again. Roy came out of the water. Bliss flipped upside down under the surface. Ben still clung to the wagon, kicking furiously until he finally broke the board completely loose from the wagon. The water sucked Roy away.

Without the counterweight of Roy, the wagon came back down, Bliss went right side up, Smitty was flung into the water, and their wild ride resumed. Luckily, Smitty still held the harness reins wrapped around his hand. As he swirled, he saw Ben trying to bust free. Smitty managed to pull himself to Bliss and climbed on. By then, Ben had broken his board free. He stepped over the front of the wagon.

Smitty realized his mistake. *I should have listened back in Harmony. We should have executed him and the others right then and there.*

Ben busted the yoke that attached the harness to the wagon's tongue. He looked Smitty squarely in the eye before he jumped into the water.

Smitty spit creek water from his mouth and clung

to his horse. *I can't believe he freed Bliss from the wagon, but I sure am glad. She would have drowned before I could have cut the other strap.*

The current swept him and his horse into the Arkansas River. Smitty knew it was up to Bliss. "Get to the bank." A long way downstream, but much closer to the shore, Smitty feared Bliss wasn't going to last much longer. He encouraged her, "You can do it." They drew near, but soon Bliss could only float with the current. Pulling Bliss by the reins, Smitty took over and swam toward salvation. "Just a little farther, Smitty, Don't give up!" he told himself.

They went downriver quickly as Smitty struggled toward the shallow water. Suddenly, he felt strong resistance. *What?* He put his feet down. *Nothing.* He forced himself only a few feet down before he felt the riverbed. Smitty popped back up. "Walk, Bliss!" Barely able to do so, his horse complied. They made it onto the dry ground and collapsed. Smity lay beside Bliss and hugged his horses' neck. "You saved us. You are one great horse."

Smitty let Bliss rest and graze for a whole day before they started back toward Cadron Creek.

***

SIXTEEN

Beside the fire, Smitty stated his opinion. "I don't know for sure what happened to Roy or Ben, but I suspect they got to shore. I want to tell you that I'm sorry, and I know I'm a stupid man."

Zachariah squirmed where he sat. He avoided a response to the statement. "Now that we don't have Ben or Roy, what should we do? Do we still need to go to Little Rock?"

"I need to report the loss of the prisoners and the wagon, file the scripts, make a claim for last year's pay, yours as deputy, and Betsy's as schoolmarm. Plus, I'll request funds to get home."

"I hope this trip is almost over." Sally asked, "How much longer before we get there?"

"I would guess it's about nine miles to the Arkansas River crossing into Little Rock. We'll be there tomorrow evening."

Ann passed out the plates. "We should get up early and get this trip over."

"I think so too." Noah agreed with Ann, not only because Ann was his wife, but also because getting to Little Rock somehow felt like it would be the end of their troubles.

The others concurred. As soon as the sun was down, they lay on their bedrolls around the fire. Ann happily gave her bedroll to Smitty and shared Noah's. No longer worrying about Smitty's fate, they slept soundly.

They followed their plan, got ready fast, and left early. The land was low most of the way then hilly and rocky just before they arrived at Crittenden Ferry Landing. The man stationed on the north side of the river told them the bad news, "The ferry is on the Little Rock side. It's not due back until morning."

Smitty asked about the other possibility, "What about the lower ferry?"

The man wanted them to wait, so he could earn the fare. "You can go check, but it's half a mile away. If it's not there, you'll have wasted your time, and I have a better place to camp."

Smitty thought they should check. "Let's go see if the lower ferry is still on this side." At the lower ferry, they saw the boat just offshore. Smitty hollered, "Ferryman, earn a fare tonight. Come back."

I'm going anyway and I'd rather be paid. "Be right there." The ferryman remained on the deck of the boat when he docked at the landing. "Seven people, three horses, and one wagon. That will be four dollars. In advance."

Smitty pointed at his tin badge. "I have to give you a court script payable in Little Rock."

"In that case, it'll be five."

"You have paper and a pen?"

"Not here, you can write it over in Little Rock." The man let down the ferry gate. When all were aboard, he secured the latch and started the pull across. To assure that they didn't run out on him, the ferryman went with them to Peabody Inn.

Smitty spoke with the innkeeper, "I need rooms for a few nights, paper, a pen, and ink." Smitty wrote the script for five dollars, handed it to the ferryman, and then started negotiations with the innkeeper as the ferry operator walked away.

Seeing that Smitty was writing court scripts and the amount of the charge, the innkeeper stated his rate at the high-end, "Two dollars a room per night."

Smitty asked, "How many beds in a room?"

"Some have two. Most have one."

Smitty decided to use the same knowledge that made the man ask for higher prices to get a fair deal. "That's the most beds per room? What about big families? What's your name? I'm filing a complaint."

The innkeeper wanted to avoid getting in trouble with the law or getting a bad reputation but still angled for the most he could get. "There's no need for that. I just remembered we do have a couple of open rooms with three beds. The rate is one dollar for each room plus a dollar a bed per night."

"I didn't hear your name."

Being an overweight man, now nervous about what he'd gotten himself into, the innkeeper sweated profusely. "John Peabody. I'm sure we have a nice room that will meet your needs. What do you want?"

Smitty stated his requirements, "One room with three beds, and another with four, two bits per bed per night for two nights."

"It just so happens that I have exactly what you want." Mr. Peabody placed another slip of paper in front of the Sheriff.

Smitty started to write. Ann knew they all stank to the high heavens. "Would it be possible to have a bath? All of us girls can share one tub of water."

Smitty knew every one of them could smell a lot better and figured all of them would appreciate a change of menu items. "Add a bath, and if you have it, a steak, potatoes, collards or some other kind of greens, and some apple pie for each of us. Plus, breakfast in the morning."

Mr. Peabody calculated. "That will make it seven dollars for rooms for two days, two bits and a dollar for seven baths, two dollars and ten cents for supper tonight and breakfast tomorrow, plus three dollars for your horses for two days."

Once the baths were ready, in both the women and men's bathing rooms, they enjoyed a long bath. They gathered in the dining room with the other guests at the inn and ate steaks of beef, baked potatoes, collards cooked with pork fat, and apple pie with thick slices of cheese. After the meal, they enjoyed soft, warm beds extremely glad to be in Little Rock.

SEVENTEEN

Smitty filed his reports, submitted claims for reimbursement of burial expense of Pete and Charlie when he had them laid to rest at Clarksville, burial of Hank at Harmony, and medical services provided by the doctors of both Clarksville and Harmony for the men injured when they captured Ben and Gus the first time.

He asked for payment of the scripts for the provisions he had purchased, passage fees, rental of Horace's wagon and Zachariah's horse. He requested replacement of the lost wagon, funds to get home, the previous year's pay for himself and Betsy, and Zachariah's deputy pay. Last, Smitty informed the clerk, "We want to press charges."

The clerk took all the pertinent information. At that time, there was nothing else happening in Little Rock that required a court hearing, so he put them at the top of an empty page. "I put you on tomorrow's docket."

After they left the courthouse, they walked the streets, looked at a small park, at homes and shops, the cemeteries, a saloon that was Little Rock's other tavern, and then went to the upper ferry.

Stephanie pointed to the ferry. "Isn't that Harry?"

Smitty looked through the spyglass he'd repossessed from Zachariah. "Sure is."

"I can't believe he already left Minnie. I don't want to be here when he gets across." Zachariah stormed off.

As they hurried away, Noah whispered to Ann, "I want to see him turn in our marriage form."

"You want to follow him?" Ann didn't think it was necessary, but she was willing to do so.

Noah nodded. "I don't know why, but I have the feeling that he's not trustworthy."

Ann turned to her sisters. "We're going to explore on our own. We'll be at the inn at dinnertime."

"May I go with you?" Sally asked. Noah turned down Sally's request. Sally thought they wanted to be alone. "Then, I'll see you at the inn."

Noah and Ann followed Harry. He did not go to the courthouse. Instead, he went to one of the houses in town, unlocked the door with a key, and walked right in. Ann looked at Noah. "That's strange."

"Let's see if he comes back out."

They watched until they had to meet the others. Harry was still in the house. With frustration, Ann stated, "We have to go."

"He must live there."

"Should we tell the others?"

"Let's not, it's not our business."

As they walked to the inn, Ann informed Noah of what she and Sally suspected, "I think something happened between Minnie and Zachariah."

"What makes you think that?"

"One, she was behaving the way I felt after our wedding night. Two, Zachariah was looking at her that way. And three, the way they both acted when Harry came home."

"That complicates things. Let's keep this to ourselves."

Noah and Ann entered the inn and heard Zachariah fussing. "I'm telling you, he has to be living here in Little Rock while he leaves Minnie alone in a dangerous place." Zachariah confronted Noah, "I followed Harry. I saw you there. Don't deny it."

Noah sat. "We never said we weren't there."

"What do you think?"

Ann picked up the peas. "We wanted to see him turn in our marriage paper."

"That's not what I meant, and you know it."

Noah spooned mashed turnips unto his plate. "We think he lives in the house he entered. He opened the door with a key, walked right in, and remained there all morning."

Stephanie passed a platter so big that she had to use both hands. "What difference does it make? It doesn't have anything to do with us."

Zachariah took the hot, juicy pork chops. "It has something to do with me."

"It does?" Stephanie asked.

Smitty motioned for Zachariah to pass the meat. "I saw you get into your blanket that morning."

"What?" Stephanie took the peas.

Zachariah thought he had been discreet. "So you all know?"

Together, Stephanie and Eli said, "I don't know."

Sally put potatoes on her plate. "I knew Zachariah slept with Minnie."

Zachariah felt embarrassed that a fourteen-year-old girl knew what he had been doing. "How did you know?"

"I'm observant. You two were as obvious as Noah and Ann, and Eli and Stephanie."

Ann looked at Stephanie. "Have you two been together?"

Eli stood up. "That's none of your business."

Across the table, Noah did the same. With an intense scowl, he looked Eli dead in the eyes. "I think it is. Do you remember what you told me? Then you turn around and do exactly what you told me not to do."

Stephanie joined the two men standing, forcefully put down the peas, and defended her honor, "Eli has never even kissed me."

Ann stood up, put her hands on her hips, and demanded that Noah explain, "Just what did Eli tell you?"

Noah told her the truth, "He said he was going to protect you from me because I was going to go too far."

Ann glared at Noah. "That's why you asked me to marry you?"

In front of every person in the dining room, who all watched intently, Noah took Ann's hand. "I asked you to marry me because I love you."

Ann looked into Noah's eyes. She believed he was telling her the truth. She stroked the side of his face. "I believe you. I'm sorry."

Smitty motioned towards the people in the room. "I think you all just put on quite a show for the locals."

Ann wanted to hide. "Maybe we should leave."

John Peabody came up behind her with an apple and a cherry pie. "Just grin, and be happy that you have an exciting life." He placed the pies on the table.

Eli started the blessing. Ann whispered, "Wait."

"Why?" Eli said, "I thought the blessing was important to you."

"At this moment, we're not a good example. I don't want others to get the idea that this is the way Christians behave; arguing and fussing and sleeping with another man's wife."

It didn't matter to Zachariah. "I've never claimed to be a Christian."

Ann chastised Zachariah and pleaded with Eli, "You still did the wrong thing. Eli, if you have to say a blessing right now, then just don't say the blessing out loud. Please."

Eli cut a slab of cherry pie. "I won't say the blessing."

Zachariah took a slice of the apple pie. "I don't know what any of you plan to do after we eat, but I'm going to see if I can find out what Harry's doing."

Smitty figured it wouldn't do any good but told Zachariah what he thought, "You should leave Harry alone and Minnie too."

When the last bite went down the hatch, Zachariah wiped his mouth and stood up. Noah got up with him. "Since you want answers and I want my marriage recorded, we might as well go together." They returned to their spying activities.

Late that afternoon, Harry came out of the house wearing a different wedding ring. A very shapely woman, carrying a baby left with him. Zachariah started towards Harry. "I'm going to beat the stuffing out of him."

Noah held him back. "That's not the solution."

"Minnie deserves better."

"Let him file our form then figure out what to do about it, and think about what that woman and that baby deserve." Noah and Zachariah stealthily followed them to a house where an older couple invited them in and kissed each one as they entered.

Zachariah believed he accurately understood what the situation was. He felt furious. "I don't think he's filing your paper today." He stormed off.

"I don't think so either." They went back to the inn to the room the men shared. They told Smitty and Eli about what appeared to be Harry's second family.

As a lawman, Smitty advised them, "He'll get around to filing that document, Noah. Don't fret over it. Zachariah, I'm telling you to leave it alone. You will only make a big mess if you stir this up, and you won't make Minnie happy by telling her."

Both men heard the words that Smitty spoke, but Zachariah still stewed over Harry's treatment of Minnie, and Noah fretted over a sheet of paper because he wanted his marriage to be complete and legal.

EIGHTEEN

At the appointed time, the group went to the courthouse. They hoped that the judge would hear the cases in the absence of Gus, defendant number one, murdered by Ben, defendant number two, who they heard confess and saw brandish the murder weapon. Also without defendant three, Roy, who along with defendant two had escaped due to Smitty's bad judgment in taking the wagon across Cadron Creek.

Judge Hall tapped his gavel. "This court will now hear the cases of the attempted murders of Eli Yates, Noah, Ann, Stephanie, and Sally Williams and the destruction of the Williams Farm, animals, and crops by Gus Hutchinson, Benjamin Rowe, and Roy Butterfield. Judge Daniel Hall presiding. Sheriff Wyman, come forward." Smitty stepped up to the judge's bench. "State your opening remarks."

"The charges are the destruction of property, buildings, crops, and livestock, and the attempted murders of Ann Williams, Stephanie Williams, Sally Williams, Noah Williams, and Eli Yates. Benjamin Rowe and Gus Hutchinson were previously tried for attempted murder of Ann, Stephanie, and Sally Williams, and Eli Yates. Also, Roy Butterfield was previously charged with attempted murder of Noah Williams. Unfortunately, they were all found innocent the first time. They've tried to murder them a second time. Therefore, we accuse Roy Butterfield, Gus Hutchinson and Benjamin Rowe of the attempted murders of Noah Williams, Ann Williams, Steph–"

Judge Hall interrupted, "Wait a doggone minute. You're saying that Roy Butterfield, Gus Hutchinson, and Benjamin Howe have all been accused of attempting to murder these people in various configurations in the past and are now being accused again? The first time they were found not guilty. Now, you're switching it around and accusing them in my court?"

"Well, yes, I guess you could say that. We also claim that the three defendants killed three horses, three turkeys, and nine chickens. Plus they burned down twenty acres of corn ready for harvest, seventy-eight acres of wooded land, a two-acre meadow along with the main house, the barn, the smokehouse, and the sugar shack, all in the meadow."

Assuming that the defendants would soon be brought from the jail, Judge Hall proceeded. "This should be interesting. Call your first witness."

Smitty waved his first witness forward. "I call Noah Williams."

Judge Hall instructed him, "Place your left hand on the Bible, and raise your right hand." Noah raised his hand wrapped in a bandage. The judge needed to look for a brand in the palm of Noah's hand to know if he had ever been in prison. "Take that bandage off. What's wrong with your hand?"

Noah gave the bandage to Ann. "A snake bit me."

He raised his right hand, displayed the smooth skin of his palm, and put his left hand on the Bible.

"Do you, Noah Williams, swear to tell the truth, the whole truth, and nothing but the truth? So help you God."

"I swear to tell the whole truth. So help me God."

"Tell me what happened."

Noah pointed at the girls. "I was working for the Williams sisters on their farm. On August 27 of 1839, I went to bed late but awoke when I heard a sound. I looked out the window of the bunkroom and saw fire." He pointed at Eli. "I woke Eli who was sleeping in another bunk in the same room. He and I knocked on the door of the girl's room and told them that we had to get out. We ran to the stairs and started down. Halfway down, a flaming can of oil crashed through the window and landed in the hall at the foot of the stairs. Immediately, a man jumped into the house through the window and ran towards the living room. The flames blocked our way, so we ran back up the stairs and looked out the front window. We saw Gus on his horse holding the Williams' music box that had been on the mantelpiece over the fireplace. He looked up at us looking out the window down at him. He tipped his hat at us before he raced away.

"We escaped the house through the bedroom window. As far as I could see, flames engulfed everything. We barely made it into the well. The next day, after the fire burned out, we got out of the well and found everything burned to the ground. We went to town and captured Ben then Gus and last Roy. The day after that, Sheriff Wyman and other folks went with us to look at the farm. We decided we would bring Gus, Ben, and Roy here for trial."

"That will be all for now. Take your seat. Sheriff, call your next witness."

Smitty called Eli who displayed the smooth palm of his right hand and swore to tell the truth. Eli started his testimony at what he believed was the beginning. "It all started when Noah came to town, went into the saloon, and ordered a meal. He was eating at the bar when Roy, Ben, and Gus, along with Hank, Charlie, Al, and Pete came to town and tried to pick a fight with Noah just because he's an Indian."

Judge Hall stopped him, "All the Indians are supposed to be in Indian Territory, and how does an Indian have the name, Williams?"

Eli answered, "He was in Indian Territory until he came to check on the Williams Farm for a friend. When he got there, he met and then married Ann."

The judge continued his line of questioning on an irrelevant topic, "Is Ann a white woman?"

"Of course she is." Eli looked at Ann, just in case she had miraculously started looking like she was not a white woman.

The judge probed further, "And you say Noah Williams is an Indian?"

Eli continued to speak the truth, "Part Indian, and part white man."

"Are you saying Ann Williams, a white woman, has married Noah Williams, an Indian?"

"Yes, but it has nothing to do with this. What Ben, Roy, and Gus did happened before that."

"When and where did they get married?"

"They married at Kuhn Bayou September 13th of this year."

They all wondered why the judge was asking questions about Noah and Ann's marriage. The judge ordered the local sheriff, "Sheriff Taylor, go pull the marriage document."

Smitty fidgeted uneasily for a few minutes then spoke up, "Your Honor, may I approach?"

"Approach."

"What is it that you're getting at?"

"Interracial marriage is illegal in Arkansas."

"That has nothing to do with this case."

"It is going to be tried as well."

"Then, I'm asking for a recess, so I can examine these laws."

Sheriff Taylor came back into the room. The judge asked, "Did you get them?"

"There hasn't been any marriage recorded for Ann and Noah Williams."

"Eli Yates, you are still under oath. Have there been immoral sexual relations between Ann Williams and Noah Williams?"

Noah stood up. "That's none of your business."

"Sit down. You're already in enough trouble, and it IS the business of this court when an Indian and a white person marry or engage in immoral sexual behavior."

Sally spoke her opinion, "There's nothing immoral about their relationship."

Stephanie silenced her sister, "Be quiet." She didn't want to complicate things by saying anything when they didn't know what was what.

"I heard that, Miss Williams. Are you saying there has been sexual behavior between them?"

"I'm not saying anything." Sally clammed up.

"Sheriff Taylor, take Ann Williams and Noah Williams to jail. Sheriff Wyman, study the law you apparently do not know. We'll reconvene tomorrow."

Stephanie exclaimed loudly, "What?"

Just as Stephanie had done, and for the same reason, Smitty commanded, "Silence! All of you come with me." He took the law books handed to him by Sheriff Taylor at the request of Judge Hall.

When out of hearing, Smitty gave everybody his or her orders, "Zachariah and Eli, I have relatives named Hall. I've never met them. My mother's sister married a man named Daniel Hall. That man is too young, but maybe this judge is her son. I might be able to get leniency as a request from a family member. Find out what you can about Judge Hall. Stephanie and Sally, let's see what we can learn about these laws." Smitty and the girls walked away.

Zachariah looked at Eli. "How are we going to find out anything about a judge?"

"Working in the store, I realized that people like to talk. If you listen, you can learn a lot. You can ask a few indirect questions and discover all kinds of things you might not even want to know."

"All right, let's try the general store."

Sheriff Taylor escorted Ann and Noah at the end of a shotgun barrel. Noah remembered how Judge Atwood had spied and secretly listened while investigating the charges against the Butterfield Gang that spring. Noah assumed somebody would be listening in his current situation, but he didn't have a safe way to tell Ann. The sheriff put Noah and Ann into cells beside each other.

When the sheriff left them, Ann asked, "Noah, what should we do?"

"Leave me alone. You're more trouble than you're worth. I only wanted to have a little fun with a white woman before I went home to my real wife in Indian Territory."

"I don't believe you. You've been acting like you love me."

"Of course I was. How else would you have been willing?"

"But we got married at Kuhn Bayou."

"Why do you think I've been trying to find Harry? I want to stop him from turning in that paper. I don't want to actually be married to you."

Ann looked at Noah and tried to determine what was happening. He steeled himself and looked back into her eyes with his best look of indifference. Noah hated to lie to her, but he didn't know the consequences of breaking interracial marriage law, so he stuck to his usual habit of trying to protect Ann against her wishes.

"Just to let you know, I don't think you're a half Indian or half anything. You're a whole Noah, and you're a better man than those narrow-minded people who came up with these idiotic laws will ever be." She walked to the cot at the far side of the cell and laid there with her back to Noah.

Stephanie took a book. "This is ridiculous. It has nothing to do with the charges we filed."

"True but we better figure out what we can about interracial marriage laws while the judge lets us." Smitty handed Sally a book, opened one himself, and started reading.

In her cell, Ann prayed loudly to be sure that Noah heard, "God, help me understand, and make sure Noah always knows that I love him."

Noah did hear her prayer, but he thought he had a way to make the judge believe that nothing had happened between them. "I don't love you. It's just too bad that I never got to have any fun with you."

Gratefully, she didn't try to talk to him anymore. The sheriff listening on the other side of the door heard every word. When Noah and Ann ceased speaking, Sheriff Taylor told Judge Hall what he had heard.

In the room, they poured over the law books until Stephanie looked up from the book. "Listen to this."

Smitty hoped she had found something that would help. "What did you find?"

"If there is or has been a pregnancy, then the law finds the defendants guilty by default. If two or more people have knowledge of the defendant's cohabitation, then the law finds the defendants guilty by default. Punishment is not more than fifty-nine lashes for the male and not more than twenty-nine lashes for the female. But if there is no evidence of the marriage and no proof of immoral sexual relations and no cohabitation, but there is reasonable cause to believe that a marriage or sexual relations have occurred, then the defendants will be sentenced to not less than one month and not more than one year of hard labor."

Smitty jumped up. "Sheriff Taylor said there isn't anything filed. We have to get that document." He raced out of the room.

Sally watched the door close then looked at Stephanie. "But they've been together."

"You don't know that. Did you see that happen?"

"No."

Stephanie informed her sister of the proper way to look at the situation, "Then you are only guessing as to what may have happened, and guessing has no place in a court of law."

Sally got the drift. "They haven't cohabited any differently than the rest of us at the farm or on the trip here. We've all been together."

"Exactly."

Smitty went to Harry's house. A woman holding a baby answered the door. To determine Harry's relationship with the woman, Smitty asked with specific words, "I have business with your husband. May I speak with him?"

"Come in. May I tell him who is calling?"

"Sheriff Smithfield Wyman."

She walked down the hall. "Harold, Sheriff Wyman is here to see you."

The words had barely left her mouth before Harry flew into the hall and rapidly ushered Smitty out the door. He begged the sheriff to keep his secret. "Please don't say anything to my wife."

"Your wife at the Kuhn Bayou Bridge or your wife in this house?"

"I mean Laura, but don't say anything to Minnie either. I do not want her coming here creating problems. What do you want?"

"I want the marriage document of Ann and Noah Williams."

"I was going to file them. I didn't think it mattered if I did it immediately or not, but I'll have it recorded right now."

"I want you to give the document to me."

"I'm not supposed to let anybody else have them. Why do you want them?"

Not wanting to explain, Smitty countered, "Why do you want two wives?"

"I don't want two wives. I just ended up with this problem. Minnie is not my wife. I never had the marriage recorded."

"So, you want to keep Minnie out in the woods while you live in town with Laura?"

"I don't want Minnie. Whichever of you was messing with her would do me a favor by taking her away."

Minnie was a sweet woman. Smitty wanted to slug the man but held back his desire. "Just give me the paper, or Laura will know all about you."

134

She still wouldn't know all about me. "I'll get them. Stay out here." He came back with an envelope.

To verify that it held what he wanted, Smitty opened the envelope. Along with the marriage record was a note addressed to the clerk of the court to accept and file the document delivered by Sheriff Wyman and signed by Harold LeBarron. "Mr. Harold LeBarron or Harry Pitts, whichever it is, is this the only copy?"

Harold replied with mounting irritation. "I never make copies. Do you need a copy? How many do you need?"

"None, this will suffice. Good day." Smitty had confirmed that he possessed the only document that could incriminate Ann and Noah.

Harold was visibly nervous. "You're not going to speak to anybody about this, are you?"

"If you don't know anything about this marriage or this meeting, then I don't know anything either."

"I know nothing. Still, anytime you need to cross the river, it's free for your entire party." Harold quickly went back into the house.

Smitty stood by the door. He heard the bolt slide into the lock and Laura ask, "What was that about?"

"He just wanted some documents." Harold gave her a quick kiss before retreating to his office to regain his composure.

Smitty returned to the inn with Ann and Noah's unfiled marriage document. Eli and Zachariah returned only knowing that the judge was originally from Tennessee and moved to Little Rock a few years back.

"He could be family. We're from Tennessee." Smitty carefully hid the marriage document and the note in his bag. "Let me read you the law." Smitty read the relevant passage to the men. "Also, whatever you think may have happened between Noah and Ann on their wedding night, or at any other time, is only you guessing. No matter how much you believe you know what happened, you didn't see anything."

NINETEEN

Sheriff Wyman and his group arrived with a plan. The judge entered the courtroom just before the local sheriff brought Ann and Noah over from the jail. "Sheriff Taylor, where are the other defendants?"

Not Sheriff Taylor but Smitty stood up and explained, "Gus Hutchinson is dead. Benjamin Rowe confessed to his murder. He showed us the murder weapon as Cadron Creek swept him, Roy Butterfield, and me into the Arkansas River. I think they are now at large, but I don't know for sure. They may have drowned."

"Since they aren't here, what do you want me to do?"

Smitty stated their request, "Hear the case. Then, if you find them guilty, sentence them. We'll find them and bring them here to serve time at hard labor, or if you find them guilty of attempted murder, the court can execute them."

"The charges are posted. However, due to the death of Gus Hutchinson and the absence of Roy Butterfield and Benjamin Rowe, I can't try the cases. Sheriff Wyman, I would have thought that you would know that the defendants have to be present to have a trial. The case I will now hear is the State of Arkansas against Noah Williams and Ann Williams for the violation of Anti-miscegenation laws. Judge Daniel Hall presiding. Noah Williams, take the stand." Judge Hall looked him in the eyes. "You are still under oath. What is your real last name?"

"I don't have a last name, but I have been known as Noah Swift Hawk."

"You will no longer hide behind the name Williams. The change of name is denied. Do you understand?"

"Yes," Noah affirmed that he understood the statement.

"Noah, did you marry Ann Williams?"

"There was a ceremony to make Ann think we were married. I planned to stop Harry Pitts from recording the marriage and then return to my real wife in Indian Territory after I enjoyed knowing a white woman."

Sally thought, *you liar,* but she knew Noah had said what they needed the judge to believe.

"Did you live with Ann Williams as man and wife?"

"We have been traveling in a group since we left Harmony. Other people have been around us all the time."

"That's not what I asked."

"We have not lived together." Noah believed he told the truth.

"You are saying you engaged in no immoral sexual relations with Ann Williams?"

In his opinion, what was between them was entirely moral. "We did not."

"You never wanted to?"

Noah continued to state the truth, "I already told you I had wanted to have relations with Ann outside of marriage."

The judge felt disgusted and angry that an Indian had tried to have his way with a white woman. "Get out of my sight. Take your seat. Ann Williams, take the stand." Ann went to the stand with eyes red from crying. "Put your left hand on the Bible and raise your right hand. Do you swear to tell the truth, the whole truth, and nothing but the truth? So help you God."

"I swear to tell the truth, the whole truth, and nothing but the truth. So help me God."

"Did you cohabitate with or engage in immoral sexual behavior with Noah Swift Hawk?"

"We've been traveling. Therefore, nobody is living with anybody, and we purposefully did not have immoral relations."

"Did you marry Noah Swift Hawk?"

Ann flung her beliefs about the law that was destroying her life into the courtroom already crowded with hostile feelings. "Yes, and not you or anybody else can tell me that there is something wrong with that."

Of her own free will, a white woman had joined herself to an Indian. Judge Hall felt sick to his stomach. "Go to your seat." Ann walked to the defendant's seats and sat with her back to Noah.

Noah knew he was hurting her. He wanted to hold her and make everything all right, but he knew he absolutely could not.

Judge Hall spoke what he believed was a righteous verdict. Their last thin shreds of hope shattered. "Ann Williams and Noah Swift Hawk, I find you guilty of interracial marriage. The penalty is fifty-nine lashes for Noah Swift Hawk and twenty-nine for Ann Williams. The marriage is annulled. Sheriff Taylor, take the prisoners and carry out the sentence."

Noah begged that Ann be spared. "I'm the guilty one. I manipulated her. She's the victim of my intentions. Give me all the lashes."

Ann realized that Noah was trying to protect her, but there was no way she was giving him up. She stood beside the man she loved. "Give me my lashes because I AM going to live with Noah, I AM going to have all kinds of sexual relations with him and fill the world with our babies, and I'll be right before God, and you'll still be wrong." In his heart, Noah smiled. Ann was magnificent as she stood for her right to love him.

The judge demanded respect, "Silence!"

Ann did not silence herself, "You can't legislate who I love or who loves me."

His face red with anger, Judge Hall stood up and leaned forward. "Silence or I'll charge you with contempt of court and add ten more lashes!"

"Then do it!"

Smitty interrupted, "One moment." He signaled to Ann to be quiet. "Before you finalize the sentence let me read the law you wanted me to study." Smitty read the passage from the law book then continued, "Since Ann is not pregnant, they have not been living in a house as man and wife, there is no evidence that immoral sexual relations have occurred, and even though Ann says she is married, there is no record. Therefore, they are not. In conclusion, I ask that the sentence be hard labor rebuilding the Cadron Ferry. That will spare Arkansas the expense as well as punish Ann Williams and Noah Swift Hawk."

Judge Hall contemplated. He wanted the woman whipped, maybe even to do it himself, but saving the state a large expense could be beneficial to his career. "I agree, but a military unit is to be dispatched with them to ensure that the work is done satisfactorily. No other person is to participate in the project or help in any way. Keep Ann and Noah separated and chained until they have completely rebuilt the crossing and ferry. If I ever find Ann Williams and Noah Swift Hawk together again, I will order maximum flogging and a whole year of hard labor. As for you, Ann Williams, you are insolent and abrasive. I don't know why any man would want to be with you for even one night. You're lucky I don't whip you for contempt of court. Sheriff Taylor, take the prisoners to jail then arrange for the military escort to leave in the morning. Court is adjourned."

As Sheriff Taylor took them back to jail, Ann told Noah, "I'm not going to deny that I love you."

Noah knew it would have been better if Ann had denied their marriage. However, in his heart, he felt the proof that nothing would change Ann's love for him was amazing, and he loved her even more. Neither of them believed that the relationship between them was immoral. They believed that they had told the truth with the one exception that Noah had denied that he wanted a real marriage with Ann. However, Noah thought that he had protected her. He was not going to get her lashed. In his mind, that was final.

Sheriff Taylor went to the arsenal to arrange the escort. All the troops were in the mess hall. "Captain Cornish, I need a unit to escort prisoners to Cadron Creek to rebuild the ferry and stay there until it is completely reconstructed. I'll give you final instructions in writing."

The information would determine whom he would send, so the Captain asked, "Who are the prisoners, and what are the charges?"

"Noah Swift Hawk and Ann Williams are the prisoners. The charges are interracial marriage."

"You're going to waste my men's time over an interracial marriage?"

To Sherriff Taylor, the charges didn't matter. "The court has ordered a military escort."

"How many men do you want? When will they leave?"

"Five men including somebody who knows about ferry construction. They'll leave in the morning."

The Captain stood up and tapped his knife on the side of his tin cup. "I need five volunteers including somebody familiar with ferry construction."

One of the men at the table stood up. "Private First Class Jeremiah Pratt, volunteering for service. I know about building a ferry. I helped build the lower ferry."

"Anybody else?" Nobody else volunteered. "Private Pratt, how long have you been in the army?"

"Almost two years, sir."

"You're promoted to Specialist, and you're leading this mission. Pick four privates to accompany you."

"Thank you, Captain, sir." Jeremiah selected the men he thought were least likely to have a mind of their own and the man he knew was a good cook, "Melvin Hatcher, Justus Keen, Henry Fenn, and John Jackson."

"Prepare to stay for several months. I'll have your final orders and provisions list..." Captain Cornish turned to the sheriff. "When will that be, Sheriff?"

"If we can go over possible construction plans with Specialist Pratt, we can make those determinations right now."

The Captain waved Jeremiah over. Jeremiah acted as if he didn't know Ann or Noah. "Why are we supervising prisoners?"

Sheriff Taylor explained, "Judge Hall wanted to give them lashes, but Sheriff Wyman got him to change the sentence to hard labor. Nobody can help them. The two of them are to stay away from each other. After they complete the ferry, they can't leave together. To tell you the truth, if I had a woman willing to be whipped because she wouldn't deny that she loves me, I would have taken her lashes too."

"He took a whipping for the woman?" Specialist Pratt wasn't surprised. That spring, he had been in Harmony when Judge Atwood had let the remaining members of the Butterfield Gang go free. He had thought Noah seemed like a decent man and not the murderous horse-thieving Indian that Judge Atwood had tried to make Noah out to be.

"No, but he sure didn't want her to suffer a single stroke. I'm sure he would have taken them all. He said he doesn't love her, but he wouldn't have done that if he didn't."

Jeremiah remembered the trial in Harmony. *Just what is the problem that white people have with Indians?* As they planned how to make the work as much like hard labor as possible, Jeremiah made no further comments about the prisoners.

Captain Miles Cornish was impressed with Jeremiah's ferry design. He decided what to do with him. "Specialist in engineering is what you should be, Jeremiah. When you get back, I'll arrange for engineering training."

TWENTY

Jeremiah supervised the preparations. They put the hens Melvin insisted they needed into crates and loaded them into the wagon with all the rest of the provisions for sustaining life. The milk cow that Melvin requested they tied to the rear. They loaded the second wagon with tools locked in crates, along with the construction materials they had to bring from Little Rock.

Smitty also got ready. He acquired another wagon to replace the one he'd lost then went to collect all the funds due as well as funds to cover his expenses to get home. Smitty paid Zachariah the rental fee due for using Tequila and his deputy pay for the trip to Little Rock. Eli and Zachariah packed fresh supplies into Smitty's new wagon and the wagon rented from Horace. Stephanie and Sally waited close to where Ann sat chained in the construction wagon. "May we ride with Ann or walk next to her?"

The soldier standing beside the wagon answered, "Miss Williams is to have no contact. Basically, she's in prison."

Stephanie stated something she had read in the law book. "Prisoners are allowed visitors." She looked at Ann and silently mouthed, "I love you."

Private Melvin Hatcher thought Stephanie was probably correct. "I'll go ask our commander."

Jeremiah listened to the request before he handed Noah over to the private under his command. "Private Hatcher, chain Mr. Swift Hawk into that wagon." He pointed to the wagon that did not contain Ann.

"Yes, sir." Private Hatcher took the completely docile Indian to the wagon.

Sally watched the soldier walk towards them holding his finger to his mouth over his lips. "That's Jeremiah."

Stephanie turned to Eli. "I wonder why that one called Jeremiah, 'sir'."

Eli whispered back his opinion, "He seems to be in charge of the whole thing."

Sally replied, "Curious." She thought, _I'll find out._

Jeremiah introduced his men, "This is Private Melvin Hatcher. He's going to be our cook. These men are Private Henry Fenn, Private John Jackson, and Private Justus Keen." With pride, he added, "I'm Specialist Jeremiah Pratt." As if he didn't already know them, he said, "Please state your names."

"I'm Sheriff Smithfield Wyman, but I go by Smitty." He pointed to each of the members of his group as he introduced them. "This is Eli Yates, Zachariah Eggleston, Stephanie Williams, and Sally Williams."

"This is a military prisoner transportation and work detail. I will permit you to accompany us only if you follow my rules to the letter. Do you all understand?" They nodded their heads affirmative. "Private Hatcher has informed me that you have asked to visit with the prisoner Ann Williams."

Smitty added to the request, "All of us would like to visit both prisoners."

Sally secretly waved to Noah. So she didn't get herself into trouble, Noah acknowledged that he saw as unobtrusively as possible. She smiled at him. He felt furious. They were taking all of them away from him. "Visitation will be during supper. Bring your meal with you. You can join us then but only two visitors per prisoner per visit." Ann and Noah heard there would be visitation privileges. They both needed comfort and silently thanked God.

Jeremiah moved them along at a swift pace. They arrived at White Oak Bayou just after noon. He led them across then issued the command to halt. "We'll have our mid-day meal here. Private Hatcher, a quick cold meal. Private Fenn, go tell the civilians if they want to continue with us, to do the same, and be ready to go on my command." Jeremiah immensely enjoyed making the decisions. _Being in command isn't hard; it's duck soup._

Melvin rationed out the ham, cheese, and bread. However, since apples were in season, and he had plenty, he allowed them to take as many as they desired. Private Fenn delivered the message. In order to be ready when Jeremiah said it was time to go, Stephanie and Sally served cold food directly out of the wagon.

Thirty minutes after they'd stopped, Jeremiah stood up and brushed the crumbs off his lap. Everybody sat within feet of him. They all saw that he was ready to get back into formation. He still called out his orders, "Everybody to your wagons." Again, he thought it felt good to be in command.

Once back underway, Sally brought up a problem, "Stephanie, how are we going to be able to visit if we have to cook?"

"I guess we'll have to take turns."

Smitty knew it was most important that the girls visit. He offered his services, "Tonight, so you two can spend as much time as possible visiting, I'll fix us another cold meal the same as we just ate."

"That's wonderful." Sally smiled happily.

They had not gotten all the way to Palarm Bayou when Jeremiah called a halt. He wanted to have the evening meal and visitation over before dark. As soon as the wagons stopped, Sally and Stephanie went over to Ann's wagon. Private Fenn attempted to send them away. "It's not supper time yet."

Sally held out cheese between two pieces of bread. "Why not? It's suppertime when we're eating. Specialist Pratt, may I speak with you?" Sally walked towards the man who could give her permission to talk with Ann.

Stephanie complained, "Private Fenn says it's not visiting time, but you told us to bring our food, and we could visit while we ate supper. We have ours."

Sally raised her meal. "It's your cook who's slow."

Jeremiah realized how intelligent the girls were. "Let them visit, but keep your eyes on them." He looked at the girls. "Don't try to give Ann anything to use to escape or whatever."

"We wouldn't do anything like that. We appreciate you letting us visit."

They hurried over to Ann who had been desperately hoping Jeremiah would let them come over. She held her arms open, so they could step into her embrace. "You're an answer to prayer. I need your hugs."

Not saying a word, they stood with their arms around each other for several minutes. The wagons were close together. Sally wanted Noah to hear. She told Ann loudly, "I just can't believe this." So that Noah would understand that she meant it for him too, Sally looked directly at Noah as she told Ann, "I love you."

Noah didn't want Sally to get into trouble by overtly notifying him that she loved him. He mouthed, "Love you," back to her as Zachariah arrived with another sandwich made by Smitty.

Zachariah told Noah, "I'm sorry this happened. I don't know what I can do for you, but I'll do everything I can. Somehow it will all work out."

"Not this time." Noah said, "There's no hope."

"Go visit with Noah." Smitty handed Eli a sandwich.

Eli felt mad at himself. "You go. I doubt he wants to see me after what I did."

Smitty went to be Noah's second visitor. "Eli feels responsible. He thinks he caused this to happen. He thinks you don't want to see him."

"It's not his fault. It would have come out one way or another. Besides, I should have considered that being part Indian would be a problem if I married Ann. I want him to visit with me tomorrow. I'm not mad at him." Then, so that he wouldn't let out a tirade of anger and grief, Noah barely said another word.

Smitty and Zachariah didn't know what to say to his silence. Before long Zachariah said, "I guess I'll go."

"I wish you wouldn't. I feel better having you here. I'm just so mad that I can't talk."

Zachariah sat again. "It's all right to be grum. I'll still stay." The three of them silently sat together until Jeremiah told them visiting hours were over. Zachariah said, "I'm here for you," then went back to his wagon.

Before he got away, Noah stopped Smitty. "Tell Eli, this is going to be a difficult time for me, and I need him to be my brother. I want him to visit me. Make sure he knows that I'm not mad at him."

"I will. Together, we'll make it." Smitty thought about prisoners as he made his way back to the area assigned to the civilians. First, he had traveled with prisoners he did not care for even the least little bit. Smitty had tried to interact with them as little as possible but had come to like Ben and had thought it was a shame that Ben had gotten himself into a position where he was most likely going to be hung, but the law was the law, and the law needed to be enforced.

Now, Smitty was traveling with prisoners who were his friends. He wanted to be with them and help them but within the boundaries of the law. However, for the first time since he had become a sheriff, he felt the law was wrong. He still believed he had to uphold the law but had done his best to mitigate its enforcement into something with which he hoped they could all live.

When he got back with his group, Smitty told Eli, "Noah said he is not mad at you, and he needs you to be his brother and to visit with him." Smitty then turned to Zachariah. "Come walk with me." They walked away into the dusk. "I waited until after we had left Little Rock to tell you what happened when I got Noah and Ann's marriage paper."

"So tell me."

"Harry is married to that woman in Little Rock. He goes by Harold LeBarron there. His wife in Little Rock is Laura, and that baby is theirs. He told me that he never recorded his marriage with Minnie. She doesn't know. Harry, or Harold, or whatever his name is, said he doesn't want her, and whoever was messing with her would do him a favor by taking her away."

Zachariah's face turned red. "It's a good thing you didn't tell me. I would've pounded him into the ground."

Smitty calmly listened to Zachariah rant and let his anger out. When he was out of steam, Smitty asked, "What are you going to do?"

"I could leave in the morning, and if she wants to go with me, get Minnie, but I told Noah I would be here for him."

"He has other people here. If you decide to leave, take enough supplies to get to Minnie. Do you want to think it over?"

"I don't need to think about it. Help me move supplies tonight. I'll leave as soon as the sun is up."

"All right, we'll do it now."

Sally, Stephanie, and Eli already had the civilian part of camp set up when Smitty and Zachariah returned. Sally asked, "Where have you been?"

"Talking." Smitty gave Zachariah the privacy he deserved and started moving supplies.

Eli wasn't letting them off that easily, "What's going on?"

Zachariah put the items Smitty passed him into a pile beside the wagon. "I'm leaving in the morning to rescue Minnie." Stephanie rolled eggs in Zachariah's clothes to protect them. Sally and Eli moved supplies out of Horace's wagon into Smitty's. So he would be ready to go in the morning, Zachariah placed his one small bundle of supplies back into the wagon he was taking. Not long into the night, Zachariah woke his friends. "I've changed my mind. I'm leaving now." Eli went for Tequila as Zachariah rolled up his bedding. Smitty attached the harness to Horace's wagon then got Tequila into the harness.

Zachariah traveled easily by the light of the almost full moon. At the Palarm Bayou Bridge, he thought about buying back their dutch oven and pot but decided against it. At Cadron Creek, Israel got up in the middle of the night and put the harness on the line for a traveler. He was surprised when Zachariah came into view. Zachariah informed Israel that Smitty and Bliss had survived and had rejoined them. They didn't know for sure, but Smitty believed that Roy and Ben had not drowned but had escaped. He explained about Ann and Noah, and that the group would probably be there late the next day or the following morning to start building a new ferry. After passing on all the news important to Israel, Zachariah continued on his way and arrived at Gay Creek as the sun came up. He let Tequila graze and rest while he cooked all the eggs, all the bacon, and all the oat porridge, and also toasted all the bread on the rocks of the fire pit. He figured he would eat it all then not stop again and arrive at Kuhn Bayou before the end of the day.

TWENTY ONE

"Where are Zachariah and the wagon? Private Jackson, Private Keen, a whole wagon is gone. Were you standing guard last night or were you sleeping?" Jeremiah demanded information from the troops watching the camp.

Private Jackson answered, "Sir, he went home. I thought we were guarding the prisoners."

Jeremiah mulled that over quickly. *Now what? I just pitched a big conniption fit in front of everybody about something that happened outside of my knowledge when I never said to do anything but guard the prisoners.* In fact, the others weren't prisoners and were free to come or go. The real issue was that Jeremiah needed to know what was happening in the camp. "Yes, you are supposed to be guarding the prisoners, but we should keep a close watch on everything. In the future, inform me of anything that's out of the ordinary. Be vigilant, and keep me informed."

"Yes, sir, thank you for clarifying our orders." Private Jackson liked having a commander who was reasonable.

Jeremiah felt that he had dodged a minor problem that he could have made into a big one. Having civilians attached made this mission different. They needed to treat the civilians respectfully but also sternly. He couldn't have things happening willy-nilly. Because it was so unusual, he needed to think about this situation carefully, determine exactly how he should run everything then pass that information on to everybody, including the civilians. He realized being in command was not going to be easy; it was going to be difficult. He went to speak with Smitty. "Sheriff Wyman, walk with me please." Jeremiah led the sheriff away from the others. "Sheriff, I require you to notify me of anybody leaving or joining your group or any other significant occurrence."

"I agree, and I apologize for not informing you last night when I knew Zachariah wanted to leave. What are you doing here? I thought you were stationed at Fort Smith."

"I'd rather the men didn't know anything about Harmony or that I had any previous connection with you but only think that we're here performing this mission. As to why I am not at Fort Smith, Lieutenant Lampson and I both asked for a transfer after what happened in Harmony. Neither of us explained the reason for our requests, but we both felt we could no longer take orders from Judge Atwood. Warren went back to Maryland, and I went to Little Rock. When I heard Sheriff Taylor say he had a mission to transport prisoners by the names of Ann Williams and Noah Swift Hawk, I volunteered. I'm not upset that they got married, but they did break the law, and they do have to serve their sentence, but I believe that I can make it better by being here."

"I'm glad you're in charge. You're a good man, and

I think you handled the situation very well this morning. Let me know what you expect, and I'll make sure we do what you ask."

"I would appreciate that. This is my first command. I want to execute it well." They returned to the camp.

Smitty gathered his group. He explained the situation then requested, "You are always respectful, but I'm asking you to be extra respectful, obey his rules, and let him know if you are going to do anything out of the ordinary." Eli and the girls agreed with no reservations.

While Jeremiah had spoken with Smitty, Melvin had cooked for the troops and the prisoners. Stephanie and Sally had prepared the food for the civilians. Both groups sat together to eat. Stephanie saw that Melvin had made bacon along with some cooked bread.

Ann ate a bite. "This is good, Private Hatcher. How did you fix it?"

Melvin smiled. It made him happy when people appreciated his culinary skills. He believed food was a pleasure that people should experience, and he enjoyed providing the pleasure. "First you mix eggs, milk, vanilla, cinnamon, and allspice. Next, you soak both sides of a slice of bread in the mixture. Last, you fry it."

"Simple but excellent. Am I allowed another one?"

Melvin put another serving on Ann's plate before anybody could say yes or no. Stephanie listened to the instructions and thought she'd like to make some the next day. The problem was that they didn't have milk.

Later that day, as they traveled, Stephanie went to

Jeremiah. "Specialist Pratt, do you think your cow will make enough milk that we could have some if we milked her for you every day?"

Jeremiah didn't think that would be a problem, but he didn't want to make a decision without all the facts. "I'll speak with Private Hatcher and let you know at the mid-day meal."

Stephanie smiled at Noah and made a little hello wave as she walked past.

Jeremiah called out his orders, "Private Hatcher, come over here." Jeremiah spoke softly to make it a private conversation, "If the civilian women milked the cow for you, and you kept every drop we need, would there be any milk left for the civilians?"

"If they give me what I need every time I ask, they can have whatever more she gives. I think she'll give us plenty."

"That will be all." Jeremiah was glad he could allow a small thing to soften the sentence without compromising his mission. In addition, it freed his man from milking duty. When they stopped for dinner, he waved Stephanie over and told her Melvin's offer, which she happily accepted.

TWENTY TWO

Zachariah exited the cypress swamp as the sun set. He was only a few miles from Minnie and considered urging Tequila into a run, but his horse had pulled the wagon for almost forty hours with only two short rests. He decided that would be as stupid as driving into a raging river. He finally arrived at Kuhn Bayou and called out, "Bridge Keeper, come out, and let me cross."

Minnie always checked out the travelers before exposing herself. She walked to the window and peeked out then flung open the door and ran to the gate. "Zachariah, you came back!" She opened the gate.

Zachariah drove across and jumped off the wagon. "I had to. I haven't gotten you out of my mind for a second." He opened his arms to invite Minnie, if she wanted to be there, into his embrace.

She was there in a blink of his eyes. "I haven't either."

Behind the cabin, Zachariah unhitched Tequila from the wagon. "I have a long story to tell you."

"Can your story wait?" Minnie took Tequila into the shed.

Zachariah gave his horse a forkful of hay. "I think so. Do you have a plan for something else to do?"

"Yes, I do!" Minnie closed the shed door, took Zachariah into the cabin, and proceeded to show him exactly what was on her mind.

TWENTY THREE

After the dinner break, Jeremiah pushed to travel the remaining fourteen miles to Cadron Creek. Night had fallen long before Jeremiah arrived and signaled that travelers wanted to cross. Since Zachariah had already told him who was coming, and it was not too dark to navigate by the light of the almost full moon, Israel already had the harness attached. He sent it over.

Jeremiah took Melvin and Ann and crossed with Eyanosa tied to the back of wagon one. He left the other soldiers to guard Noah, who no longer had his horse.

While the civilians crossed over, Jeremiah explained to the ferryman why they were there. Israel already knew the prisoners were Ann and Noah, and why, but he listened carefully as the commander of the mission explained, "The road and crossing have to be open at all times for military movements. Therefore, these prisoners will rebuild the ferry. I'll determine where to set up permanently tomorrow. Where do you want us to camp tonight?"

"There's no place to camp except the field, so you might as well start setting up permanently. Move as far to the back as you can, so other travelers will have space if they need to stop."

Jeremiah backed into the top inner corner of the

field. He directed Melvin to put together a meal while he examined the area. Melvin went into the forest in search of wood. Jeremiah decided they would erect a fence inside the wood line to allow the animals to have some protection from the wind or sun if needed.

He knew neither Ann nor Noah would run away and leave their family, so he decided to place the civilian wagon next to the woods with the military wagons positioned diagonally away from the woods at both ends. With a gated fence across the front of the wagons, they would have a corral for the cow and horses.

Jeremiah thought they should erect the two military tents in front of the corral, and use the large one as the mess tent and meeting room and the smaller one as a dormitory for the troops and prisoners. The civilians could put up their tent in the same area. He decided there was only enough time to park the wagons, run a rope around them to contain the animals in the grassy area in the middle, prepare a meal, and then retire for the night.

Smitty's wagon and the cow that swam over while tied to the rear arrived. Jeremiah told Smitty, "Pull the wagon in with the woods at the right side and butt it up to my wagon at the front."

Bliss walked into the forest to pull the wagon as far forward as Jeremiah wanted it. Eli unharnessed Bliss. The cow lowed for relief from her full udder, so Stephanie got the milk bucket and milking stool and saw to the cow.

Eli walked to the edge of the forest. He didn't want Melvin to shoot him not knowing who or what he was. "It's Eli coming into the forest for wood."

Sally was ready to cook when Eli and Melvin returned. The last wagon, with Noah, Justus, John, and Henry pulled up. As requested by Israel, Jeremiah directed them to back up to the woods as close as possible, directly behind and perpendicular to the civilian wagon. The field opened on both sides of the last wagon. Both of the military wagons could easily pull straight out but blocked in the civilian wagon completely. John unharnessed the horse and let him go to the grass between the wagons with the other horses and the cow. Stephanie asked, "Is it time to visit?"

Jeremiah refused, "Not tonight, it's already late and dark." Jeremiah kept the prisoners in their separate wagons on the opposite sides of the camp.

Since the men were all occupied and not paying attention, Ann kept mouthing, "I love you," to Noah. It drove him crazy. He knew they weren't supposed to have any communication between them. He wanted to tell her he loved her, but he knew, if caught, there would be severe consequences. He also knew he was going to have to leave Ann, and he wanted to stop loving her. He looked away. Before he knew it, he was looking at her again. Ann never took her eyes off Noah. She didn't want to believe that he didn't love her. She knew his desire to protect her. She wanted to believe he was protecting her the only way he thought he could. She was going to tell him she loved him anyway.

TWENTY FOUR

When they woke, Zachariah told Minnie everything. He explained how the floodwater had taken away Smitty, Ben, and Roy at Cadron Creek. He related the story of Ben confessing to the murder of Gus while being washed down the river, about Ben and Roy escaping, and the horrible news about Ann and Noah. Last, but most gently, he told her about Harry.

"I should have known. Harry said he loved me when I married him. Well, when I thought I married him. Then he immediately said, as my husband he could do anything he wanted with the money my father had left me. We came here, built the bridge and cabin, and set up using that money. He was here most of the time back then. He left to file documents when we had any, which didn't happen very often, but it always took him a long time to get back. Then he started leaving even when he didn't have anything to turn in. Harry's barely been here for the last few years. I should have realized that something was wrong. Looking back, I know I did, but I didn't want to admit it to myself. He said he had also become a clerk of the Little Rock Court, and there was business he had to attend to in town. I chose to accept that explanation. Now, I know what business he was attending to in Little Rock."

"I'm sorry that he treated you that way. I have some more very hurtful news to tell you."

"With you here, I can hear it."

"Harry told Smitty that anybody who took you away would be doing him a favor because he didn't want you. I'm sorry he said something so hurtful."

"I've known he doesn't want me for a long time."

"But I do. Remember how I said I didn't have a life in Harmony, and I wanted my life to start, but I didn't know how to make it happen?"

"I remember."

"Mine started when you gave your love to me. I know we barely know each other, but I feel like I know you completely, and you know me. This last year and during the trip to Little Rock, I've realized how fragile life can be and how unsafe the world is. I want to take you to the safest place I know, my home in Harmony. I want to have a life with you, love you, and treat you like the wonderful woman you are. I want to marry you, and we can walk together to the courthouse and see the marriage recorded."

"And you gave me back my life when you gave your love to me. I want to go to Harmony with you and be your wife, but first, I want to go to Dover and make sure there is no marriage filed for Harry and me. When I marry you, I want it to be right."

TWENTY FIVE

That same morning, Jeremiah started to establish the camp. Some commanders might have made the prisoners build the camp, but Jeremiah believed the sentence of Noah and Ann was only to construct the ferry. He got his men started. "We'll fell cedars to make a fence, and since we need more grass for the animals, we'll enlarge this field. John, you guard Ann and Noah. The rest of you, get your tools and come with me."

Eli saw the soldiers cutting down cedars and went to speak with the commander, "Specialist Pratt."

Jeremiah continued to saw. "I'm busy."

"We'd like to have the branches, so we'll cut them off if you'll let us have them. Also, since we'll be staying here, we should help build the camp."

Jeremiah stopped sawing and looked at Eli. "Do you have your own tools?"

"We do."

"I'd appreciate your help. Get your tools. Take all the branches you want."

Jeremiah was surprised when all four of the civilians arrived with tools. "Stephanie and Sally, you don't have to help."

Smitty knew Jeremiah was wasting his breath. "Don't bother trying to keep them from helping. You won't be able to do it."

Sally didn't understand why anybody would think a farm girl shouldn't work. "We're completely capable of cutting branches off cedar trees."

Eli added his two-cents-worth, "She's telling you the truth."

Stephanie explained why she wanted to help, "We're not going to sit around all day doing nothing. I couldn't stand being that bored."

Jeremiah decided there wasn't any sense in trying to stop them. "All right, go ahead."

Except for the prisoners and the one soldier guarding them, they all worked in the woods. Henry figured Sally couldn't be more than thirteen or fourteen. He wondered why she would work so hard for tree branches. He asked her why.

Sally explained, "The aroma of burning cedar wood is heavenly, branches make a good bed, we use them to make medicine, and we eat the cones."

Henry asked, "What kind of medicine?"

Before anybody had time to answer Henry's question, Melvin interjected, "How do cedar cones taste?"

Stephanie explained, "The medicine is for wounds. It helps take away pain and soreness and helps wounds heal without infection. I can't describe the taste of cedar cones, but I can say they taste good."

Sally bragged about Noah, "Noah taught us all about it. He's very smart. You should take some branches to sleep on. There's going to be more than enough for everybody."

Henry went to Jeremiah. "Sir, they said it's more comfortable to sleep on cedar boughs. May I have permission to use some?"

Jeremiah figured that sounded reasonable. "Go ahead." He spoke up loudly, "If any of you want to take cedar boughs, go ahead, just be sure you get all insects and other creatures out of them first."

Sally decided to push her luck, "May we give some to Ann and Noah?"

"You can take them into camp, but Henry will take the branches to the prisoners after examining them."

An hour before noon, Jeremiah issued instructions to Melvin and Henry, "Go to camp. Send John out to help with the trees. Melvin, you start the meal. Henry, you keep an eye on the prisoners."

Sally went with them. In camp, Henry explained to John where to find the others then took over guard duty. As Sally's fire filled the camp with the pleasing cedar aroma, she asked, "What are you making for dinner?"

Melvin sniffed the air. "I'm thinking."

Sally informed him, "I'm going to boil some smoked beef. When that's almost done, I'll add rice, dried vegetables, and cedar cones. I'm also going to make corn pone."

Melvin broke a cedar branch and tossed the pieces into the fire he had made close to Sally. "I've never tried cedar cones. Did you like the french toasted bread you made this morning?"

"I sure did. I don't know why we never thought of that."

Melvin came to a decision. "I'm going to make the same dinner you're making."

"You want to add our food together and cook enough for everybody."

Melvin didn't know how Jeremiah would feel about it. "Maybe I shouldn't."

"Suit yourself, then." She broke off branch tips with the cones attached and put them into an empty pot.

"Now what are you doing?"

"I'm going to make some cedar poultice. It's not just good for healing wounds. It's also good for sore aching muscles." Melvin broke off big pieces from a branch that he hadn't thrown into the fire. Sally told him, "You're doing it wrong." Melvin looked at her. "You only use the very tips. Like this." She snapped off short tips with the berries.

Melvin's muscles were already stiff. He wanted to make the medicine correctly then use some. "Anything else?"

"I'll explain how to make the poultice if you want."

"Thanks, Sally, you're the best."

"If we can find the right ingredients, I can also show you how to make a good painkiller."

"What do you need? I'll try to find some."

Sally looked towards Melvin. His handsome, dark brown eyes seemed to ask her, "Don't you want to do whatever I ask of you?" For the first time in her life, she felt curious and contemplated his physique. Of all the soldiers, she thought that Melvin looked the best. At five and a half feet tall, he wasn't much taller than she was, and she liked his short black hair that looked like her father's hair. She wondered if he was much older than she was. "We need willow trees. How old are you, Melvin? You know a lot about cooking." Sally plucked cedar cones. *If I was guessing who was an Indian, I'd pick Melvin, not Noah.*

"I'm nineteen. I learned about cooking in my parent's tavern."

"Where is it? How long did you work there?"

"It's in Richmond, Virginia. It's called the Halfway House. My family started it before my mother was born. I worked in the tavern all my life until last year when I came out here. I thought I didn't want to work in a tavern. I told myself that I wanted to do something more manly, so I left my family and came out here. I didn't have a job, so I joined the army. What they gave us to eat wasn't very good. Every meal, I described what I would have done to make it better. Captain Cornish finally said, 'Melvin, you're on cooking duty. Make what we eat better,' so I ended up cooking again and realized I do like cooking."

Sally decided they shared a mutual interest. "I do too."

Melvin could see that Sally was much younger than he was, but she seemed very sweet. He wondered how young she was, but he didn't want to upset her. "You look just a little younger than me. Where did you learn to cook so well?"

"I'm fourteen. I also helped my mother cook, that is, when she was alive. Since she died, I've done a lot of cooking with my sisters."

"I'm sorry your Ma died. You have good ideas. I'm glad to be sharing what we know."

"So am I." Sally was happy to be sharing and getting to know Melvin. She thought he was an awfully nice person.

TWENTY SIX

By dinnertime, they had the cedar trees on the ground almost devoid of branches. Jeremiah knew they were just about ready to drag the trees to camp. "Justus, go get the animals. We'll use them to pull these trees to camp."

John watched Stephanie drag cedar branches away. He wanted to talk with her, and this seemed like an excellent opportunity. "I'll go."

"Go on." Jeremiah didn't care who got the animals.

Smitty spoke up, "Bring Bliss and the harness."

"Sure." John hurried and caught up with Stephanie. "Let me help you with those branches."

"All right." Stephanie let the branches drop.

"I'm getting our animals. We're going to use them to pull the trees to camp. Smitty asked me to tell you to bring Bliss and her harness." John pulled all the branches and made small talk. In camp, he informed Melvin, "We're getting the animals."

Melvin put down the cedar branch from which he was removing the little blue cones. "You need help?"

John wanted to keep Stephanie's attention. "No."

That suited Melvin fine. He was happy to stay next to Sally. "Dinner is almost ready, so come right back."

John carried the harnesses to the corral. Stephanie asked, "What are their names?"

"This one is Storm because he's as black as a storm and this sorrel one is Chester. I don't know why."

"Nice names. Sally, do you know why Smitty named his horse Bliss?"

"I don't," Sally replied.

John walked to the cow with a larger harness. Stephanie was surprised. "Are you bringing the cow?"

"She's strong, and she's pulled for us before."

"What's her name? I hate to call her 'cow' when I milk her."

Melvin revealed their sad condition, "We have a nameless cow."

Sally cocked her head and put her finger to her chin. "We need to think of one."

Melvin looked at Sally. *She looks so cute.* A smile spread across his face. "I think so too."

John and Stephanie started back into the woods. John thought, *even if we're leading a string of animals, maybe a walk beside the creek would be romantic.* "Let's walk back along the creek. I think it must be a nice walk."

The last time she was there, Stephanie hadn't gotten close to the creek out of fear of falling into the raging waters. "All right." The two of them enjoyed a pleasant walk together leading the horses and the cow. John felt that his time in Stephanie's company was very enjoyable. Too quickly, in his opinion, they arrived. A short time later, they pulled the logs into camp with Chester, Storm, Bliss, and the nameless cow.

Melvin informed everybody, "The food is just about ready."

Jeremiah invited the civilians into the mess tent for dinner with the prisoners, "Come on. Let's see what good things Melvin and Sally have fixed for us."

As the corn pone finished cooking, Sally brought up the topic of the nameless cow, "We need to name the cow."

Jeremiah saw no reason to do so. "We do?"

"Yes, we do. I want to call her Peppermint. I like the cow, I like peppermint, and I think Peppermint is a cute name." Sally waited for any responses. It wasn't supposed to be visiting time. Ann was glad to be sitting with her family, so in case Jeremiah took it as a transgression, she did not reply.

Nobody else offered an opinion, so Noah spoke up, "I think Peppermint is an excellent name."

Sally reminded Jeremiah of his sister. He decided there wasn't any harm in going along with her small request. "Naming the cow Peppermint will be acceptable."

Sally put a hot cast iron frying pan full of cooked corn pone by the civilians. "Great! I'll tell her after dinner."

"Let's eat. You can all have visitation time together, except you two prisoners can't talk to each other, of course." Everybody sampled both batches of beef stew and corn pone prepared by Melvin and Sally. Jeremiah declared both equally good then issued the afternoon's orders to his men, "Melvin, come to the forest when you're done cleaning up. Justus, stay here and guard the prisoners. This is what I'm going to do going forward. When I whistle like this." Jeremiah stuck his thumb and pointer finger into the edge of his mouth and let out a loud whistle. "I'll follow it with the name of anybody I want to go to camp. Melvin, you know it is always your job to prepare the meal. The other person will start their shift on guard duty."

All Jeremiah's men replied, "Yes, sir."

Sally wanted to remain with Melvin. "I'll clean up our dishes."

The rest of them went back to the woods. Justus started his shift watching the prisoners as Melvin and Sally enjoyed each other's company and cleaned up. Noah heard Sally and Melvin talking about making the painkiller. He hadn't seen any willow trees on the way to Little Rock. Visitation was over, so he knew he shouldn't speak, but Sally needed information. "Sally, if you can't find a willow tree, look for a cottonwood tree. You get the inner bark the same way."

Justus called an immediate halt to the conversation. "It's not visiting hours."

Sally turned towards Justus. "But I don't know what a cottonwood tree looks like. Can't he tell me?"

Justus stuck to his decision, "No."

Melvin stood behind Sally and patted her shoulder. "Don't worry, Sally. I know what they look like." As they went to join the others, Melvin carried a hatchet and a large sharp knife. Sally brought their pouch. They walked through the forest looking for either a willow or a cottonwood tree. They didn't see either.

When they got there, Melvin reported to Jeremiah,

but John had a plan. "Melvin, work with me." Sally worked with Stephanie. Melvin worked with John on the tree felling detail until it was time to return to camp to start the evening meal. Jeremiah signaled to Melvin to go to camp. Since Melvin and John knew exactly where Sally and Stephanie were working, they walked over. Melvin said, "Sally, I'm going to walk back to camp. Do you want to keep looking for the tree?"

"I'd love to." Sally walked away with Melvin.

John's plan had worked out exactly as he had hoped. "I guess it's you and me, Stephanie. You want to hear a joke?"

"Sure."

As John implemented his plan to pursue Stephanie with laughter, Melvin and Sally walked to camp beside the creek. Melvin pointed to a tree over a hundred feet tall covered in brilliant, yellow, triangular shaped leaves. It had deeply fissured whitish colored bark covering its six-foot wide trunk. "That," he paused, "is a cottonwood tree. Aren't the leaves of fall beautiful?"

Sally stood close to Melvin. His hand looked inviting. *Is he holding his hand slightly away from his side so that mine will fit in his?* She didn't dare. "It's magnificent!" They gazed at the tree for a few minutes. "May I use the hatchet? I'll show you how to gather the part we need."

Melvin thought it over. Sally wasn't a prisoner who should never have a potential weapon. She had nothing to gain by attacking him, and she had been around him with very sharp cooking knives. He handed her the hatchet. "Show me how."

174

"We don't want to hack up the tree. We want the tree to recover, so we chop only as deep as the outer bark." Sally chopped out a six inch square of bark. "Knife please." She held out the hatchet to Melvin who swapped it for the knife. "The part we want is this inner bark." Sally carefully scraped the pink from the back of the bark in her hand then every bit still clinging to the tree. "We can harvest from several places in a tree this big. Just don't make a ring all the way around. Will you chop the outer bark while I get the inner bark?"

"Of course I will." Melvin was happy to help such a pleasant young woman harvest the inner bark from the giant cottonwood. They arrived back in camp with a large batch of the pink substance in the pouch. Sally showed Melvin how to make the tea and poultice. Melvin showed Sally how to make his smoked chicken soup with dumplings and his apple cobbler using all three large pots and all three dutch ovens.

Jeremiah had realized that it would be easier to cut off the branches in camp than in the forest and then drag them separately to camp, so the people in the forest came back to camp pulling four trees with the branches still attached.

At the supper table, John sat beside Stephanie. Eli walked into camp unhappy about what had become apparent to him. "Stephanie, move down the bench." He put himself between Stephanie and John.

When everybody was at the tables, Sally and Melvin passed out cottonwood bark tea and warm poultice. Sally asked Jeremiah to allow Noah to speak,

"May Noah explain about the cottonwood medicine and the cedar poultice?"

Since it was supper time and visiting hour, Jeremiah allowed it. "Go on and tell us."

"I guess you're a little sore. The cottonwood will dull or even stop the aching. Just drink it like tea. The cedar mashed into a warm poultice you put in a cloth to hold it against any area you've cut or scraped or that's aching. Not only does it help with pain, but it keeps a wound from getting infected."

Jeremiah decided it would be best to be cautious. "I don't know for sure what it will do. Don't give it to Ann or Noah, and none of you men can use it."

"If that's what you want." Sally took it back from the soldiers.

Melvin handed over the batch he was about to put on his scratched arm. He didn't mention the batch already on his aching back or confess that he'd drunk some of the tea earlier. Melvin realized that he should have considered all the possibilities and not tried it without asking for permission, but he didn't see Sally as deceitful. He wondered if Sally would tell on him.

Smitty ate apple cobbler. "Your Private Hatcher is a talented cook."

Jeremiah knew Melvin was a good cook, but he suspected that Melvin was putting on his best show for the sake of Sally. Jeremiah noticed every meal that Melvin had gone over and sat beside Sally, even after they had worked together to prepare the meals. "Yes, he is, and I think Sally's dinner recipe was excellent."

Smitty made a suggestion, "Perhaps we might be able to persuade the two of them to be our full-time cooks."

Everybody looked at Jeremiah. Even though Ann and Noah were supposed to remain separated from the others and have limited visitation, it just wasn't practical or possible. Everybody ate together. Not wanting her sister pressured into anything, Ann spoke up, "Don't you think it should be Sally's choice?"

Melvin looked at Sally and hoped. She spoke the words Melvin wanted to hear, "I'd love it."

Melvin smiled. He was glad Jeremiah had picked him for the mission. When the prisoners went into the sleeping tent for the night and Sally had kept Melvin's secret, he was very relieved not only from worry but also from the pains in his body because he had benefited from the ministrations of both the tea and the cedar poultice.

"Ann, you sleep on that side of the tent. Noah, you sleep over on this side."

Ann cringed. She was a prisoner and had to do as told, but sleeping in the tent with five soldiers she barely knew upset her. Before Ann could speak her unhappiness, Noah rejected the plan, "Ann is not sleeping in a tent in front of soldiers."

Specialist Pratt erected a curtain. "None of us is going to bother her. She has privacy behind the curtain, and it's safer in the tent than outside."

Jeremiah was in command, Noah was a prisoner, and that was that. There was nothing Noah could do about it, and he didn't want them thinking he cared. However, he was very mad that he had gotten Ann into this position. "I don't care anyway. She's more problems than she's worth." Noah lay in his designated area on the bed of cedar boughs that his sisters-in-law had managed to get for him and stewed in his anger.

TWENTY SEVEN

They talked about the day's work over breakfast. Henry suggested, "We could prevent travelers from entering all our area by putting the fence all the way around the camp and not just around the enclosure for the animals."

Eli quickly calculated. "That would add only five more posts and ten more crossbars."

Melvin passed around another batch of french bread. "We're going to need a lot more wood for cooking and staying warm. The trees around this field would be best for both those uses. Hardwood burns hotter and longer. If we cut the oak trees at the top of the field and move the wagons over the stumps, we can enlarge our area. Not only will we have the wood we need, but also the animals will have more grass."

Israel planned to make sure the field and fence ended up something he wanted and had joined the men in time to hear Melvin's suggestion. "It would be good for me if you enlarge this field. Would you cut enough trees from the upper end to leave the entire current grass field for animal grazing?" He stopped for a second. "And would you run a fence for an animal enclosure around the whole field?" He paused again before he meekly added, "And for shade a little way into the woods? The newly created camp area would then only need a barrier across the front, if at all."

Jeremiah considered. *It's better to accept good ideas than to reject them just because they aren't my original plan.* "Make it so."

Noah offered, "I'll help do the work."

Justus held out his plate for more breakfast. "You have to be up to something. Nobody would offer to do extra work when they're going to have to build a whole ferry and two landings."

Jeremiah didn't believe that Noah had an ulterior motive. *I doubt Noah would hurt anybody. Still, he could probably take out everybody with an axe but not with a saw. I don't want Noah loose, and I don't want to put any of my men in danger.* "Only with a saw, not an axe, and I'm going to chain you to me."

Henry pointed out, "Jeremiah, you'd be chaining yourself to a person who might want to kill you to escape!"

Jeremiah believed he knew enough about Noah that he felt safe. "Israel, may we have your permission to move our camp into the road? We'll completely block the way through, but maybe nobody will come along until we have completed the task."

"I want you to do what I suggested, so we'll take a chance. Go ahead."

There weren't many trees to cut down to make the new area, but they were hard oaks and a hickory, and the trees were much bigger than the cedars. The men sawed in teams. Stephanie and Sally cut off the branches after the first tree went down. At first, Ann wasn't going to help but eventually felt too bored with nothing to do. She could reach the tree while still chained to the wagon, and she would be with Stephanie and Sally. She walked towards them.

John let go of his end of the saw and picked up his rifle. "Whoa, Ann." Ann stopped in her tracks.

Jeremiah asked, "Where are you going?"

"I thought I would help. You can leave me chained to the wagon. I can reach these branches and cut them into firewood for you. Stephanie, Sally, and I work together very well."

Smitty offered his knowledge of the women, "The three of them can make a stack of firewood faster than you would ever figure. I've seen them do it."

John put down his rifle. "We don't have another saw."

Henry said, "The more people we have working, the sooner we'll get the work done. If they stay over there, you could give her an axe. She wouldn't be close to anybody but her sisters and they're on the wrong side of the branches to worry about her throwing it at us."

Jeremiah knew they were eventually going to have to let both Ann and Noah use all the tools to build the ferry. He decided to let Ann use them now. "Stephanie, go to the wagon and get an axe."

They all went to work. The giant trees landed on top of each other in the field and created a massive pile of tree trunks, branches, and multi-colored leaves strewn across the new field and the original field. Some branches slammed deep into the ground. Others stuck high into the air as if they were a tree all on their own. Many branches lay broken and scattered. All shades of green, orange, yellow, and red leaves littered the fields. After taking down only three large trees and a few smaller trees, they had cleared an extra fifteen feet from the road all the way to the wood line at the rear of the field.

Justus looked at the massive tangled pile of trees. "It's going to be forever before we have the field back."

That night, Jeremiah ached. Eli, Smitty, Stephanie, and Sally had used the tea and poultice with no ill effects. Jeremiah also noticed that Melvin was not stiff like the rest of his men. He figured it was safe. "You have permission to apply the cedar and drink the tea."

Israel sipped a cup of the tea. "If I contribute supplies, may I join you every day?"

Jeremiah believed he was probably lonely. "Yes, get with Melvin about what to contribute."

Sally knew Noah had to ache. She got a batch of cedar poultice and a cup of cottonwood tea before she walked to where Noah stood chained to the wagon. She put the cup inside the wagon and wrapped her arms around him for the longest time. Noah needed the hug. He was happy to let her. He knew how much her family meant to Sally, and he knew she felt that he was her brother. He hated that he was going to hurt her. Finally, she let him go. "I brought you this." She held out the cedar in a handkerchief.

Noah knelt down. "Across my shoulders please."

Sally never held back her feelings. As she put the cedar under the top of Noah's shirt, she told him what was on her mind, "Don't believe anything that judge said. We are your family. I know you don't have a wife in Indian Territory. You are not fooling any of us by pretending that you don't love Ann, and you need to stop it. You're hurting her."

Trying to convince her, Noah stood up and looked Sally in the eyes. "You don't know everything. I was pretending that I care about her."

Sally handed Noah the hot tea. "There was nothing to gain by pretending that you care about us, but you think you're helping now by pretending that you don't. Noah, trust God to get us through this and keep us together."

Noah held the cup of hot tea. "I can't."

"I'll tell you what Stephanie said to Ann. You are not God. It is not your job to control everything. Let God do his job and stop trying to do it for Him."

Noah changed tactics and gave his real reason, "I can't do things that will get Ann whipped."

"There's the right thing to do and the wrong thing to do. Make the right choice. You can let Ann know you love her without laying it out for everybody to see."

Noah wasn't able to find a place to hide from his fear. He denied his feelings, "You need to get it into your head. I don't want her." He sipped his tea to avoid looking at Sally.

Smitty hung back, but he had promised to deliver a

message. When it looked as if Noah and Sally were no longer having a tense conversation, he joined them at the wagon. "I told Zachariah I would give you a message. First, you should know that I confirmed that the woman in Little Rock is Harry's wife. I told Zachariah that she is and that Harry said he didn't want Minnie. Not only that, but Harry said if anybody took Minnie away, he would be doing Harry a favor. Zachariah went to get her. He asks you to forgive him for leaving. He hopes you'll understand. He thinks you know what a man does for the woman he loves."

Noah did, but in his case, he had to give up the woman because he loved her. "Good for him. I hope the world leaves them alone."

Smitty heard the bitterness in Noah's voice. "I'm not a Christian, Noah, but I think God said He overcame the world. Even though everything is stacking against you and these girls right now, God has a plan for you to overcome this."

Sally pointed out that Smitty affirmed what she had told Noah, "You see? I told you so."

Noah knew he didn't want to let any of them out of his life. He looked at Ann across the camp. The yellow, orange, and red fall leaves of the felled trees in the field appeared to be ablaze with the red light of the setting sun. As he looked across the fallen trees, Noah felt the real barrier separating them just like the simulated fire between them. He didn't know how he could keep her in his life.

Jeremiah ended the conversation, "Visiting time is over."

"Come with me." Eli led Stephanie away from everybody. "Stephanie, I've been thinking. Ann and Noah only had a week together. I used to believe we would have all the time in the world but maybe we don't. I love you so much. Even though I haven't told you, I think you know it. I don't want to wait. I'll do everything I can to make you happy. If you'll have me, let's go to Little Rock and get married."

"I love you too. I've been waiting for you to ask me, so I could say yes, but I hate to leave Ann and Noah out of our wedding. Let's talk to the family tomorrow and see what we can figure out. I'll talk with Sally and Ann. You speak with Noah."

"You talk to Noah. I'm sure he's mad at me and doesn't want to talk to me."

"He said he wants you to talk with him. Now, I think you should kiss me. I've been waiting so long."

Eli longed to do so. "I love you, and I want to. I think about kissing you all the time, but I know I wouldn't be able to just kiss you. We should wait until we're married. Then I'll cover you with kisses." They joined the family without sharing a kiss, but both looked forward to the arrival of that day.

Ann lay alone chained in her wagon whispering a prayer, "God, help me be strong. Make sure Noah knows that I love him. Comfort us all. Show us what to do. Thank you that we have our wonderful family here with us, and thank you for Jeremiah Pratt. God, Noah needs you very much, be there for him. Thank you for Melvin. We could be eating nothing but gruel, but you gave us Melvin and Sally to make delicious meals. Thank you for Henry, John, and Justus; all good decent men you put here with us to bless us. Keep us all safe as we work and sleep. In Jesus name, I pray. Amen."

Henry was nearby on guard duty. He heard Ann thank God for him. He had never thought of himself as a blessing. He spent his shift thinking about that prayer. He decided he would prevent Ann from escaping, but he would protect her as well.

Noah woke drenched in dew. A thought popped into his mind. *I will drench you with the dew of Heaven until you acknowledge that I am the most high, I do as I want, I rise up, and I throw down. No one opposes my will.*

He prayed, "God, forgive me. I know everything is in your hands. Before anything happens to any of your children, you have to give your approval. I don't know why this is happening, but I'm going to stop struggling against it. If it's your will to let me have Ann, Stephanie, Sally, and Eli, please let it be. If it's not, I'll accept it." Noah wanted to believe. Unfortunately, he didn't know how to give the situation over to God, he couldn't see a way it could work, and he didn't know how to stop struggling. He felt that life was hopeless.

Noah got out of the wagon, walked to the end of his chain, and added logs to the fire. He looked at Henry then scooped up a little dirt and climbed back into the wagon. He reached his hand over the side and allowed the dirt to drop onto Henry's hand.

Henry woke. "Oh, no!" He looked around. Nobody was awake, but the fire blazed. He stood up and looked into the wagon. Noah lay in the wagon sleeping. Henry was extremely relieved that he hadn't been found asleep at his post, but he chastised himself. *Don't let that happen again.*

That morning, Jeremiah chained Ann to a tree to work with Stephanie and Sally. He chained Noah to a tree on the other side of the field. They all started the hard task of chopping up the trees in the field.

Stephanie spoke to her sisters, "I have something to tell you. Last night, Eli asked me to marry him."

"That's wonderful." Sally was going to have both Noah and Eli as her brothers. She dropped the briars she was pulling and hugged Stephanie. "How did it happen?"

Ann hacked the roots of the briars. "Sally, that's between her and Eli. I'm very happy for you and Eli. I'd hug you, but we'd be in trouble."

Stephanie relayed her dilemma, "It's just that Eli wants to go to Little Rock and get married right now, but you have to stay here, so I don't want to do it. He says we don't know how long we have, and he doesn't want to wait."

"He's absolutely right. Noah and I only had a few days together. Go and get married, and take Sally."

Sally pulled briars to the massive pile they planned to burn. "This brings me to what I was going to tell you, Ann. Noah loves you no matter what he's saying. He's afraid you'll be whipped."

"Did he tell you that?" Even though Ann didn't believe what Noah kept saying, she wished he would assure her that he did love her.

"Not exactly, I told him he should let you know that he loves you, but he said he couldn't. He said he isn't going to get you whipped. I told him I know he loves you, and that he doesn't have a wife in Indian Territory, but he said I didn't know everything."

"That's not saying that he loves me."

"But he does. He was willing to be whipped eighty-eight times to protect you from even one lash. If he didn't love you, he would have let you be whipped."

"If he loves me, he should have let me take twenty-nine lashes and then met me somewhere, so we could go someplace safe and be together."

Sally walked to another patch of briars. "I guess people have different ideas about what love requires."

Stephanie expressed her opinion as she followed with Ann. "I think it proves how much you both care. You would both take a whipping because you love each other. I hope Eli and I have that much love."

"I hope you never have to be in this position. Tell Noah this evening then go to Little Rock and make Eli our brother."

They saved three long sections of tree trunks that once flattened at the tops would make seats around the fire pit. To use as worktables, they kept the big ends of the trees to pull into position with the horses later. It was a long, tiring, backbreaking day.

During the evening meal, Eli held Stephanie's hand and told Noah, "We have some news to share."

Noah looked at Stephanie glowing. He figured he already knew. "Share your news."

"I asked Stephanie to marry me."

Stephanie told Noah what he knew he already knew, "And I said yes."

"Congratulations to both of you." Noah hugged them together against him. "Be happy, and don't let anything get in the middle." Noah silently prayed. *God protect them and don't allow anything to happen to them as it has to Ann and me.*

Eli stepped back. "That's why we want to marry now. We don't know if something will interfere."

Noah looked across the camp. "I understand too well."

Stephanie relayed her desire and problem, "But I want for us all to be at our wedding."

"That's not going to happen, so go to Little Rock, and get married. Savor every second God gives you with each other."

Eli changed the topic to what had been eating him up, "I'm sorry for causing this to happen to you and Ann. You don't have to forgive me. I just want you to know how very sorry I am."

"It's not your fault. I know most white people hate Indians, and that they would make me leave if they caught me here, but I didn't know they made a law against marriage. James didn't tell me about that."

Stephanie brought up the subject Noah dreaded to discuss, "Which brings me to something else I want to say to you." Noah tried to brace his heart and mind. "You need to stop lying about your feelings. You are not doing the right thing. I know you think you are, but you're not. After you build this ferry, we can meet you at Point Remove Creek or the cave at home."

Noah wished it was that easy, but he hadn't gotten through even one year in white man land without getting his skull cracked, which had almost killed him. He had then been accused of stealing his own horse, which could have gotten him hanged then almost been burned up alive in a fire. He had barely escaped a lashing for marrying Ann and was now serving a hard labor sentence. The odds were definitely against him. He couldn't do something that might get Ann whipped, imprisoned, or in an even worse situation. That was not love; it was selfishness. "I hear what you're saying, Stephanie. It's too risky."

Stephanie beat at his heart. "So, you think it's better to sentence her to a life of sadness without you. She'd rather be whipped if she can have a life with you."

Noah commanded Stephanie to stop, "Leave me alone, take Eyanosa, and go get married."

"I'm not trying to hurt you, Noah. I care about you. I know you love each other." Stephanie reached out to comfort him.

Noah turned his back to the two of them. "Specialist Pratt, make these two leave me alone."

"Don't bother. We love you, Noah." Stephanie and Eli walked away. Noah climbed into the wagon. He felt confused, upset, angry, lonely, and incredibly sad.

Across the camp, Ann and Sally told Smitty that Eli had proposed to Stephanie, and now they wanted to go to Little Rock to get married. When Eli and Stephanie joined him, Smitty congratulated them. He offered to let them take Bliss but told them that they had to notify Jeremiah. Smitty then gave them ten dollars, as a wedding present, so they could go to Little Rock, get married, and get back.

Eli sat beside Jeremiah for breakfast. "Specialist Pratt, Stephanie and I will be taking Eyanosa and Bliss to Little Rock today."

Stephanie walked to Jeremiah with the pot of coffee. "Is there anything we can get for you while we're there?"

"Why are you going?" Jeremiah held out his cup.

Stephanie poured coffee into the cup. "Since you want to know, we're going to get married."

Jeremiah put down his cup and took the plate of scrambled eggs from Israel. "I'm not surprised, congratulations and best wishes to you both. Is there a reason why you wouldn't want to bring the preacher here for the ceremony?"

Eli held his cup towards his couldn't-be-soon-enough-wife. "I don't think a preacher will come out here, and we thought we'd stay in town a few days."

"If you change your mind, go down Main Street to 12th Street, and turn right, then go past Mount Holly Cemetery to the first house on the left. Ask for Thaddeus Pratt. He's a preacher and my uncle. I think he'll come here if you tell him that I sent you."

"We'll think about it." Eli patted the spot beside him. "Sit here, Stephanie."

TWENTY EIGHT

As Eli and Stephanie got their things together, Eli brought up his latest thought, "It would be nice to have the ceremony here, but I want to have some time for ourselves."

"Maybe we could get married in town, stay a few days, then come back here, and have another ceremony."

"Or we can get the license and the preacher, come back here for the ceremony, and then go back to Little Rock for a few days."

Stephanie closed their bags. "I would like that if it's what you want."

"I do. I want to have our wedding with the whole family." Eli rolled together their bedrolls with a tarp and a rope. He walked over and let Jeremiah know their plans. "We're going to get the license and your uncle if he'll come. We'll come back here for the wedding. Afterward, we'll go back to Little Rock for a few days."

As Stephanie and Eli rode away, Ann thought it was wonderful that they would all be together, and Noah felt a few rays of happiness in his currently miserable existence.

Two days after Stephanie and Eli left Cadron Creek, they walked into the courthouse in Little Rock.

Eli told the clerk why they were there, "We want to apply for a marriage license."

The man behind the desk recognized Eli. "Aren't you the brother of that Indian?"

"I'm not Noah's brother, but he is a friend."

The clerk asked Stephanie, "Is he your brother?"

"Neither of us is Indian. We're both completely white."

"A marriage license will be two dollars." Eli handed the man two coins. The clerk walked out of the room, out the back door, and over to the sheriff's office. "Any of those other folks with that Indian even partly Indian? Two of 'em wanna get married."

Sheriff Taylor didn't even look up from his desk. "Give them the license. The rest of them are white."

Eli and Stephanie waited thirty minutes for the clerk to return with the license. "Had to find the form."

After they left the building, Stephanie commented, "I doubt that he couldn't find the form for that long."

"All that matters is that we have the license. Let's go find that preacher."

They made their way down Main Street, turned, and walked up 12th Street past the cemetery then knocked on the door of the next house. A middle-aged man, a few inches under six feet with salt and pepper hair and a clean-shaven face, opened the door. Eli told the man what they wanted, "We're looking for Reverend Thaddeus Pratt."

"I'm Thaddeus Pratt."

"Jeremiah told us to come see you."

Thaddeus invited them in, "What can I do for you?"

"We hope, maybe, you'll marry us at Cadron Creek." Eli stepped inside the man's home.

"You're with the woman who married the Indian?"

"Ann is my sister. Are you against a white woman marrying an Indian?" Stephanie followed Eli into the house.

"I have nothing against it at all." The Sunday service was over. The Reverend didn't need to be in town for a week. "If we need to go now, you can tell me all about what happened on the way, but you're welcome to stay here, and rest before we leave."

"It would be nice to have a bath and sleep in a soft bed tonight then leave tomorrow." Stephanie looked at her soon-to-be-husband to see if that would suit him.

Thaddeus agreed before Eli could decline, "Excellent! I'm glad you'll stay for supper, a bath, and the use of my spare beds." He ushered his guests into the sitting room.

Eli sat in a soft, overstuffed chair. "Tell us about Jeremiah." They spent the afternoon talking about Jeremiah, Ann, Noah, and themselves while sipping delicious English tea. Late in the day, they ate supper after which they enjoyed hot baths. Stephanie snuggled into what felt like Heaven in the form of a bed and wondered if Thaddeus might be able to help Ann and Noah.

The night passed slowly for Eli. He wanted to spend his whole life with Stephanie and somehow

Sally, Ann, and Noah, but he felt something was surely going to go wrong. In the morning, he suggested a slight change of plan, "I think we should get married right now and have it recorded before we leave."

Stephanie walked to the breakfast table with Reverend Pratt. "Would you be able to marry us that fast?"

"We only need two witnesses. My neighbors have done this before. I'll get them after breakfast. We'll have the ceremony and then file the documents." It wasn't long before Thaddeus left the house. He returned quickly with Rudolph and Flossie Andrews. Everybody went into the sitting room. Thaddeus directed them to their places, explained the procedure, and handed Stephanie and Eli each a piece of paper with the words they should say. "Are you ready?"

Stephanie smiled at Eli. "Completely."

Eli replied, "Absolutely."

"Then, let's begin. Before these witnesses do you, Eli Yates, take Stephanie Williams to be your lawfully wedded wife, to love her and care for her with all her faults and strengths and offer yourself with all your faults and strengths, to help her when she needs help, and turn to her when you need help as long as you both shall live?"

"I, Eli Yates, take you, Stephanie Williams, just as you are, as my wife and the person with whom I will spend my life."

"Before these witnesses do you, Stephanie Williams, take Eli Yates to be your lawfully wedded husband, to love him and care for him with all his faults and strengths and offer yourself with all your faults and strengths, to help him when he needs help, and turn to him when you need help as long as you both shall live?"

"I, Stephanie Williams, take you, Eli Yates, just as you are, as my husband and the person with whom I will spend my life."

"Then, I pronounce you man and wife. You may kiss your bride." Eli took Stephanie in his arms and finally kissed her.

When Eli let Stephanie go, she lightly licked her lips. "MMM." They wanted more, but the time was still not right.

"Ruddy, Flossie, come sign."

Reverend Pratt's neighbors signed just as they had in the past. "Congratulations. We wish you a wonderful life."

Stephanie thought Flossie looked exactly right. "Flossie, you wouldn't happen to have a dress I can borrow, would you?"

"Come over. We'll look." Stephanie followed them to their house. A short time later, she returned with a package.

Thaddeus put the two forms in his vest pocket. "We'll take these documents to the clerk of the court on our way out of town." With bedrolls and bags tied on the horses, they rode to the courthouse. Thaddeus called out to the same clerk who had given Eli the license the day before. "William, I've got a marriage."

William took the pieces of paper. In his log, he notated the date and time he received the marriage documents. He signed the certificate of marriage, and the license then filed the license in the cabinet but handed the marriage certificate to Stephanie. "Done and done."

Thaddeus declared them as married as can be. Eli felt a huge relief knowing his marriage to Stephanie was secure.

As he walked with his bride out the courthouse door, Eli informed Thaddeus that he needed to get a tent large enough for six people.

TWENTY NINE

Thaddeus headed east. Eli spoke up. "When we were here the last time, I saw the tentmaker on the other side of town."

Thaddeus assured him, "This man is a better tentmaker."

Inside the shop, Eli wrote the man's name and the date on the court script on which Smitty had previously written: payable for one waterproof tent large enough for six people and had signed Sheriff Smithfield Wyman.

The shop owner placed a large bundle beside the counter. He ducked back into his storage area and got an india rubber wagon cover, which he set on the tent. "These come together. You can't buy just one." He then, of course, added the cost of the two items together. It was still a reasonable amount.

Eli entered the amount and slid the paper across the counter top. "You know where to redeem this?"

"I do. Much obliged for your patronage."

There wasn't enough space for Eli to get on Bliss with the tent and wagon cover, but he didn't mind. He was happy about it. He got on Eyanosa with Stephanie and wrapped his arms around his wife. When Stephanie turned her head towards him, he kissed her lips then started back to Cadron Creek with Reverend Thaddeus Pratt.

THIRTY

Five days after they left Cadron Creek, Stephanie, Eli, and the reverend who would marry them in the presence of their entire family rode into camp. The wagons were parked in the field over the short stumps of the trees they had cut down. The wood from the chopped-up trees had been stacked into a high wall at the top edge of the newly cleared space. Eli was surprised. "I thought there would still be plenty of trees to chop when we got back."

"Israel insisted we work from sunup until sundown. He said we had to clear the road. We weren't done until just before dinner today. After we ate, everybody went to look for trees suitable for the ferry. When it got close to suppertime, me and Sally came back to start cooking. The others should be back soon."

Stephanie looked at the center of camp. "And you flattened the logs. I think we can easily fit twelve people around the fire."

Sally left her cooking duties and helped Eli unload. "Are you my brother now?"

"Yes, but we're having the official ceremony here."

Sally hugged him. "I'm so glad."

"And I'm happy that you're my sister." When Sally let him go, Eli led Bliss and Eyanosa into the field on the lower side where the other horses and the cow grazed on the newly accessible grass.

Sally felt happy. Now, both Eli and Noah were her brothers, exactly as she wanted it to be. She knelt beside Stephanie, and the huge bundle on the ground that she hoped was a tent.

Stephanie unfolded the purchase from Little Rock. "This is an india rubber tent."

Sally had never heard of such a thing. "What's india rubber?"

"I asked the same thing when we bought it. India rubber is made almost the same way we make maple sugar, but they gather the sap from trees that grow down in South America in the country of Brazil. They process it into what they named rubber. They call it rubber because you can rub pencil graphite away with it. One of the other things they do with it is to let it congeal in canvas to make a strong, flexible cloth that doesn't leak."

Sally looked at the sky. "I'm glad you're already here with it. I'm sure we're in for rain."

Eli came up from the field, and Melvin walked over from the mess tent. Together with Stephanie, Sally, and Reverend Pratt they set up the tent. The civilians moved their bedrolls and the cedar boughs inside. Melvin stood by the piece that still lay on the ground. "Where does this part go?"

Eli joined him. "It's a wagon cover. I want to put it on over the canvas already on the wagon. I don't want the wooden wagon bows to damage it." They unfolded it beside the wagon. Eli stepped up into the wagon. "Humm, I guess I'll have to lower the canvas to get ahold of it then pull them both over together. I need your help, Melvin."

Melvin climbed into the wagon. Stephanie, Sally, and Reverend Pratt lifted the cover towards the men. The two in the wagon pulled. Even though impregnated into good, strong canvas, the rubber stretched. Eli was concerned. "Stop, it might rip."

The four contemplated. Melvin had an idea. "Maybe we can flip it over with the inside facing up, tie this edge onto the wagon bows, and lay the rest on the ground. We can leave this side of the current canvas tied but put the rest on top of the rubber cover. If we roll them both up together with the canvas sticking out at both ends, we should be able to pull it up by the canvas and not stretch the rubber."

"That way, we'll also put the canvas back on at the same time and protect the inside of the rubber." Eli got out of the wagon. The four proceeded to implement Melvin's plan.

Not many minutes later, Stephanie pulled closed the puckering strings at the front end. "I don't think rain will be able to seep in anywhere."

Sally pulled the other end closed. "Good. My blankets ended up pretty soggy at Kuhn Bayou."

Since it wasn't raining yet, they sat around the fire and waited for the others. Jeremiah returned to camp and saw his uncle. "Uncle Thaddeus, it's good to see you. I appreciate you coming all the way out here."

Ann wanted information. "The meal is ready. Is it visiting time?"

"This is a special event. Speak with everybody you want then they can all go talk with Noah."

Ann quickly made her way to her family. She hugged Stephanie and Eli. "Are you my brother?"

"Yes, I was afraid something would go wrong, and I wanted it all complete while we were in Little Rock, but we're going to have a ceremony here."

"I hope you're not upset." Stephanie didn't want to add any more unhappiness to her sister's life.

"Of course not, that was a wise thing to do. I'm happy that Eli is officially part of the family."

Sally spoke her feelings, "It's my dream coming true. I knew this is supposed to be our family, with Noah too, of course. It's what I dreamed about on our way to Harmony after Gus burned down the farm."

Every day, Ann felt Noah's sadness and anger. She sent the family to take him joy then watched Noah hold them in his arms. Even though she couldn't hear what they were saying, she could see that Noah was happy. That made her happy.

Jeremiah proudly told his uncle about his promotion then took him to check on the horses. He wanted to explain his dilemma. "I'm trying to walk a thin line here. These people don't deserve this, but I have a job to do. The ferry needs to be built, and they have to do it." Reverend Pratt slowed his pace, so they would have plenty of time to talk. Jeremiah looked over Storm and Peppermint. "I'm supposed to keep them apart. Then, I have to make sure that Noah and Ann don't go away together. I can't follow them for their entire lives. It's a stupid order. It's hard on all of us. I can tell it also bothers my men. It's obvious that these are all decent people. I think I'm going to remove the visitation restriction and let them talk freely, except between Ann and Noah. The orders are to keep those two apart. There are no orders about the rest of them. I already don't post a guard at night. Ann and Noah are in the tent with us, and they aren't going to try to get away without the rest of their family. Although, I do have their wagon blocked in."

Reverend Pratt inspected his horse then Chester. "I believe you'll find the proper balance. I think God put you here because you're trying to be a blessing to this family and do your job well. You should start your new policy tomorrow for the wedding. That would seem reasonable. Then leave it that way."

In camp, Ann visited with Israel and Smitty as she watched Noah talk with Stephanie, Sally, and Eli. She was glad that he had a smile on his face. He turned and looked at her. She sent him a kiss through the air. She believed he felt it touch his lips before he looked away.

Stephanie and Eli quietly told Noah everything that Reverend Pratt had told them about Jeremiah. They confessed that they had a quick marriage ceremony and had it recorded before leaving Little Rock. Since they wanted the visit to be a happy time, they purposefully did not mention Ann because it always upset Noah.

Jeremiah and his uncle walked back and called everybody into the mess tent. Eli, Stephanie, and Sally visited with Noah during the meal and on until the rain started. Jeremiah then declared the meal and visitation over. Israel ran to his cabin. Jeremiah ushered his prisoners into the military dormitory tent. All his men followed right behind them.

Eli sprinted over and held open the flap of their new tent. The others took turns dashing over. Smitty ran in last. They still had space. "I approve, especially since the tent came with the waterproof wagon cover."

Jeremiah planned to march everybody into the forest to work. However, in the morning, he changed his mind and instructed Ann, Stephanie, and Sally to stay in the camp with Melvin and Reverend Pratt to prepare for the wedding. He told the rest of them to get the tools and follow him into the forest.

Noah walked again chained to Jeremiah. He described how he could cut down the cedars he needed without technically having anybody else's help. "I can use the large part of the tree for the dock, and you can use the small end for fence posts and rails. I would have worked with Ann, but she isn't here, and it isn't possible to saw alone. If you let me saw with Eli, I can be sawing off my end of the tree as he is sawing off his end of the tree but in the same place at the same time."

Henry followed close behind with a large, two-man, crosscut saw across his back and an axe on each shoulder. "Cutting only small trees for what we need and doing it all ourselves is going to make our fence take longer to build, and we'll have weaker posts."

John knew they had enough tools since Smitty, Eli, and Israel toted the same complement of tools as

Henry. He himself lugged several smaller saws. "We should be able to take the trees we need. If Noah can use the part that's left, or we can use the part he doesn't use, it's not our fault."

With four rifles hung across his back and one in his hand, Justus brought up the rear behind Noah and the commander of the mission. He stated what he believed Jeremiah should consider, "This is security fencing that needs to be built quickly."

Jeremiah agreed to the plan. At the largest of the trees they had marked the day before, he left Eli and Noah, a crosscut saw, and a couple of axes. He also left Justus, who sat on a bank of wet dirt with the axes beside him and a half-cocked rifle in his lap. Smitty worked with Jeremiah to cut down a tree for the fence that happened to be large enough to get logs for both projects. Henry and John worked on a third tree large enough to acquire the same two parts.

Eli reminisced as he and Noah pulled the saw back and forth under a shower of rainwater left on the branches of the cedar they were cutting. "Remember catching those turkeys?"

"We had a lot of fun. Those turkeys probably would have killed us if we had tried to get them all. It's a horrible shame that Gus burned them up. I wish we had left them in the woods."

"We didn't know he was going to set the fire. If it had worked, it would've been great raising turkeys. Do you remember shooting the deer standing beside Arabella?"

"The girls cooked the back strap. It was delicious. That night I watched Ann pour tea and thought she was so beautiful and very gracious."

"Back then we barely knew each other. Now, we're going to be brothers."

"I wish it could work out that way but it won't."

"They can't follow you forever."

"Ann wouldn't be safe. Stop talking about our family."

Eli found out something important. *Noah does believe we're a family.* When the tree Noah planned to use as one of the longest posts of the dock met its demise, the ground bounced under their feet. The monster lay on the ground dying as Noah used the axe to chop off its limbs. He removed the branches along the section of its trunk where he needed to cut to acquire the long piece he wanted. Together, Noah and Eli cut the tree into two pieces. Noah discarded the smaller end of the tree, which Eli claimed for the fence.

Jeremiah and Smitty lopped off the branches on the fence end and discarded the useless larger end. John and Henry did the same. The fence builders ended up with three sections from which they could make several posts and many rails, and three of the four huge logs that Noah and Ann needed also lay on the ground. After the trees were down, everybody cut branches until noon. Then, right there in the forest, they gathered to eat the dinner sent with them so those in camp could get ready for the big event.

THIRTY ONE

In the camp, Melvin asked for ideas about what would make a lovely wedding in the woods. It wouldn't have mattered so much to him, but he liked working with Sally, and he knew it was important to her. On top of that, he didn't feel like he was there guarding criminals. He felt like he was with friends.

Sally sat beside Melvin. "I've only been to one. We probably shouldn't do the same thing. I know how to make spiced beef with picante sauce, and we have a smoked beef roast."

Stephanie knew the dish. "I think that's a great idea. I'll help you get what we need." They walked to the wagon.

While waiting for Sally and Stephanie to bring over the beef and other ingredients, Melvin, Ann, and Reverend Pratt discussed what the U.S. Army could contribute. Melvin proposed: baked beets, roasted rutabagas with onions, fried carrots, and potato fritters.

As she placed the beef on the table, Stephanie accepted the dishes as good doings for the meal.

Ann requested permission to get what she needed to make her addition to the wedding feast. "Would you go with me, so I can look through our wagon for Imperial Cake ingredients?"

Melvin picked up his rifle and escorted her over. He stood outside and watched Ann rummage through the wagon. "How do you make Imperial Cake?"

"First, you thinly slice a quarter pound of citron, chop up half a pound of almonds and a pound of raisins. Then, you cream together a pound of butter and a pound of white sugar. Next, you beat the whites of eight eggs separately from the yolks. After that, you mix it all together with a pound of flour, and then you bake it until it's done."

"Sounds good. Have you got everything?"

"If you would let me have eight eggs and enough milk fat to make the butter, then I'll only be missing citron and almonds, but we have hickory nuts, and we have sunflower seeds. Maybe I could use one of them. What do you think?"

"Almonds taste very different than either of those. It might be better without the nuts. We haven't used many eggs or much milk lately, so you can have the eggs and milk you need." Ann tried to hand the raisins to Melvin. He refused to take them, "Sorry, Ann, I need to keep to protocol. Losing control of my ability to fire my rifle isn't going to happen."

"That wasn't my objective. I wouldn't make problems. Especially, not on the day my sister is getting married."

"I'm just following protocol." He called out, "Come help Ann carry these cake ingredients."

Ann handed Sally and Stephanie the sugar, raisins, and hickory nuts then got out of the wagon and picked up the bag of flour. Melvin escorted them into the mess hall. Only Ann and Melvin knew his primary objective was to move the prisoner securely.

Ann knew she couldn't go to the cabin, but there was something important to arrange. When Stephanie wasn't close by, Ann whispered to Sally, "Would you feel comfortable asking Israel if he would let Eli and Stephanie use the cabin for the night?"

Melvin heard the question. He thought it was inappropriate for a fourteen-year-old girl or a preacher to ask about that kind of thing. "If Reverend Pratt will keep guard, I'll go ask."

Reverend Pratt agreed to take the job. "I surely will." As soon as Melvin left, the Reverend lay down Melvin's rifle. He was sure he didn't need it.

Melvin knocked on the ferryman's door. "Mr. Cotton, do you have a room the soon-to-be-wedded-couple could use for the night? It's an important part of marriage."

Israel almost laughed. It was funny the way Melvin had stated the request. "I only have one bedroom, but I can stay in your camp and let them stay in the cabin."

"Excellent, sir, the wedding will be an hour before sundown." Israel was at his cabin preparing a surprise dish for the meal. Melvin knew that Israel already knew the time, but the comment gave Melvin a tactful way to close the conversation and leave.

"I'll come to camp with what I need for the night."

Back at the camp, Melvin whispered, "Ann, it's all set."

"I'm very grateful, Melvin. I guess the appreciation of a prisoner doesn't matter, but I do appreciate you asking for me."

"You're welcome. Your appreciation does matter, but that's not why I went."

"One more favor. Do you have a ten-gallon tub or something large for bathing?"

"I'll get what we have." He left to retrieve the tub while the Reverend, who had picked up the rifle when he had heard Melvin outside the tent, continued to stand guard.

Sally handed the picante sauce to Stephanie to pour over the slices of beef that Stephanie had placed in the dutch oven. "What are you planning to wear?"

"I knew I didn't have anything here. Flossie, who was one of the witnesses, looked about my size, so I asked if there was any way possible that I could borrow a dress and send it back to her with Reverend Pratt."

"Did she let you borrow one?"

"She did. I'll show it to you."

That afternoon, when the men came back to camp, Stephanie had already finished her bath and sat in the civilian tent with rags tied in her hair to make ringlets. In the tent with her, she had Sally and everything else she needed for the ceremony.

Melvin delivered a message, "Eli, there's a tub of hot water waiting for you in the military dorm."

Ann quickly added, "Jeremiah, I hope you don't mind if Eli uses your tent to get ready for the wedding."

Reverend Pratt interjected, "I told them they could."

Jeremiah unloaded his tools into the wagon. "We don't need to be in there until tonight. I'll get my men to inspect it before then. Eli may use the tent to get ready."

Ann breathed a sigh of relief. "I appreciate you allowing us to do this and letting me help. It means so much to me."

Noah spoke up, "Is there anything I can do?"

Everybody looked at Jeremiah. He knew Noah and Ann were going to work side by side when the work on the ferry began. "If there is, then let him help."

Ann didn't know if that included being around her, but she wanted it to be so. She spoke the first words that she had said to Noah since they had left Little Rock. "Come help me decorate the mess tent with cedar and holly."

Jeremiah knew he couldn't let them be unsupervised. "Henry, accompany them."

The three of them picked up an armful of prickly branches covered in bright red holly berries and less prickly cedar branches covered with their small blue cones. They went into the mess tent. Ann wanted to hug and kiss Noah with every fiber of her being, but she only did what she thought she would be allowed to do. She spoke words, "Noah, I appreciate your help."

"I want to do what I can to make the wedding nice."

Ann held a cedar branch. "Help me attach this." Noah casually walked over, stood beside her, and reached up to attach the decoration high in the tent.

Ann was so close. He wanted to touch her. His arm brushed hers as he tied the branch. Ann felt it like a shockwave. It was only a tiny sensation but magnified a thousand times by her love for him. He fought his desire to sweep her into his arms. To be so close but apart crushed them, at the same time, neither wanted to separate. Ann whispered only, "Noah."

Her question screamed into his mind. "God help us." He turned and held her. "I love you."

Henry finished hanging his branch. He turned back towards the room. "Break it up. You're going to get me into trouble. Noah, I know you woke me up that morning, so I'm not going to say anything, but leave now, and don't do that again."

Noah only held Ann in his arms for a few seconds. He didn't want to, but he tried to let her go. Ann held on tight. "I can't do this, Noah. It's killing me."

"Me too." He pulled her arms away from him. "We can't have each other." He left while he could.

Bitter tears wracked Ann's body. Henry thought, *this is ridiculous, there's no reason they shouldn't be allowed to love each other.* Ann pulled herself together and finished decorating the tent with the help of Henry.

"How bad are my eyes? It would be best if I don't come out of the tent with puffy red eyes."

"We'll give it a few more minutes. I'm sorry, but I have to follow orders."

Ann could see that Henry was distressed. "Don't be upset. You did what you're supposed to do. We were the ones who were wrong."

"No, ma'am, I don't think you are, but I still have to do my job."

"I appreciate that thought. It's good to know everybody isn't prejudiced and blind."

After a short while, Henry decided they were safe. "I think your eyes are all right now."

The pleasing aroma of the good food and the decorations of green, red, and blue from the forest filled the tent. Smitty informed the others that Eli was ready and wanted to know if he should come out or if he should wait. Since Sally had already told everybody Stephanie was ready, Reverend Pratt gave him the answer. "Tell Eli to come on."

Eli walked to the makeshift altar in wedding attire left in the tent with a note telling him to put it on. He faced the tent where Stephanie waited. Sally stood at the door and waited for Reverend Pratt's signal. The Reverend waved for Stephanie to come. Sally opened the tent door. "You look so beautiful. Go marry Eli."

Stephanie stepped out of the tent. Her long blonde hair hung in soft ringlets that cascaded down her back. She wore Flossie's dark blue dress with white lace open at the neck and shoulders. The dress plunged down at the front but closed above her breasts. Slightly too long, the dress trailed out behind her as the ground pulled it out to make the extra length into an attractive train. In her hands, she held a bouquet of cedar with blue cones that complimented her dress and echoed the pale blue of her eyes. Eli always thought Stephanie was beautiful. At that moment, she completely captivated him.

Stephanie filled John's eyes too. "That's a beautiful woman."

Melvin watched Sally slip into the back of the group. "They all are."

Reverend Pratt started the ceremony. "Family and friends, we are gathered here today to join these two in holy matrimony. If there is anyone who knows of a reason why these two should not marry, speak now, or forever hold your peace." Reverend Pratt paused. Nobody objected. "At this time, Ann is going to read a message from the Bible."

Ann moved to the front. "Eli and Stephanie, always remember what love can be.

"Song of Songs 4:9-16. The man: The look in your eyes, my sweetheart and bride, and the necklace you are wearing have stolen my heart. Your love delights me, my sweetheart and bride. Your love is better than wine; your perfume more fragrant than any spice. The taste of honey is on your lips, my darling: your tongue is milk and honey for me. Your clothing has all the fragrance of Lebanon. My sweetheart, my bride, is a secret garden, a walled garden, a private spring; there the plants flourish. They grow like an orchard of pomegranate trees and bear the finest fruits. There is no lack of henna and nard, of saffron, calamus, and cinnamon, or incense of every kind. Myrrh and aloes grow there with all the most fragrant perfumes. Fountains water the garden, streams of flowing water, brooks gushing down from the Lebanon Mountains.

"The woman: Wake up, North Wind. South Wind,

214

blow on my garden: fill the air with fragrance. Let my lover come into his garden and eat the best of its fruits. Song of Songs 4:9-16 from the mouth of God." Ann closed the Bible then made her way to her seat with her eyes on Noah.

Noah wished he could remain in the moment. As he had said the morning after he had married Ann, she wasn't a woman you would forget. The message from Song of Songs had brought their wedding night to full remembrance. Since Ann could not love Noah with her body, she had loved him with her words. Noah looked into her eyes. They both knew that love still filled them.

Reverend Pratt continued, "The bride and groom will take their vows. Do you, Eli Yates, take Stephanie Williams to be your lawfully wedded wife, your constant friend, faithful partner, and love from this day forward?"

"In the presence of God, our family, and friends, I offer you, Stephanie Williams, my solemn vow to be your faithful partner in sickness and in health, in good times and in bad, and in joy as well as in sorrow. I promise to love you unconditionally, to support you in your goals, to honor and respect you, to laugh with you and cry with you, and to cherish you for as long as we both shall live."

The Reverend turned to Stephanie. "Do you, Stephanie Williams, take Eli Yates to be your lawfully wedded husband, your constant friend, faithful partner, and love from this day forward?"

"In the presence of God, our family, and friends, I

offer you, Eli Yates, my solemn vow to be your faithful partner in sickness and in health, in good times and in bad, and in joy as well as in sorrow. I promise to love you unconditionally, to support you in your goals, to honor and respect you, to laugh with you and cry with you, and to cherish you for as long as we both shall live."

"What God has joined, let no man pull asunder. I pronounce you husband and wife. You may kiss your bride." Eli happily kissed his bride. "I present to you, Mr. and Mrs. Eli Yates. Let us celebrate in the mess tent."

Ann already sat at a table when Noah entered. He sat beside her. Jeremiah pointed across the tent. "Sit at a table over there."

Noah pleaded, "Let me sit beside Ann on the night her sister is married. I'll be good. I promise."

Henry could have told everything. "You're only going to make the situation worse if you don't."

"I know. I promise." Noah waited for permission. Jeremiah finally nodded his consent and moved away but sat where he could keep an eye on them.

Ann whispered, "What if I'm not good?"

Noah told Ann what she needed to know, "Be good, Ann. I want to sit here with my wife, and my love, and remember our garden."

She spoke with tenderness and love in her eyes, "I'll be good. I remember." Under the table, her foot touched the side of his.

For a long time, everybody laughed, talked freely,

ate deliciously spiced beef, baked potatoes, beets, onions, corn, rutabagas, freshly baked bread, butter, cheese, and baked spiced pears from Israel's pear trees. Last, they ate the only version of Imperial Cake Ann was able to make, which turned out quite good with hickory nuts.

During the meal, Israel told Eli the plan, "I'm going to stay over here tonight. You and Stephanie use the cabin."

Eli was pleasantly surprised. "That's so wonderful!" They celebrated, shared their happiness, and let Noah and Ann sit close together to talk, mostly to each other. After a few hours, Eli whispered to Stephanie, "Let's try to slip away." Talking to different people, they maneuvered themselves close to the door. When nobody was looking, Eli disappeared with his bride. Stephanie started towards the tent. Eli stopped her. "No, my love, my beautiful one, we are spending the night in the cabin."

"Then let the North Wind blow us to our secret place. Milk and honey are under my tongue. Enter into your garden."

THIRTY TWO

When Stephanie and Eli walked into camp, everybody was in the forest except Reverend Pratt. Stephanie handed him the dress once again wrapped in brown paper. "Thank you so much for coming all the way out here to Cadron Creek and giving the family the gift of being together at our wedding."

Reverend Pratt was not the same size as Eli, but Eli didn't know who else could have lent him the clothes. "Do the clothes left for me to wear belong to you?"

"They do." Reverend Pratt put them into his bag with the dress. He spoke blessings over the two newlyweds then started back to Little Rock.

Stephanie watched him swim his horse across Cadron Creek. "I wonder why he has clothes that don't fit him."

"I don't know, but I was glad to use them."

"And you looked so very handsome in them." Stephanie kissed Eli. She thought his lips felt wonderful touching hers.

They strolled into the woods towards the place where Eli had worked the day before. The logs they had previously denuded lay abandoned where they had dropped the previous day, but they heard the sound of sawing drifting past. It wasn't long before Stephanie and Eli found Noah and Ann pulling the saw back and forth across their current victim.

Henry, both guarding and sawing, worked out of hearing range several yards away. Henry hoped neither Noah nor Ann would try to get away because he didn't want to shoot either of them. However, he did stay in rifle range, with his primed and half-cocked rifle beside him, in case either of them tried to make a break for it.

Stephanie stood beside Ann. "We'd be glad to take a turn."

Ann refused, "I appreciate the offer, but our sentence is hard labor with no help. There's already been too much cutting of trees that seems like help, and I don't want Judge Hall to decide we didn't serve our sentence."

Eli took Stephanie's hand. "We're ready to cut the branches off the fence end as soon as it comes down."

Stephanie sat on a bed of pine needles not far from her sister. "God really provided for you when he put Jeremiah in that mess hall in Little Rock. Thaddeus told us that Jeremiah was supposed to have already left that day. God made everything happen exactly the right way for us to have Jeremiah in charge."

Noah mulled that over. "I've felt that God isn't here, but maybe you're right. Maybe God is in this with us."

"I've been too mad to talk to Him, but when I couldn't stand it anymore, even if it was only for a second, Noah's arms were around me."

"You hugged her?" Stephanie was surprised.

"Yes, I can't stand us being so close but apart. I also

know that Ann is not my wife, and we can't be together in the end."

Ann did not agree. "God joined us together, Noah. Judge Hall can't pull that asunder. That's what Minnie said. I don't care if there's a piece of paper in a drawer or not. You're my husband, and I'm your wife."

"But we still can't be together. Men will find us, they'll whip us, and give us a year of hard labor someplace much worse than this, and they'll do it every time. I don't want to do that to you."

Ann tried to come up with a solution. "We can live in Indian Territory."

"Maybe Sally, Stephanie, and Eli don't want to live there. Are you going to leave them?"

"I will if I have to. Would you two forgive me?"

Stephanie said, "I'll go with you if Eli will."

"I would have to leave my father. Then he would have lost both my mother and me."

Eli had gotten them into this unintentionally. Now, he was preventing any chance of him being with Ann. "You see, Ann, it's too complicated. In the end, we won't be together."

Stephanie said, "We can't see it, but God will provide the way."

"I hope and pray that He does." The tree started to lean. Ann warned everybody, "Stand back."

Noah yelled, "Timber," then gave the tree a push. The giant cedar made a loud snap then dropped to the forest floor. Ann and Noah walked over and sawed a branch at the dividing line between the dock and fence sections of the tree.

Stephanie and Eli worked to remove a branch from the fence portion of the tree. Eli knew that he had upset Noah and changed the topic of discussion, "Have you finalized your construction plans?"

At that moment, Noah didn't want to talk to Eli, but he went ahead and explained, "On each side, we're going to dig six six-foot-deep holes each eighteen inches around. We'll use cedar posts eight-foot or longer that we'll adjust to the correct height to build the landing's frame. We'll do the same on both sides of the creek. It's going to take a ton of logs to make all the planks we'll need to cover the landings.

"Jeremiah has a plan about how to make the dock so that Israel can raise or lower it as the water level rises or falls. If the creek is flooding, Israel will be able to pull the ferry onto land with a chain and winch attached to a post that we'll set in the ground far up from the creek. Jeremiah said that we have to build a ferry big enough for a wagon and a team of four oxen. We'll also have to dig two holes at least ten feet deep in the creek for the ferry mooring posts."

"Sounds like a hard but good plan." Eli pulled away the branch he and Stephanie had finished cutting.

Stephanie again changed the topic of conversation, "It's good that Judge Hall doesn't really know us, isn't it?"

Eli positioned the saw. "What do you mean?"

"He thinks he has given out a horrible sentence, but it's not any harder than Noah and Ann can handle."

In the place where they had removed a few

branches, Ann pulled the saw her way then let Noah pull it his way. "Even though we're capable, it is hard work, and we have to do it without any help."

Stephanie asked her sister for validation of her opinion, "But we would have been willing to help Israel anyway. Wouldn't we?"

To Ann, it didn't feel like anything she wanted to do. "I guess we might have. Maybe it's because we're being forced that I hate it."

Noah paused. "I think the hard work is a blessing. The real punishment is separating me from Ann. The hard work gives me something else to focus on." Noah whispered to Ann, "It is so very hard not to touch you."

"I think so too, but I'm very happy that we can talk and that you stopped telling me that you don't love me."

"I'm trying to protect you. If I'm doing the wrong thing, it's because I don't know what the right thing is."

Ann believed that the answer was simple. "Running away from me definitely is not right. After this is over, meet me somewhere, and we'll figure out where to go."

"There is no place we can be safe together, and trying will get you whipped. If only I was taking a chance, I would surely want to attempt it, but I couldn't face myself if I purposefully did something that got you whipped, imprisoned, or worse. Let's just cut this tree and stop talking about this."

After a long day of hard labor, they returned to camp dead tired. The following day, they again suffered through the backbreaking, mind-numbing, endless monotony of sawing. Day after day onwards, they cut trees, removed the branches, and hauled the logs to the creek until all the logs Noah thought they needed for the west-side-dock lay beside the creek, and all the logs Jeremiah thought he required for the fence lay in the camp.

At that point, sawing in the woods with everybody working around them ended. Next, with only each other and one soldier guarding them, Ann and Noah trudged to the creek to work. Both of them sharpened their axes for an hour. Noah walked to one of the biggest logs. He swung the axe. The short stub of a branch flew into the air followed by chips of various sizes. In a short time, he had leveled several of the branch stubs. "Let me test yours." Noah held out his hand. Ann gave him her axe. Chips flew in every direction. He handed her back the axe. "When it gets dull, stop and sharpen it again."

Noah had already been impressed by the tireless work of Ann as they sawed. Now he saw something new. Because he and Eli had done all the wood chopping since he had been at the farm, he saw Ann chop a tree for the first time. He looked at her sleek, perfectly shaped body. He watched her strong muscles swing the axe and hit the branch nub at the perfect angle. To Noah, Ann chopping wood looked like a ballet of grace. She moved with perfection. She was strong, tireless, beautiful, and distracting. He decided he was going to chop off his arm, his leg, or something by not paying attention to what he was doing. "I'm going to work on that tree over there." He went to work where he wasn't facing Ann. However, when he stopped to sharpen his axe, he again looked at Ann and took in her beauty. He wanted to spend every second he could looking at the woman he wanted. At the same time, he hated to be reminded that he was going to lose her.

For many days they worked to prep six large logs for the frame, several logs of smaller diameter for the platform base, two huge eighteen-foot logs for mooring the ferry, many logs for the cross planks, and all the logs for the ferry. They followed the same basic process to debark the logs at the creek that the others used in the field by the camp to make fence posts and cross rails.

Noah and Ann sat together and sharpened their drawknives. Noah stood up beside the front end of the log. Ann walked several feet down the log behind him. They chipped the knives through then drew the blade down the tree under the layer of bark. It wasn't long before Ann, for the hundredth time, had the same problem Noah repeatedly faced. Ann decided she had better work on a different tree, so she didn't injure herself by looking at the man in front of her instead of paying attention to where she was pulling the very sharp tool.

Just outside of camp, Jeremiah started the fires to heat a massive iron drum of black goop. During the days that Noah and Ann debarked the trees by the creek, the men in camp lowered batches of fence parts into the hot creosote. After the creosote had come up to temperature, they put out the fires but left the wood in the drum to draw in the preservative as it cooled. Creosoting and debarking continued for many days. Ann and Noah debarked all their trees, split off planks, shaped, and stacked them. Many of the planks Noah made started correctly sized but then, with some of his help, the fibers of the wood turned, and they became too thin, or they broke unexpectedly. Long after all the fence posts and rails sat creosoted, Ann and Noah continued to make planks.

Noah sabotaged the work to slow the construction, but the day still arrived when all the planks they needed were ready to creosote. They sealed up the drums, rolled them to the creek, set up again, and started the fires. The fall days were cool, but Ann and Noah were not. For days and days, they slaved by the fire, painted layer after layer of hot tar on the debarked logs too big to put into the drums, and treated the massive piles of planks in the drums.

When all the wood was ready, they felt getting away from the heat to dig holes would be a relief, but the ground was mostly a rock pit that happened to have some dirt in it. They pried and dug out rock after rock. The holes ended up much larger than the required eighteen inches around. Then, the same rocks they dug out, they put back around the posts to hold them in place while they replaced the dirt. Eventually, Ann and Noah packed the final shovel full of dirt around the last post planted on land.

THIRTY THREE

The prisoners stood in Cadron Creek and tried to make holes in the bed of rocks. As they jabbed at the creek's bottom, their shovels clacked against the rocks but didn't penetrate between them. Both prodded, stomped, and tried to work their shovels under the edge of the rocks that blocked their progress. Noah finally got the shovel a tiny bit under the edge of the rock he was attempting to remove. He pushed the handle down. Nothing happened. Ann tried to help him but to no avail. Noah decided to try a different side of the rock but achieved the same lack of results. He tried a third position. "Ann, I got the shovel way under! Help me push down."

Side by side, with all four hands, they pushed the handle down.

SNAP!

Their faces hit the cold water. The rest of their bodies followed their faces into the creek. Ann sat up. Although she was glad they had been close to the bank where the water was not deep, and that they had remained where they hit the water, she was very unhappy that she was completely soaked. Ann looked at Noah sitting beside her in the creek. He whispered, "I wish I could help you get warmed up."

Henry was on guard duty and had seen their dive into the water. "Let's go. We don't want you to get sick."

Noah felt around then held up the shovelhead. "Found it!"

The two wet people shivered as they walked back to camp. Henry followed them to the tent. Noah stopped him. "Ann should go in first." Ann stepped into the tent. Noah closed the door. "Ann, so you don't drip on anything, leave your wet clothes by the door. When you're in your area, we'll come in."

"All right."

Henry waited outside the tent. Even though he didn't need to, Noah firmly blocked the door until Ann could get behind the curtain that Jeremiah had erected.

"I'm out of view."

Noah stepped into the tent with very blue lips. He stripped as fast as he could. "May I get under my covers to warm up a little bit?"

"I guess that's all right. I'll lie on my blankets while you two each get warm in your separate beds."

Henry heard Noah's teeth chatter for several minutes before he heard the sound of Noah's breathing change into the sound of a man sleeping. Soon, he heard Ann asleep as well. Henry knew Ann was wearing down. He wanted to be the blessing that Ann had called him in her prayer when they had first arrived. He decided to let them sleep, sat up so he didn't join them, opened up his book, and read until he heard Melvin and Sally come into camp to start supper.

Noah and Ann had been asleep for quite a while. "You better get up now."

Noah got into a set of dry clothes. "I feel refreshed. How long did I sleep?"

"A few hours."

"That was very nice." When Noah was completely dressed, he told Ann, "I'm ready. Are you?"

Ann stepped out. "Maybe it was worth taking the swim to get the wonderful nap."

Henry gave his report to his commander when Jeremiah returned to camp. "The shovel broke, and the prisoners fell into the creek. I let them warm up, each under their own blankets. I remained on guard duty in the tent with them. Since they have to fix the shovel before they can get back to work, I let them sleep." He didn't mention that he was worried about Ann.

"That's fine. Thank you for reporting the incident."

Henry wasn't the only one who had noticed the haggard look on Ann's face. Noah informed Jeremiah, "We need to replace the handles of both shovels." To let Ann rest, Noah halted the work in the creek by spending days carving long handles with the much harder wood of the hickory tree they had cut down when they had enlarged the field.

Jeremiah knew what Noah was doing. He didn't mind. He knew they both needed to rest. He also knew he had to have a reason he could report to Captain Cornish and Judge Hall as to why they spent a few days in camp.

When Noah completed the handles, the two

prisoners returned to their task under the watchful eyes of Justus. With a shovel that was able to withstand and apply more force, they eventually pried out the rock. Noah breathed a sigh of relief, "Finally."

Their happiness was short-lived. The water immediately washed away all the surrounding creek bed and exposed a rock even larger than the one they had just removed. They dug and dug and dug to get it free and once again dislodged most of the surrounding creek bed. Every time they started a hole, the water caved in the sides. After many days of very hard work, they had made no progress. The creek bed was lower, but there still wasn't a hole.

That evening, the group discussed how to dig a hole in moving water. John proposed digging the whole creek bed down ten feet then building it back up around the posts. Even though Noah and Ann were supposed to be doing hard labor, Ann thought digging the whole creek bed down ten feet was ridiculous and impossible. Thankfully, Jeremiah knew the replaced dirt and rocks would be loose and wash away. He rejected the plan.

Israel knew the creek the best. He suggested they pile rocks and dirt above, down the side, and below the area where they needed to sink the posts. That would temporarily make a dam to keep the water out of the area where Ann and Noah needed to work and leave a channel for the water to pass.

Noah thought it over. He believed that would work, but he didn't want to leave his family. Even though Noah knew he couldn't make it last forever, he wanted to make the project take as long as possible. On the other hand, he knew the continual very heavy labor of digging in the rocky bottom of the creek was wearing Ann down. "Plus, if we take the dirt from the other side to build the dam, we could shape the bank so that the ferry could pull right up to the road, and we wouldn't have to make a second landing."

Not having to cut more trees or build a second landing was definitely Ann's choice. She wanted to get the job done and secretly escape to the west with Noah. "I like that plan."

They looked at Jeremiah. "I do too. Make it so."

After days of standing in water, getting colder by the day, Ann needed her feet out of the water and into several pairs of socks with her feet propped up by the fire. "My feet are completely waterlogged. I don't think they'll ever be warm again, and I can barely walk."

Noah hobbled to the fire. "Mine are the same." He sat across the fire from Ann and put his feet up to warm them. Later, when everybody sat in the mess tent eating another scrumptious meal prepared by the Melvin and Sally team, Noah mentioned the problem that he hoped would create another excuse to let Ann rest. "Jeremiah, we need warmer clothes, and we need to work on dry land for a while to let our feet heal."

Expecting they might end up with this problem, Jeremiah had already prepared. "John, get the bag of clothes we brought." Jeremiah explained, "Assuming we would probably still be here when the weather got cold, I brought warmer clothes for you two." John returned with the bag. He handed it to Jeremiah who passed both Noah and Ann short, heavy, canvas overcoats lined with a thick layer of wool, along with wool pants, wool shirts, wool socks, scarfs, gloves, and hats. Jeremiah also went ahead and authorized Noah and Ann to spend a few days with their feet by the fire before they had to return to their work in the creek.

The second day Noah and Ann sat in camp, those building the fence each placed one piece into the last section of the fence. Israel inserted the last rail into the hole of the last post. They maneuvered the post into plumb, shoveled in dirt, and tamped it in with an iron rod. In appreciation for enlarging the field and building the fence, Israel prepared a celebration supper.

Two days after the fence completion, Noah and Ann went back to work in the creek. At the end of the week, they had diverted the water and returned to digging, this time in a dry creek. Making holes in the creek bed was the hardest work Ann had ever done. Her back ached. Her feet and legs hurt from trying to force a shovel into the rocks. The cedar poultice and cottonwood tea didn't help enough. In an effort to keep working, she consumed large amounts of cottonwood tea. That made her stomach hurt. She thought she wasn't going to survive. Everybody in camp was worried about her.

Noah tried to do as much of the work himself as he possibly could. The work wore him down as well. Still, he told Ann, "You fill in around the posts. I'll finish digging the last hole."

Ann knew Noah was working too hard trying to help her. She turned towards him but couldn't even see his head above the top of the hole. She thought the hole was deep enough. She walked over and held her hand down into the hole to pull him out. "Noah, please come help me keep this post straight." Noah took her hand, put his foot on a boulder at the bottom of the pit, and started to rise. The ground swayed to the right. Ann stumbled. Noah dropped back into the pit. Ann got to her feet. "What was that?"

Noah grabbed Ann's wrist. "Pull me out now!"

The ground heaved. Ann flew backward. Noah no longer held her wrist.

John stood up, cocked his rifle, pulled the set trigger, and strategically placed his finger on the firing trigger to take out whatever gigantic thing was coming their way. The earth moved violently. John tumbled sideways. His finger squeezed the trigger and sent the lead ball into the invisible enemy.

Ann rolled towards the open hole. In front of her eyes, the hole slammed shut. She didn't know if she had pulled Noah out or not. If he was inside, her heart was buried with him. As the earth flipped her about, the dam broke. The rush of water attempted to wash her into a newly created pit that swallowed the creek and caused it to run backward. Ann crashed into a post. She clung tightly but heard the screams of the destroyer. *Let go, be with Noah in death. Nobody can keep you apart there.* She also heard the whisper, *trust me, and hold on.*

The soldiers and civilians tried to run from the camp to the creek. They knew Ann and Noah had to be in deep holes and feared that they had been buried alive. The earth threw them to the ground. They scrambled back to their feet and took off again. Eli was the first to arrive. Long thin ropes of Ann's black hair swirled and attempted to tie her head to the post to which it was pressed.

Ann's mind screamed, *let go, go to Noah.* The water reversed again and rushed back. Eli and Ann both saw that it carried a body barely flailing against the current. The deceiver ordered, *Grab him. Save him.* Ann's creator whispered into her heart, *you'll be ripped into the current, and Noah will drown trying to save you.* Ann knew that was exactly what Noah would do. She held on, saw Eli jump into the raging water, and knew she had listened to the right voice.

Jeremiah arrived as Noah washed past with Eli going downstream just as fast. Justus came up beside Jeremiah. "Aren't you going after them?"

"If they don't drown, they'll be back."

The rest of the group arrived at the creek as the earth ceased its thrashing. Stephanie took in the scene. Only Ann was visible. "Where are Eli and Noah?"

Jeremiah pointed. "Eli is down there somewhere trying to save Noah." Stephanie and Smitty ran. If they needed to help, they wanted to be there.

Sally started towards her sister. Jeremiah stopped her. "I'll go out and get her." He had barely stepped into the creek before he realized his feet would not touch the creek bed all the way over, and the rush of water was too strong to swim against it. "Ann, get to the upstream side of the post." He looked at his men. "Get a rope."

Israel had the best idea. "Let me get my ropes and harness." He didn't wait for permission.

Ann was sure if she loosened her grip to move that she would not be able to hold on. She stayed where she was and prayed, "God, help me hold on, and help Eli save Noah."

Jeremiah lassoed the post to which Ann clung and tied the other end to a landside post. Israel attached the sliding harness, tied Jeremiah in, and handed him the short end of the feed rope. "Tie Ann to you. We'll pull you back."

Secured in the harness, Jeremiah swam into the creek as Israel fed out the retrieval rope. Jeremiah pressed his body against Ann's back. "I'm going to tie you to me. Don't let go until I tell you." Ann nodded that she understood. He forced his hand between her waist and the post. Splinters embedded themselves in the back of his hand. He pulled the rope through and tied it back to himself. "I've got you. Let go." He waved to the people on shore. Sally, Justus, John, Henry, Melvin, and Israel pulled them in. In lockstep, with Ann tied in front, they walked the last few steps out of the creek onto land.

As soon as she was untied, Ann turned and hugged Jeremiah. "Thank you for coming out to get me."

Downstream in the middle of the creek, Eli grabbed Noah's arm, pulled it over his shoulder, turned away, and brought Noah up onto his back. He brought Noah's other arm around his other side under his arm. Eli tried to keep the water out of his mouth as he sputtered, "Hold your hands together."

It took all of Noah's remaining strength to keep his arms clamped around his brother-in-law as Eli swam for the shore. They went downstream as fast as Smitty, Roy, and Ben had gone. With every breath, they drew the water that rolled over their faces into their mouths. As he hauled Noah, who was so exhausted that he would never have made it on his own, Eli spat muddy water and tried to draw only air into his lungs.

At the shore, Noah was too tired to climb out. Even after the rush of water subsided, the men lay against the dirt bank. Stephanie and Smitty caught up with them. Smitty retrieved Noah from the water. Noah had one thought on his mind. "Is Ann safe?"

Stephanie drew Eli up. "She was clinging to a post and had six people there to help her."

Noah wasn't sure if he felt grateful or wished he had drowned. If he had died, he wouldn't have to live his life without Ann. However, Eli had just risked his life for him. "Eli, I just can't thank you enough for pulling me out of the creek. I'm sure you saved my life."

"You're very welcome." The four rested on the shore before making the long walk back.

Ann stood beside the full creek. She could barely stand the thought of all the lost work. "Now, we have to rebuild the dam, dig the holes again, and straighten out the posts."

Jeremiah eyeballed what he could see above the

water. "Leave them as they are. Except for that one, I can barely tell that the posts are crooked, and now the ground is packed around them better than you could ever get it." An aftershock rocked the earth. "Not again!" Everybody braced, but nothing more followed. "We don't know how many aftershocks there will be or how strong they will be. Let's go back to camp. You can rebuild the dam tomorrow."

As they walked to the camp, Jeremiah decided ten feet was much too deep of a hole. "I don't want your hard labor sentence to turn into a death sentence if another hole should collapse. When you dig the last dock posthole and the mooring postholes, six feet will be deep enough."

They all hoped it was over when they went to sleep that night, but a tremor awakened them during the night. As a safety precaution, Jeremiah kept everybody in camp the next few days.

All the dirt of the previous dam had washed away. When Noah and Ann started back, they had to dig out more of the bank on the far side of the creek. It was much easier moving the dirt from the bank than digging holes in the rocky creek bottom. However, the water was much colder than the first time they built the dam. They could only move dirt a few hours before they had to warm up at the fire. With the easier work, both Noah and Ann recovered from extreme exhaustion to merely very fatigued at the end of every day. To make it easier, they dug the last dock hole where they had made the previous one. In case the earth moved again, they planted the post as soon as it was ready.

236

Eli sat beside Noah. "I've been wondering how you're going to fit an eighteen-foot-long log into a hole only six-feet-deep."

Noah passed Eli the bowl of beans. "We're going to cut the poles four feet shorter. Then we're going to rig ropes and pulleys to the trees, raise the posts, and drop them into the holes."

Ann butted into the conversation, "We don't know if it will work."

Eli passed the bowl to Ann. "Sounds like it should."

Even though they had only two mooring post holes to dig, the holes had to have a much larger diameter than the dock postholes. They fought and wrestled the rocks. They didn't know how there could be so many large rocks in one place. They returned to the same level of exhaustion as before the earthquake. When they finally had a hole dug, it was a huge relief.

Everybody went to the creek to watch Noah and Ann set the huge post that would moor the ferry at the end of the dock. Noah tried to hold the pole at the hole while the horses pulled the ropes attached to the pulleys. They couldn't keep the bottom in position and raise the upper end. Even though everybody tried to be respectful of the hard time Noah and Ann were having, it was such a funny spectacle that they all laughed under their breath.

Ann decided they needed to try something different. "Maybe we can attach a rope to the bottom and have one horse pull to hold the post while the other rope attached at the top raises the pole."

"I'm all for trying. This isn't working."

The others stood on the bank as Noah and Ann worked in the dry creek bed and tried to direct the bottom of the pole to the hole. At the same time that Noah used ropes tied to the reins of Eyanosa to get him to pull the bottom of the pole in the proper direction, Ann directed Bliss to pull the top of the pole. Noah orchestrated the work, "I need the bottom of the pole to come towards me. Bliss needs to go more to the right."

Ann pulled the right rein with one hand and directed the pole with her other. Bliss moved right. The top rope lost tension, slid up the post, and came completely off. The giant log crashed into the creek across the dam. "#*% $$! I'm sorry! I shouldn't have said that. This is just so frustrating! I don't know how that horrible person of a judge expects two people to be able to do this. I'm just too tired to pay attention to everything."

Noah walked over and assessed the damage. "I agree completely, including the first two words." The rest of the day, to not flood the dry area or wash out the hole they had worked so hard to dig, they used the horses to raise the log very slowly as they repaired the damaged dam little by little.

The first thing the next day, so that the ropes wouldn't slip, Noah notched the post at the top and the bottom. Eyanosa and Bliss pulled as commanded, Ann and Noah directed the lower part of the post towards the hole. As they looked down to see how the pole was lining up, the top of the pole went past the tipping point. In a big arch, the giant log swung towards the earth and Bliss. Smitty yelled Bliss's command to run. Ann dropped the ropes to Bliss's reins. The horse darted forward as the giant log crashed behind her.

Smitty turned towards Jeremiah. "That's it. I will not put my horse in danger any longer. That log could have killed Bliss or any of us. Let us help set these posts, or this isn't getting done."

Jeremiah issued orders to John and Justus, "Bring Chester and Storm in the harnesses. We should have been using them anyway." When they returned, Jeremiah took the reins of the two military horses. "Everybody, go back to camp. Do not come down here or even look down here." Jeremiah kept every witness contained in the camp with no visibility of the work at the creek then tied the pull ropes to the military horses' harnesses and the control ropes to their reins. "You don't say anything about this, and I won't either. Everybody else can say they never saw one drop of help because they aren't here to see anything. Keep your eyes on the pole bottom, and call out instructions. I'll direct the horses, and I'll watch the top of the pole."

After more struggling, the post finally slid into the hole. All three called out, "Hallelujah."

With hope, Noah added, "Now that we know how to do this, maybe the next one will be easier."

Unfortunately, but not unexpectedly, the last hole wasn't any easier to dig. Days later, the second mooring-post hole was ready. Noah, Ann, Jeremiah, Storm, and Chester once again struggled to maneuver the giant log into the six-foot-deep hole. After much aggravation, the post finally went into the hole. Emotionally worn out from the struggle, Jeremiah ordered that they quit for the day.

The next day, the whole group returned to the creek to watch Noah and Ann, on their own, direct Chester and Storm to pull the last post into plumb. Ann stood beside the post with the level and tried to hold the giant log straight. Noah filled in the space around the posts with rocks he rolled over that, to the exhausted man, seemed like moving giant boulders. As he went, he filled in around the rocks with dirt that he forced down with the tamping rod. Every post was set, but Ann was down to a frazzle.

The following days, Noah told Ann to do nothing but stand beside him and hold the shovel or the tamping rod while he repeatedly added and tamped down the dirt. They both prayed the posts would become well set. Noah also hooked up the heavy logs of the dock foundation but allowed Ann only to lead the horses as they hauled them into position. At the creek, he used the horses and carefully positioned pulleys to link the logs with the posts like cabin corners. Ann stood beside the horses and directed them as instructed. They pulled over and built the frame with a set of smaller but still large logs.

Noah spent an unusually long time installing the log that was only visible when standing in the creek. He walked past Ann on his way to the shoreline. "Go inspect the last log. It's the most important thing and something you must always remember."

Ann didn't think one made any more of a difference than any other log, but she went to examine it anyway. She called back to Noah, "I need to use your knife to get this exactly right." With an enormous smile, Ann walked to Noah and retrieved the knife.

Half an hour after they would have quit for the day, she made her way up the bank out of the dry creek bed. Noah wished he didn't have to wait until the next day to see what Ann had done to the log. He wanted their work to be a permanent part of the ferry dock, and he hoped that she had made it so it would remain forever. He wanted them both to know, no matter what, that one thing would never be gone.

Noah hurried through breakfast. He rushed Henry, who was to be their guard the first part of the day. Ann was ready to get to work as quickly as Noah was. Noah stood at the end of the dock. "It's perfect." He looked at the words they had deeply etched into the logs.

"Noah Swift Hawk loves Ann Williams forever. Ann Williams loves Noah Williams forever." They shaped two boards to fit tightly, painted the shaved places with creosote, nailed the first one down across the frame, and covered their declaration from the view and knowledge of everybody else. No matter what happened in the future, they both knew it would always be true.

THIRTY FOUR

Noah and Ann shaped board after board to fit against the previous board, creosoted the shaved places, and nailed them into place. Two months after they had arrived, they completed the final details of the dock that was the landing beside Israel's cabin. At the front edge of the adjustable platform, Noah knelt at one side then the other. He bolted the heavy metal "C" clamp, hooked to a large gauge metal link chain through the first plank and the large log at the front of the dock. Each chain ran back to land then through a pulley attached to a post buried deep into the earth. Noah secured the second chain. "They're attached. Try it out."

Straight up would be the position during very high water. "I'm going to try to raise it." Ann turned the wheel. The front end of the landing rose. "It's working!" With the same winch, Israel would also lower the platform so that he could pull the ferry out of the creek to its place on land. She turned the wheel the other way. The landing lowered smoothly all the way down to what would have been water level if the water had been in that part of the creek. Ann walked over, took hold of Noah's hand, shook it up and down three times, held on for a few seconds, then let it go before their guard noticed. "You do goooood work."

"You do too. Let's go get Jeremiah." They walked to Justus. "The dock is finished."

All three returned to camp and told Jeremiah the news. Everybody went to the landing. Jeremiah turned the wheel to raise and lower the platform. "I think we should test it with weight, but it would be difficult with one of our wagons. They're not easy to get out."

Noah pointed at the logs he planned to use for the boat. "It just needs to support the weight that will move across it. We can roll those logs on for a test."

Jeremiah didn't know if they would be enough. "How much do you think they weigh?"

Using knowledge learned working at Yates Mercantile, Eli quickly calculated. "Cedar wood, twelve feet long and a foot or thereabouts around, would be about five hundred and fifty pounds each."

Jeremiah issued orders to the prisoners. "Noah, you and Ann get the logs, and test your work." They rolled the first log onto the platform. No problem manifested. Everything remained fine when the second log rolled on. The platform creaked but held when they added the third one. When the final log rolled on, the chains snapped. They swung past Ann and Noah with deadly force, slammed into, and buried themselves in the ground. The front of the platform dropped. The logs rolled into the dry creek bed. Ann and Noah instinctively turned to each other away from the chains that swung past. Blessedly, they were between the chains.

They clung together. One, or both of them, could

have gone out of the world. At that moment, Noah didn't care what anybody thought. "My God, we could have been killed." He kissed Ann in front of everybody. Ann drank that kiss into her soul.

"Stop that. Move away from each other right now," Jeremiah demanded compliance. "I'm going to have to report this."

Noah let Ann go and stepped back but looked into her eyes. She saw how much he loved her, wanted her, and needed her.

Sally begged, "Please don't. They were almost killed."

Stephanie stood in front of Jeremiah and locked eyes. "This whole thing is wrong, and you know it. They've worked on this landing and your fence for days on end. They've stayed away from each other, and I'm sure they will while building the rest of it, not only that, but they have to go separate ways when this is over. Isn't that enough?"

Jeremiah couldn't let them get away with a blatant violation. He put them on notice, "If there are no other incidents, I won't report this. If there is, I'll have to. So don't make me."

Henry knew this was not the first time, but he did not divulge that information. *I hope they can do it.*

Thinking he would be able to comply, Noah assured him, "The situation overcame me, and I acted without thinking. I won't do it again."

"I'll behave properly too." Ann turned back to Noah. "Let's get the logs back on land."

After the horses had pulled the logs back to the place where they planned to build the ferry, the whole group again reasoned together. Even though the boat was going to be narrower than the dock, it was going to be just as long. Only the main logs that would be the ferryboat's base still lay beside the creek with only a few boards. They hadn't felled enough trees. Ann and Noah were going to have to saw down many more cedar trees to make the ferry, and they were going to have to do it without any help under the excuse of making fence posts.

Next, they tried to come up with a solution to the problem of supporting massive weight on the adjustable platform. Eventually, the group realized they were not going to come up with an answer.

Since they were all there, and he needed to talk with all of them, Smitty brought up what had been on his mind, "I want to leave in the morning. We've been here a long time, and the ferry isn't even started. I don't want you to be upset with me. It's not that I don't care. It's that I should go home to Mara."

Noah assured Smitty, "I won't have any hard feelings. It's not your sentence, and there's nothing you can do to help anyway."

Smitty still felt he should justify leaving his friends in a bad situation. "Mara is probably worried to death. It's been more than two months since we left Harmony. I was only supposed to be gone one month, and I still have over a week more of travel to get home. I know it's a big nuisance to get the wagon out, so I'll take Bliss but leave the wagon. You can bring it home when you come."

Eli pointed out the flaw in the logic, "Noah's going to take Eyanosa in a different direction. Without Bliss, we can't get the wagon anywhere."

Jeremiah no longer felt he needed to keep the wagon hostage. "We can take down the mess tent and move the logs from around the fire, so you can get the wagon out."

Sally brought up another consideration, "I don't want to sleep under the stars with no place to get out of the rain. What are you planning to do with the tent?"

Smitty felt guilty, and he knew they needed the shelter. "You keep the tent until you get home." He hated to leave his friends in this situation, but he knew there wasn't anything his presence would change. He went to the wagon to determine what he should do with its contents.

Ann talked with Stephanie, "I'm not going back to Harmony when this is over. I don't want a life without Noah. I'm going with him whether he likes it or not. You, Eli, and Sally can have the farm. You can rebuild it, and stay there if you want, or you can come with me. Maybe Smitty will buy the farm. Talk to Eli and Sally, and decide what you want to do. If you do want to come with me, ask Smitty if he'll buy the farm. I'm sorry, but if he's going home in the morning, you have to decide tonight."

Stephanie's thoughts of the farm were painful. "Our beautiful house is gone. Even if we built another, it wouldn't be the same. As far as I'm concerned, we can abandon the farm. I'll ask the others."

First, she talked to Eli, who said, "I still don't want to leave without Pop. I want to find out if he'll go with us before I decide anything."

Afterward, when alone with Sally, Stephanie told her Ann's message. Sally's answer was, "I absolutely do not want to split up the family under any circumstances. I'm mad that Noah still says he's going to leave us."

Stephanie then got them together. "I completely understand that Ann wants to be with Noah. I wouldn't want to be without Eli. Noah and Ann will have to go at least to Indian Territory or possibly even further west."

Eli was firm in his decision. "I don't feel like I have to live in Harmony. This trip has shown me how much there is to discover, but I'm not leaving my father."

Sally angrily related her frustration, "I hate Arkansas, their stupid laws, stupid courts, and stupid people. People who really do something wrong get away with it. Folks like us, who did nothing wrong, suffer. Everybody here wants to hate Indians. I don't even want to live in this state with these people."

"So, if Tom will go with us, you'd both go to Indian Territory or even all the way to the Pacific Ocean?"

Together, Eli and Sally said, "Yes."

Stephanie asked about the other important item to consider, "Do you care if we sell the land or not?"

"Sell it as far as I'm concerned. It reminds me of things I would rather forget. I thought I didn't want to ever forget, but I do."

"It's not my land. Do what you want."

"I'm going to tell Ann she should tell Noah to meet us in Harmony at the cave with the skeleton or Rock House Cave. That would be better. We could camp in there and wait for him to get there the long way around. I'll ask Smitty if he wants to buy the land. If Tom will go, but Smitty doesn't want the land, we'll try to sell the farm to somebody else. If Tom doesn't want to go, we'll figure out what to do at that time."

After Stephanie's wedding, unless Ann was in the dormitory for the night, Stephanie was able to speak with Ann any time she wanted. Later, since he didn't see how any harm could come out of it, Jeremiah had even decided that everybody could talk to anybody at any time. That was if everybody was up for the day. Stephanie went to Ann who sat at the fire waiting to hear what had been decided. "Sally doesn't want to live in Arkansas at all anymore. She is very insistent that whatever we do it has to be all five of us. Eli still doesn't want to go without his father, so we have to go to Harmony and find out if he'll go with us. We don't know if he'll be willing to go with us or not. If you still want me to ask him, I'll ask Smitty about the land tonight."

As they spoke, Jeremiah started his prisoners to the tent. Ann had to go. "I guess we'll only be able to know what's going to happen as we go. I appreciate you talking with everybody. Go ahead, and talk to Smitty. Let me know what he says tomorrow." Ann hugged Stephanie and kissed her cheek. "Good night. I love you to the moon and back. Tell Sally the same."

Stephanie went to help Smitty at the wagon and to tell him her proposition. "Smitty, I want to talk with you."

"I'm listening."

"None of us want our land anymore. We want to offer you the option to buy it."

"I don't like to make a decision like that without talking it over with Mara. However, I know in this situation that isn't possible. How many acres of land? How much do you want?"

"It's a hundred acres with an excellent creek. This spring there were twenty acres cleared for crops. Now, the fire has cleared all of it. But I don't know the fair price for burned-up land."

"The price set out by the Federal Government is one dollar and twenty-five cents an acre for uncleared land. Cleared land has more value, so I'll give you one hundred fifty dollars, the tent, and all the supplies. Except I'll keep what I need to get home, the wagon, and Bliss. You and Eli can come with me to Kuhn Bayou and transfer the deed."

"I think we have a deal, but I want to make sure that's acceptable to the others and find out if I can use a couple of horses."

The next morning, Stephanie passed on Smitty's offer to Sally, Eli, and Ann who all told her to do it. Stephanie found Noah and told him the whole plan.

Noah reminded her that his opinion didn't matter. "Do what you think is best. I'm not going to be able to be with you."

"We're not going to let you leave us."

"It's not up to us."

"Ann is going to follow you." Stephanie walked away. She got Eli and went to tell Jeremiah that they wanted to sell their land to Smitty and could transfer the deed at Kuhn Bayou. They asked if they could use the two military horses to go with Smitty to Kuhn Bayou and back. Jeremiah said he would think about it.

Meanwhile, Jeremiah let Ann help Stephanie and Smitty carry all the supplies that Smitty was leaving into the tent. Henry and John took down the mess tent while Justus, Eli, Jeremiah, and Noah moved the sitting logs, and Melvin and Sally prepared breakfast. After breakfast, everybody pushed the lower military wagon far enough out of the way for Smitty to back up then pull forward out of the enclosure through the open gate at the front. Even though he believed they would come back, Jeremiah decided he should not let civilians ride away with military horses, so Stephanie left in the wagon, and Eli rode away on Eyanosa.

THIRTY FIVE

After two uneventful days, Smitty, Eli, and Stephanie stood on the Kuhn Bayou Bridge. Smitty called out, "Open the gate."

Zachariah and Minnie came out of the cabin. Stephanie greeted them, "Hello, Zachariah. Hello, Minnie."

Zachariah worked the lock. "What brings you three here without everybody else? Are Sally, Ann, and Noah all right?"

"They were all fine when we left. Ann and Noah are still working." Eli urged Eyanosa off the bridge.

Minnie felt these people were friends, friends who had come specifically to see her. She felt so happy and wanted to know everything. "Come in, and tell us all about it." They parked the wagon and got the horses settled in for the night then went inside.

Stephanie cuddled up to Eli and drew his arm around her waist. "We got married."

Minnie wanted to make her friends comfortable and pulled out a bench for them to sit. "Congratulations."

"How did you accomplish that?" Zachariah asked.

Eli answered, "We brought Jeremiah's uncle, Reverend Pratt, out to Cadron Creek."

Minnie came back from the kitchen with the coffee they had on the stove. "So why are you here?" She put out china cups for everybody and poured.

Smitty took a cup. "I'm going home. Eli and Stephanie came with me because I'm going to buy their land."

Zachariah looked at Stephanie. "I didn't know you were going to sell your farm."

Stephanie selected the prettiest cup. "It just came up."

"We remembered that you could transfer the deed." Eli pointed to the sign.

"I can write it up, but it's always Harry who files everything." Minnie sat beside Zachariah.

"That complicates things." Stephanie put sugar in her coffee.

So he could have time to think about what he wanted to do, Zachariah changed the subject. "Tell us everything that's been happening at Cadron Creek."

Minnie was so happy to have real visitors. "I'll get you something to eat." She went to the kitchen and came back with the pot of beef soup she had been cooking. Eli, Stephanie, and Smitty told them everything that had happened at Cadron Creek.

Since they had finished the tasty soup, Zachariah stacked the bowls. "We felt the earthquake but it wasn't strong enough to damage the cabin or bridge. Minnie, I'll help you with these dishes." In the kitchen, Zachariah whispered to Minnie, "That's good land. A fire cleared all of it and fertilized the land. We'd have to build a house, but it would be our place. We could make a living farming the land. I know how to be a farmer and a carpenter. I'm sure my parents will help. Maybe we can buy the farm. What do you think?"

With that one offer, Minnie understood that Zachariah truly wanted to marry and love her for their entire lives. "It's a very good idea, but even if they'll sell it to us, we still have the problem of transferring the deed."

Zachariah kissed Minnie. "I love you. We'll figure it out." They walked back into the front room. "Smitty, would you be willing to let me buy it?"

"It's good land, and I'm happy to buy it, but I would have to get somebody else to work it. What's your plan?"

With much pride and affection, Minnie said, "Zachariah wants to build us a home and be farmers together."

"I offered them one hundred fifty dollars in cash, an excellent brand new six-man india rubber tent, and most of the supplies that were left. It's about two hundred dollars all together. You'd have to pay me the fifty dollars and them the one hundred and fifty."

Zachariah hoped he could strike a deal. "I know this is asking a lot. Can you give them the one hundred and fifty cash, and let me pay you the two hundred over time?"

"Hold on a minute, please. Zachariah, come in here." Minnie led Zachariah back into the kitchen. "I've kept back some of the money all these years. I have two hundred and forty-seven dollars."

"Minnie, my love, I appreciate the offer, but I want to provide a home for you. I don't want you to buy it for me. You keep your money."

Minnie loved Zachariah more by the minute. She had an incredible realization. *It's actually ME he wants.*

Zachariah sat across from Smitty and looked him in the eye. "What do you say, Smitty?"

"I'll do it for you, but we still have the problem of transferring the deed."

Stephanie had an idea. "What if you did all the paperwork, took it to Dover, and said Harry is sick, so you brought everything for him?"

Zachariah added, "I don't think Harry will deny it when we know about him having two wives."

Minnie got a sheet of paper, ink, and a pen out from behind the counter. "I know how to write just like him. I can write a note from him asking the clerk to file the deed transfer."

"Wait a minute." Smitty rifled around in his bag. "Here it is." He pulled out the envelope with Ann and Noah's marriage document as well as the note Harry had given him.

To the clerk of the court,

Please accept and file this document delivered by Sheriff Smithfield Wyman.

Harold LeBarron,
Associate Clerk of the Court; Little Rock

Minnie brought up a point of concern, "I don't know if he goes by Harold LeBarron in Dover."

Zachariah told her, "Make your note too."

"This one is real. We use this one. That way it is completely legal." Smitty put the note on the table and rummaged through his bag again. He pulled out the money he had collected in Little Rock and counted out one hundred and fifty dollars. He placed it in Stephanie's hand. She gave it to Eli.

Eli handed it back. "Honey, it's your money."

"You hold it. It will be safer if you have it."

"I'll carry it for you until we get back to Cadron Creek, but it belongs to you, Ann, and Sally."

After eating breakfast the following day, Zachariah and Minnie told the others that they had decided to abandon the cabin and go to Harmony when they left Dover. The five of them started moving everything from the cabin into Zachariah's and Smitty's wagons.

Eli had planned to go back to Little Rock with Stephanie for a few days, but they had never gone. Except for Reverend Pratt and the Andrews, he didn't like Little Rock. He decided staying at the cabin would be much nicer. "Since you're leaving, would it be all right if we stay in the cabin for a few days?"

"Sure. I was going to leave the door unlocked anyway." Minnie set blankets and pillows on the counter. "Take these. I'd leave the bed, but we'll need it." She smiled at Zachariah.

"This is very generous." Stephanie picked them up.

"It's getting cold. Take Harry's coats."

Stephanie didn't want to be greedy. "Are you sure you want to give all this away?"

"I'm not going to leave Harry one thing. He used my money to set up this place. I'm taking my investment back. You need coats. I want you to have them." Minnie passed Stephanie and Eli the coats then added gloves, hats, and scarfs before deciding to give them all of Harry's winter clothes. "Now that I've thought about it, I don't want to look at anything that belonged to Harry, may he rot in Hell." Minnie threw every piece of Harry's clothes into the pile to leave.

Stephanie hugged Minnie. "We didn't know we would be out here this long. Not that it would have made a difference because we lost everything, but now we have warm clothes. I'm so much obliged."

When everything was packed, they said goodbye. Smitty, Zachariah, and Minnie headed west to Dover with the two wagons and everything from the cabin. Eli and Stephanie stood beside the empty shell. Stephanie snuggled close into Eli's arms. "I'm glad we can have some time to ourselves. Let's not hurry back. I want to be alone with you. I have an idea of something we can do." They went into the cabin and put the blankets and pillows on the floor beside the fire blazing in the fireplace.

Eli entreated his wife, "Let me look at you here by the fire, my beautiful one, my love." In the light of day, Eli beheld the full beauty of his wife. Later, as Eli held Stephanie in his arms, he brought up the subject of his father, "Honey, what should we say to Pop?"

"First, we should tell him that we got married and apologize that we got married without him, or maybe since we don't want to hurt his feelings, and we've already gotten married twice anyway, we could get married a third time in Harmony."

"I like the idea of getting married again, and I appreciate your concern for my father's feelings."

"Of course, darling, he's also my father now. I care about him, and I do not want to leave him behind. If he doesn't want to leave Harmony, I'm staying there with you. Ann and Sally will have to decide what they'll do. I don't want to lose them, but even more, I don't want to be without you."

"I don't want to lose you or your family either. I hope Pop will go west with us. He doesn't have anything other than the store, and he can start another wherever we end up. I feel horrible about creating this situation by saying in court that Noah is an Indian. I should have known after what happened in Harmony that it would be a problem. I wish I could take it all back. Even though Noah says he's not, I'm sure I made him mad because I won't leave my father."

"Those are ridiculous interracial marriage laws. I just do not understand why anybody cares who other people marry. They don't even know us, and we won't ever be around them. Now, we have this mess. Ann and Noah have to work so hard. I'm really worried about them, especially Ann, and worst of all; they were told they aren't married."

"It's absolute nonsense. I like having Noah as my

brother. I don't want to hurt him. I don't want him mad or upset with me, and I love your sisters. I don't want them mad at me either. It's a horrible mess that I'm sorry I made, and I wish I could make it go away."

"One of the things I love about you is that you care about how people feel. I know you would never intentionally hurt anybody. This is not your fault."

"And one of the things I love about you is that you always make me feel like I'm a good man." Eli kissed the person who meant so much to him then brought up another topic on his mind.

"Honey, I was thinking, with all this uncertainty, maybe we should be careful and not make a child until we get this situation figured out. Would you be unhappy about that?"

"No, I agree. We have no idea what's going to happen. But let's not wait forever."

They stayed at the cabin the next few days sharing their love. On the fourth day, they left the bridge's gate locked open and started back towards Cadron Creek. All around, tiny duckweed leaves colored the entire surface of the swamp a brilliant green. Bald cypress needles lay strewn over the duckweed. Stephanie and Eli casually rode along, enjoying the beauty.

Without warning, an alligator surged up from under the duckweed. Its bone-crushing jaws clacked when it missed Eyanosa's leg. The horse bucked and kicked at his attacker as the alligator slid onto the boardwalk. Stephanie and Eli tumbled to the causeway and rolled toward the water where they could not win a battle against such a powerful adversary. Eyanosa charged away with the shotgun in its holster.

They scrambled to their feet. *Now what?* Eli quickly took in all their positions. "Run to Eyanosa."

Stephanie stood paralyzed with fear. "I'm afraid to go past. It will get me."

The giant swamp creature eyed dinner and lunged. Stephanie screamed. Eli kicked the alligator in the head. "I think I can run faster than it can." Long sharp teeth turned towards Eli. "Go!" Since his life depended on it, Eli sprinted away with all that was in him. "Get the shotgun and shoot it!" The monstrous carnivore pursued its fleeing prey.

Stephanie had to get the rifle to save Eli. Out of the alligator's view, she darted to the far edge of the causeway then took off running. "Please, God, help us!" Stephanie had heard Noah training his horse to respond to his whistles. She hoped beyond hope that Eyanosa would come to her. She whistled and whistled as she raced farther and farther away from Eli. Eyanosa heard the whistle, but instinct told him to get away from his attacker. Stephanie knew she was running out of time, but she kept trying. The only hope they had was for her to get the shotgun.

The whistle wasn't Noah, but Eyanosa finally understood that Stephanie was calling. He turned back. She swung up onto the horse. "Go." She kicked her heels into the horse and pulled the shotgun from its holster. They flew up the causeway. The alligator drew closer to Eli. Repeatedly, she kicked her heels into

Eyanosa's sides. "Go! Go! Go!" Eyanosa narrowed the gap. She had to get there in time. The alligator was almost upon its prey. Even though Stephanie was still too far away, she aimed for the monster that chased the man she loved. "Go! Go! Go! Go!"

The rapid clicks of claws on the wooden boards drew closer to Eli. He knew he wasn't going to be able to continue the full out sprint much longer. *It's going to hurt so much. I hope it kills me quickly.* He felt himself start to slow. *It has me. God, take me to you.*

Stephanie saw the alligator barely a foot behind Eli. *They're too far.* "No!" She refused to let it happen. "God, I'm begging You; help me make the shot!" She dropped the reins and merged into synchronous motion with Eyanosa. With both hands on the shotgun, she drew a bead …pulled the firing trigger …a head exploded.

THIRTY SIX

The alligator's body crashed to a halt. Eyanosa continued towards the monster. Stephanie knew she did not hit the mark on her own. "Thank you, God!"

Eli heard the blast, but death might still be trying to gobble him up. He persisted in his flight. Stephanie hollered, "It's dead," then jumped off Eyanosa and ran past the carcass to Eli. They threw their arms around each other. Adrenaline coursed through their veins. They shook uncontrollably. "Thank God that you're a fast runner."

"And that you're an excellent marksman."

"I was so afraid."

Eli comforted her, "We're all right, honey. We're safe." When they were finally calm, they walked over to look at the loser of the battle.

Stephanie kicked alligator brains. "No alligator ought to tangle with my man."

"Don't kick away the brains. I need it to tan the skin."

"You want to tan it?"

"I've never tanned an alligator, but I don't know how we can get all this stuff and that alligator to Cadron Creek."

"We can walk and carry the blankets, pillows, and

clothes. We can put the alligator and what we can't carry on the horse."

"You sure you don't mind walking?"

"I've walked to the creek once. I can do it again. I wonder if Eyanosa will let us put this monster on him."

Eli slit the alligator, pulled out its innards, and slung them into the swamp. Eyanosa backed away as they pulled the alligator towards him. Stephanie tried to hold the horse, but Eli couldn't pull the giant alligator alone, and Eyanosa would not go to it.

Stephanie proposed another plan, "Maybe if we wrap it in a blanket, he'll let us put it on him."

"Can't hurt to try." They pulled the alligator wrapped in blankets up beside the horse then got Eyanosa down on his knees. The two of them dragged the alligator-filled-blanket over Eyanosa's back. "Up boy," Eli urged Eyanosa to his feet. They put the few pieces of clothes that they couldn't carry on top. Hand in hand, keeping a close watch on the swamp, they resumed the walk to Cadron Creek.

Three days later, Eli and Stephanie walked into camp with something wrapped in a blanket draped over Eyanosa.

Sally exclaimed, "Oh, no! Is somebody dead?"

Melvin saw the tail hanging below Eyanosa's belly. "Unless your person has a long tail, I think you have an alligator."

"That's what it is," Stephanie affirmed his guess.

Eli removed the bundle from on top of the carcass. "Stephanie shot it as it tried to chase me down."

Sally asked with concern and curiosity, "What happened?"

Stephanie wanted to get the bundles of clothes, blankets, and pillows into the tent. Eyanosa was very glad when the four of them removed the heavy monster and let him go to the field. They took the alligator carcass to the mess tent and laid it on the table as Eli explained what happened.

"We'll need both tables, so we better put him someplace else." Melvin revealed his practical joker tendency, "I'd probably get in trouble if I put it some place funny, but I'm tempted."

Sally joined the joking, "We could put it like its creeping into the tent."

Eli positioned the legs to make it appear to be walking. "Or coming up from the creek."

Melvin pointed to the center of the camp. "How about crawling over the logs by the fire? Wonder how long it would take somebody to notice."

They laughed and picked up the beast. Stephanie said, "Or sneaking in under the wagon."

They frolicked, carried the alligator, and pretended that it was crawling. The four of them laughed so intensely that they didn't realize the others had arrived back at camp. Jeremiah came around the side of the tent to the door and pulled the flaps back. Ann, Noah, and the other soldiers stood behind him looking into the tent. Across their backs, Eli and Melvin carried the alligator with its head blown to shreds. Sally and Stephanie waved its front claws and laughed.

Melvin made the turn back towards the door, "Or

put it under the bed of..." He saw Jeremiah standing in the doorway.

Eli continued the alligator dance and the train of thought, "Under the bed of Jeremiah." He swung past the door, bumped into Melvin, saw boots in the doorway, and then peeked out from under the belly. "Oops, that was the wrong thing to say."

Jeremiah warned them, "You better keep it out from under my bed."

Eli recanted his plan, "Yes, sir, never under your bed."

Melvin spoke up, "I wouldn't have let him, sir."

"Whose bed were you about to suggest?" Jeremiah looked sternly at Melvin.

Melvin tried to recover, "Ahhh, Umm, Henry's."

Henry wasn't going for it, "Right under my pine boughs?"

Melvin changed his story, "I meant John."

"That's what he meant. I heard him say it earlier." Sally tried to protect her friend.

Jeremiah let them off the hook. "Not to worry. Carry on with the alligator dance. It's quite entertaining."

Melvin resumed his military demeanor. "Sir, I think we should just put it where you want it."

Jeremiah entered the tent. "In the corner where we can see it." Stephanie and Sally let go of the legs. Melvin and Eli took it to the corner. "Mr. and Mrs. Yates, you have some explaining to do during supper. We want to know how you acquired the alligator." The others crowded around the alligator to get a good look while Melvin and Sally put supper on the table. Stephanie and Eli told their story while everybody ate. After cleaning up the dishes and pots, since Sally wanted to learn how to skin an animal and tan its hide, she followed Eli to the alligator.

Melvin wanted to stay close to Sally. "May I help?"

"Be very careful not to cut any holes. Slice the skin off like this." Eli demonstrated the proper way to pull the skin and slice through the membrane that held it to the muscles.

Sally helped to carefully skin the beast. "Melvin, do you know any recipes for alligator meat?"

"No, but we can experiment if Jeremiah will let us."

Sally imagined the meat would not be very flavorful. "I think something spicy."

"Good thinking. As big as it is, it's probably old and tough. I learned a new dish called Jambalaya. I'll ask if we can make it."

Ann asked Stephanie about the other matter, "Were you able to transfer the deed?"

"I don't know. They're going to try to transfer the deed in Dover. Smitty gave me the money, but Zachariah is buying it. He plans to pay Smitty back."

"I hope it works out. I'm sure Zachariah will take good care of the farm."

"Aaaaand Zachariah and Minnie plan to get married."

Ann had never meant to upset or hurt Zachariah. "I'm glad he found love."

Stephanie asked, "How are you? You were so tired when we left."

"Much better now that we're not digging. That was the hardest work I've ever done. If Noah hadn't done so much of the work, I think it would have killed me."

Stephanie hugged her sister. "I knew he was doing that. He's such a good man. I'm glad you're better."

Sally, Eli, and Melvin completed their work. Except for the blown-up head, the alligator skin came off in one whole piece with the claws still attached. The eyes were gone from the head as well as the skin immediately behind the place where they should have been. Still, Eli was happy with the integrity of the skin and started the tanning process. Before he went to bed, Eli rubbed salt into the skin and rolled it up. So that it would be safe from wild animals, and so it would stink up the camp as little as possible, he hung the skin and the carcass high in a tree by the creek. He washed away all the alligator blood and guts with lye soap, put on a different set of Harry's clothes, and then snuggled beside his wife in the tent.

THIRTY SEVEN

Weeks later, Noah and Ann had cut down and debarked the second batch of trees. They started making boards. Noah repeatedly split planks so thin they were unusable. He broke plank after plank as he pulled them apart. After days of ruining boards, they had to cut down more trees. He pounded the wedge and broke yet another. Ann spoke sharply to him. "What are you doing? You're ruining all the wood."

Noah snapped back, "They're just not splitting right. I'm sorry that we'll have to spend more time together doing this."

Ann had seen Noah get more irritable every day. It occurred to her that he was trying to stay with them as long as he could. "If you say so."

Eli saw all the wasted wood and thought of something. "Jeremiah, I know we're not supposed to help Noah and Ann, but I don't think there is any reason why I can't have the planks that they can't use. It's not helping them."

Jeremiah stood beside the stack of wood. "What do you want to do with the boards?"

"I want to make handcarts for when we leave."

Jeremiah appreciated that Eli hadn't just taken the rejected planks. He also knew that they really did need something. As they ate alligator, again, he gave his permission.

The consensus about alligator meat was that the jambalaya was best, actually good. They had eaten it several times. Some of the other times, they'd struggled to eat the alligator portion of the meal. Even though it had extended their rations significantly, Jeremiah finally told them to throw the rest away.

Noah spoke up, "Would you allow me to make smoked alligator strips? I have no money, and I'll need meat."

"Is it still good enough?"

"I think so, if the meat is smoked."

"Only when you're not working on the ferry."

Noah looked at Sally. "If I show you how and only take a fourth of the meat, will you smoke everything that's left?"

"Of course!"

Sally and Noah got started that night. They made the racks using some of the planks Noah had ruined. Melvin helped. He said because he wanted to learn something new. Eli, Stephanie, Ann, and Henry also joined them. The following days, thin strips of the alligator that had tried to eat Eli smoked on the racks.

Ann and Noah cut down more trees and split them into planks. Stephanie and Sally helped Eli build the carts. Time after time, the rain washed the dirt down into the spaces between the rocks around the posts. For weeks, each time the dirt settled, Noah and Ann had added more, tamped it in, and repeated the process.

On December 5th, they gathered at the creek. Noah dug a small breach in the lower side of the dam to allow the creek slowly to reclaim the area denied to it for so many weeks. After the creek again flowed around the posts, the dirt holding them remained in place. Noah jumped on the dock. Nothing budged. The posts, securely planted in the creek bed, stood firm. They claimed success.

Even though Noah continually sabotaged the work, on December 19th, he hooked the six-foot-wide, twenty-four-foot-long ferry into the pulley system. The whole length of the boat they had attached treads that covered the planks at the center of the deck and made a safer walking surface for humans and animals. A second layer of boards ran the long way down the ferry from one end to the other end and reinforced the floor where a wagon's wheels would roll across. It had railings and foot-high-sidewalls designed to keep things from sliding or rolling off the ferry. Hinged ramps at both ends also kept everything inside and provided for entrance and egress. It floated on one twenty-four-foot-long log that ran down the center and two twelve-foot logs on each of the sides.

Jeremiah swept his hand from Israel towards the winch wheel. "Since you'll be the one working this system when we're gone, I think you should work the winch." Israel stepped over to the winch he would use to pull the ferry out of or into the creek. He turned the wheel. The wrought iron wire rope that replaced his hemp rope wound around the take-up wheel and unwound from the other side to let the line out. It pulled the wire across the creek, and then through the pulley, which drew the ferry forward.

The boat splashed into the water and bobbed beside the mooring posts. Jeremiah ordered all aboard. Israel unlatched the gate and lowered the ramp to dock level. He and all the others got onto the ferry. With all aboard, Israel raised the loading ramp and locked it into place. He engaged the winch and turned the wheel.

"We're underway." Israel was very happy with the ferry. "I think this is the best system ever. This big wheel makes it so easy to turn the winch."

Under his breath, Noah muttered, "I wish it had sunk." However, the tight fit of the boards and the large logs upon which it floated had made it a sturdy boat.

Jeremiah ordered further testing, "Lower the loading ramp. Let's see how it aligns on this side."

Israel lowered the ramp. It met the perfectly terraformed dirt bank a third of the way up from the water. "Hits just right and it should be fine as the water rises."

Jeremiah didn't have any doubt that it would work in both directions, but he told Israel, "Close it up, and see if this thing goes the other way."

Israel raised the ramp and locked it in the up position. He turned the wheel the opposite way. The ferry reversed its movement. They arrived back at the dock. Israel attached the mooring ropes to the posts and then lowered the ramp. They walked onto the dock and back onto land. Israel was jubilant. "Except for raising and lowering the adjustable dock, it's perfect!"

Noah asked hopefully, "Don't we have to stay here until we figure that out?"

Jeremiah wanted to be back in Little Rock for Christmas. "No. I'll take the problem to the army engineers." Much to Noah's dismay, Jeremiah released the prisoners. "Everybody is free, but it's already late today, so leave tomorrow."

That made Noah miserable and extremely mad. Trying to hold back this day, he had dragged out the project as long as he could. That moment, the inevitable had finally occurred. The time had arrived when he would have to leave the people he had come to love.

That night, Jeremiah unlocked both Ann and Noah. "This doesn't mean that you are allowed to go to each other or leave with each other."

With the leather belt that locked around her waist and the metal chain gone, Ann felt light as a feather. She watched Jeremiah unlock Noah. "Go see the Indian with the rope to the moon and back."

The soldiers assumed Ann was telling Noah to go to Indian Territory. Noah had heard all three girls say they loved each other to the moon and back many times. He knew what she meant. She was telling him to go to the cave on the farm and that she loved him to the moon and back.

He wished it was that easy, but Tom wasn't going to give up his store. Eli wasn't going to leave Harmony, and Stephanie was going to stay with him. Therefore, Ann and Sally weren't going to leave Harmony, and that meant that he had lost them. He had to go his own way, and he hated it. He hated that Eli had mentioned that he was part Indian. He hated that Eli was keeping him from being with Ann by not wanting to leave Arkansas. Hate, anger, and sorrow about the whole thing filled him.

Noah didn't understand why God let him find this family and then took them away. He thought God was being cruel. He hadn't done anything wrong. He blamed God for making him an Indian. If he had been born something else, his life would not have been destroyed. He was so angry that he could have bitten a cottonmouth snake, and *HE* would have poisoned the snake.

Noah knew he wouldn't be able to handle saying goodbye. He waited until everybody slept then packed his bedroll and clothes and crept out of the tent. He went to the mess tent, got his share of smoked alligator, his rifle, some lead balls, wadding, and powder. He hung his knife on his belt. He put all his arrows in the quiver he had made and left them with his bow on the table for the girls to have what was left of the cedars from their farm.

Since there was no need to have a guard on watch anymore, Noah was surprised to find Henry by the horses. "I figured you'd be leaving tonight. I wouldn't have been able to say goodbye either. I'm sorry this happened to you. It's a long way to Indian Territory. However, you do have time to get safely to the bluffs south of Little Rock. There's a trading post in a box canyon where you could spend the winter."

"I might check that out. Thank you for keeping my failure to resist Ann a secret. You are a good and decent man. I wish you all the best in life." Noah mounted Eyanosa and rode away towards Little Rock.

In the morning, Ann stepped out from behind her curtain and looked towards Noah's place. He was not in the tent, and his bedroll was gone. "Where's Noah?"

Jeremiah shrugged his shoulders. "He must have left during the night."

"Why'd he do that?" Ann hurried out of the tent.

"What's wrong?" Stephanie saw Ann's tears.

"Noah left last night. He didn't even say goodbye. He's just gone."

As her sisters held Ann in their arms, Sally thought, *he didn't say goodbye to me either!* She was very upset that her family had come apart again.

Eli got the four handcarts they had made. He loaded their food, the alligator hide he was tanning, the tent, and all their other supplies.

Melvin walked over with the bow and arrows. When he handed them to Ann, she knew she would never see Noah again. "Jeremiah said I could give you all the food that we won't need to get back to Little Rock. I hope it will be enough for you to get home."

"We don't have a home to get to, but I appreciate the food very much. I won't ever forget you or everything I learned from you about food and cooking." Sally kissed him on the cheek but felt she'd like to have a real kiss.

Melvin feared he might not be a gentleman. He knew he should not be thinking about kissing a fourteen-year-old girl. He grabbed one of the carts. "I won't forget you either. Let's get the rest of the supplies." He walked to the mess tent. Sally followed him. Melvin put food into the cart. "What do you mean, you don't have a home?"

Sally was shocked. "You don't know? This whole time you haven't known the whole story?"

"I guess not." Melvin didn't know that there was anything, except that Ann and Noah had married, and he had already decided that to go through all this because two perfectly decent people got married was idiotic, narrow-minded, and wrong.

"We were taking some men to Little Rock for trial because they burned down our house, twenty acres of ripe corn, the sugar shack, smokehouse, and the barn with our horses, chickens, and turkeys inside. Only a few days into the trip, the one we saw throw a flaming can of oil into the house, tried to strangle Ann with the chain that held him to the wagon. That night he was murdered. We didn't know who did it until Ben confessed as he and Roy floated away with Smitty in this very creek from right at this crossing when the water was too high and fast.

"Later, after we safely crossed, the rest of us continued to Little Rock and found Smitty. When we got there, we went to report the murder, the loss of the prisoners, and to file charges against Ben and Roy. Judge Hall didn't care about any of that. All he cared about was that an Indian man had married a white woman. There's nothing wrong with Noah. I'm glad he married my sister. Besides, he's as much a white man as he is an Indian man. So anyway, that's why we don't have a home."

"I'm so sorry, Sally. I wish there was something I could do to help." Melvin wanted to hold and comfort her. He repeatedly told himself she was only fourteen-years-old.

"There's nothing to be done. We're trusting God to work something out, but it means a lot to me that you want to help. I hope when I find my husband that he'll be just like you."

"Whoever he is, he'll be a lucky man." Melvin pulled the cart full of Army supplies over to Ann who stood beside the other carts already packed to go. "I'm sorry about everything that's happened to you. I hope, somehow, everything turns out right." He walked away.

Israel helped break camp. "I'm going to miss having you here. You've done so much more to improve this place than necessary, and I appreciate it. You can have free passage any time you come this way."

Henry, John, and Justus finished their duties. They fastened Peppermint, the named cow, to the wagon and got the chickens into their cages and onto the wagons. Melvin sat in the seat of the wagon feeling heartbroken about riding away from Sally. Jeremiah walked over to Ann, Stephanie, Sally, and Eli. "I hope I was able to make this ordeal the best it could be. I wish you all the best. Ann, I have to tell you, when this started, I didn't think there was any way it would be possible because I thought a woman couldn't do this. You are one remarkable lady. I hope God will make things right."

Henry paced back and forth until just before the second wagon started across, then, he went to Ann and spoke to her quietly, "I never told you this. Do you understand? You should know that I told Noah to spend the winter at the trading post at the bluffs below Little Rock. In the spring, you might find the west more tolerant."

"You've been such an incredible blessing. I'm so grateful that you didn't tell on us when Noah and I hugged in the tent."

"Some things are wrong, and some things are right. I want to do the right thing." He walked away and joined the last of his unit on the ferry. Israel took them across. The soldiers headed back home to Little Rock behind Noah. Ann, Stephanie, Eli, and Sally went the other way.

THIRTY EIGHT

Sally pulled her cart along Military Road towards Harmony. "I guess we're meeting Noah at the cave."

After receiving the bow and arrows, and after what Henry had told her, Ann believed that was not what Noah planned. They had all told him to meet them there. He had always said that he would not. It broke her heart. "I don't think he's going there. Henry told me he suggested to Noah to go to some trading post south of Little Rock. He left in that direction."

"We should be going that way." Sally stopped walking.

Stephanie, however, did not stop. "We have to go separate ways. There's only one thing we can do; we have to go home and hope he's going to the cave."

Eli stated his opinion, "I don't think he will."

"Why not?!" Sally refused to move.

Eli understood Noah's thoughts. "Because he thinks he's protecting us by staying away."

Tears once again streamed down Ann's face. "I think Eli is right. I don't know what to do. This is horrible. I don't want this to be happening." Now that she was with only her family, Ann let herself cry without holding back. The other three stood in the middle of the road and held her.

After several minutes, Sally gently but firmly commanded, "Ann Williams, go get Noah. If you don't, I will!"

"I don't know how to find him."

Eli reasoned it out. "The only trading post below Little Rock that I've heard of is the one at Pine Bluff. There's a ferry across the Arkansas at Point Remove Creek. We could cross the river there and then head south to Pine Bluff, but it would be a long trip, it's winter, and we don't know for sure that he'll even be there."

"Then we better get moving." Sally started walking. She would not allow any other option. In her mind and heart, that was the only choice.

Ann wanted to protect her family from going through another ordeal like the one they had just endured. "I don't want to make you go to Pine Bluff. Go home. I'll find Noah. That way, if we get caught, we'll be the only ones punished."

Sally assured Ann that was not going to happen. "I'm going with you, and you won't be able to stop me because I'll keep on following you."

"It will be safer for all of us if we stay together. Either way, we have to go this way first." Eli resumed walking towards Point Remove Creek.

Two days later, they arrived at the Arkansas River crossing. Even though it was going to be difficult pulling the carts, they'd decided to make the trip to Pine Bluff together, but they didn't want anybody coming along later and figuring out that they'd crossed the Arkansas. Eli remembered that the ferryman had barely looked at them on their previous trip and felt sure that the man didn't remember them as the people traveling with the prisoners. He decided he could negotiate without having to worry. The girls silently waited with the carts as Eli told the ferryman they needed to cross the river.

"Three dollars."

"That's the wagon rate. We don't have a wagon."

"You have four carts. They take up space."

"That's ridiculous. We're only paying footman rates."

Realizing that he wasn't going to convince Eli to pay whatever he asked, he changed his tactic. "I'll take the four of you and your carts across at a foot person's rate for each of you, and I'll only add the charge of four extra people for the space taken up by your carts."

"Nobody else is crossing, and there's plenty of space."

"Then, you're not going across." They stared at each other until the ferryman offered a compromise, "Two pennies less for each cart."

Eli's father had taught him to negotiate a fair and reasonable deal for all parties. He felt that they had arrived. "Take us across." Eli gave the man seventy-six cents. They rode across the river, all happy with the charge.

When they were on the road on the south side of the river and out of earshot, Ann praised Eli, "Good negotiating."

"I try."

The temperature dropped as they walked, but precipitation didn't threaten to accost them. At the end of the day, they didn't take the time to put up the tent. Instead, they positioned the carts to block the wind and huddled together under all the blankets in all their clothes. The weather changed during the night. A light snow covered them as they slept. As soon as they woke, Stephanie, Sally, and Eli got out from under the blankets. Ann didn't move. It was cold on the other side of the blanket, but it wasn't the temperature or snow. Ann feared her life would forever be devoid of warmth from the source she wanted.

Eli prodded her, "It looks like more snow is coming. We don't want to be stuck outside, not be able to get warm, and freeze. We need to move quickly."

Ann's heart already felt frozen. As far as Ann was concerned, her body could freeze with it. However, she wouldn't take a chance with the lives of the others for anything. Winter solstice was only days away, and daylight hours were short, so she complied.

They traveled south no longer on Military Road but still on a good road cleared of stumps, leveled to the general slope of the ground, and wide enough for a wagon. Trees crowded to the very edge of the road allowing only dappled light through that failed to melt the thin covering of snow on the ground. They arrived at Perryville with nothing left of the day.

"In case somebody comes asking, we shouldn't all be seen together. You girls, go see if you can find an inn or someplace to get a room." Eli handed Ann a Spanish Piece of Eight but kept the rest of the money because that was what the girls wanted. They trusted him and felt that they would all be safer if the money was in Eli's possession, and he did the negotiating. The girls went in search of a warm place to spend the night.

Eli felt comfortable in a small town store, so he walked into Perryville Mercantile. It looked very much like his father's store but with more traveling items. "Hello."

A woman, getting nicely plump with graying hair wound up in a bun that was coming apart, greeted him with a smile. "Welcome. I'm Hazel. What can I do for you?"

"I need a good, large, waterproof tarp and some big, thick, wool blankets. Do you have any three-point blankets or larger?"

"A few. Where you heading?"

"Little Rock. What's the best way to go? Are there any places to get more supplies on the way?"

"Travel directly east on the road out of town across the Fourche La Fave River. The people of this town built the bridge. We let everybody cross without charge. Go over the Maumelle Mountains and across the Maumelle River. There is a charge to cross that river. The town of Maumelle is the next place to get supplies, so get everything you need here. When you leave Maumelle, stay on the same road going east. After Maumelle, there isn't any place to get supplies before Little Rock."

"Where can I get supplies after Little Rock?"

"If you stay on the south side of the river after you go through Little Rock, you can go south on Arch Street to Sheridan, take Sweet Home Pike south to Pine Bluff, or go back west to Hot Springs on Rock Creek Pike. If you're going on to the north, you have to cross back across the Arkansas River. On the north side, you can take Pike Avenue east towards Clarendon, or go due north towards Des Arc. It's a very long way to any of them. You better stock up good in Little Rock."

"What about the weather this time of year?"

"It's usually very cold. Sometimes it snows, especially over the mountains. I'll get you a good, large india rubber tarp. How many three-point blankets?"

Their one-point blankets, already split into halves, were small, and Eli didn't know how cold it was going to get. He figured if all of them snuggled together inside a couple of three-point blankets wrapped all the way around, that they would surely be warm enough. In addition, they could lay the smaller blankets under them for more insulation between them and the cold ground. He decided they should be sure. "Four pairs."

"Anything else I can get you?"

"That's all unless you have peppermint sticks."

"What kind of shopkeeper would I be if I didn't have peppermint sticks?"

"I'll take four sticks." In case Eli's family had not found a place to stay, he inquired about one more thing, "I'd like to spend the night in a warm bed. Is there an inn or some other place here in town?"

"Adeline's is the only place. Stay on this road going east. It's right before the bridge."

Eli paid for his purchases but received the information he needed without charge. He believed that no one trying to follow them would have any idea where they were going beyond Little Rock.

Outside the only place they had found to spend the night, Ann told her sisters, "Sally and I will stay in one room. You and Eli have the other." Ann went in and made the arrangements without giving her name. When Eli arrived, they enjoyed hot baths, ate a delicious meal, and then slept cozy in warm beds.

THIRTY NINE

While his family had traveled to Perryville, Noah had ridden Eyanosa to Little Rock. He remembered that Jeremiah had said Reverend Pratt's house was beside a cemetery and not far from Main Street. When he found the one he thought was the correct house, Noah knocked on the door.

Reverend Pratt opened the door. "Bless my soul!"

"May I come in? I have some questions I need to ask."

"Of course, come on in. Since you're here, you must have finished the ferry."

"Unfortunately, yes, and now I've been forced to leave my family. That's where my questions come in."

"Ask away."

"When Ann and I got married at Kuhn Bayou, were we married? Who knows how many days it would have been before Harry turned in that form."

"If you made a vow before God that you were taking Ann as your wife, and she took you as her husband, also before God, then you're married as far as God is concerned. If it's recorded within thirty days, the state recognizes that you're married from the date of the ceremony."

"So, are we married even though the document

was destroyed, and an Arkansas judge ruled that the marriage is annulled?"

"I would say yes because I think it's what God witnessed not what Judge Hall or this state decides."

"That's what Ann said. I promised to be with her until death, but now I can't. I've broken a vow to God, but He let this happen. I don't think He cares about me anymore, but it still bothers me that I promised God I'd do something, and now I can't keep that promise. If He is there, He's not going to like that."

"God understands this is not your choice. I'm sure He's not upset with you, and I'm certain He does care about you."

"I love Ann, her sisters, and Eli, but I can't have them because I'm part Indian and because Eli won't leave his father. I'm so mad that I've been thinking about finding Judge Hall and scalping him after slowly skinning him and then doing the same to everybody else who came up with that stupid law."

"You have a right to feel angry. However, God would be upset with you if you did scalp or skin anybody, and so would I. I'm sure Ann wouldn't approve either."

"You don't know Ann very well. She might be on her way here to do that very thing."

"Noah, you need to understand. Bad things happen because we live in a fallen world. If it weren't for God holding things together, it would be a lot worse. We should think that it's incredible that things are this good in a world in this condition, not how could something bad happen. Also, you don't know what God is working out. You just have to trust Him. Maybe your future won't include them because He has a different plan for you, or maybe He's going to bring you back together. This is what God says about this type of thing in Jeremiah 29:11-14; 'I alone know the plans I have for you, plans to bring you prosperity and not disaster; plans to bring about the future you hope for. Then you will call to me. You will come and pray to me, and I will answer you. You will seek me, and you will find me because you will seek me with all your heart. Yes, I say, you will find me, and I will restore you to your land. I will gather you from every country and from every place to which I have scattered you, and I will bring you back to the land from which I had sent you away into exile. I, the Lord, have spoken'."

"But I have been praying. I'm praying with all my heart, but I don't hear Him answer me like I used to."

"Sometimes He says yes, sometimes no, and sometimes wait. It's harder to hear when He's saying no or wait."

"I hope He's only saying wait. Ann wants me to meet her even if it means she is whipped. She said the vows we made were for better or for worse, but how could I do something that would get Ann whipped?"

"Sometimes the choices are hard. Did you promise Ann, or God, that Ann wouldn't get whipped?"

"No, but surely God doesn't want Ann beaten, and I don't think I could stand it."

"Do you think you love Ann more than God loves her?"

"Well, no."

"Then don't you think you should be doing what you promised God you would do and trusting Him for the consequences?"

"I should, but I'm afraid to take the chance. Anyway, I appreciate you talking with me. It's helped me a lot." Noah stood to leave.

"Why don't you stay here with me today? You and Eyanosa can use a rest."

"I would like that." Noah sat back down in the soft chair and talked until suppertime. After they had shared a meal, Noah soaked in a hot bath then climbed into a warm, soft bed, all of which helped him to sleep.

FORTY

The next morning, Noah got ready to leave. "I appreciate you letting me stay here, and even more you talking with me."

"You're welcome. I hope you find the answers God wants you to find."

Noah sat on Eyanosa and tried to decide. Could he trust God and go to the cave in Harmony? Noah imagined Ann's hands tied to a post while they ripped the skin off her beautiful back with a whip. Even though he believed that Ann would stand up with a bloody, shredded back, walk right over to him, and then in front of all of them say something like, let's make babies; he knew that he couldn't allow that to happen. He decided what to do. With tears, as clouds started to gather over the Maumelle Mountains, he started down the road to Pine Bluff.

FORTY ONE

Eli and the girls left Perryville early, paid no fee to cross the Fourche La Fave River on the public bridge then headed towards the Maumelle Mountains. After hours of traveling, Stephanie stopped to observe the clouds ahead. "I hope those clouds don't mean a bad storm is coming."

Eli remembered what the shopkeeper had told him. "Hazel said that snow falls on the mountains this time of the year. We should go back to Perryville."

Sally didn't want to pull her cart all the way back to Perryville then return to where they stood before they could go farther. "We're already a long way away. We'll be over the mountain before those clouds amount to anything."

Ann agreed with Sally, "We're more than halfway to the mountain. I hate to backtrack such a long way."

They agreed to continue forward. By the time they started up the mountain, the sky was a solid sheet of dark gray that grew darker as they climbed. It wasn't long before Eli knew they had to take cover. "We need to find a cave if we can. If we can't, we'll at least have to find a sheltered place to set up the tent."

They walked and searched as the conditions drastically worsened. At a dense stand of pines that offered some protection from the gusting wind, they set up the tent. With all their possessions inside the tent, they huddled together with the large blankets and the tarp wrapped around them as they ate alligator jerky for the evening meal. Outside the tent, the snow whipped ferociously across the mountains. Sally was sure they were in trouble. "I'm sorry. We should have gone back."

Ann lay down to sleep and draped her arm over Sally. "Don't worry. It probably won't amount to anything, and we'll already be partway up the mountain when we leave tomorrow." Sally put her arm over Stephanie, who put her arm over Eli, who put his arm back over all of them. Ann closed her eyes. "Love you all to the moon and back."

Since her arm was already around Stephanie when the sun rose, Sally hugged her. "Merry Christmas." They got out of the blankets so that everybody could hug everybody then they opened the tent flap. A foot of snow lay on the ground. They ventured outside anyway. Large fluffy flakes drifted slowly to the ground and gave them plenty of time to examine the intricate patterns. Stephanie blinked a snowflake off her eyelash as she looked up. "Now what?"

Ann looked into the sky with her sister but couldn't determine anything. "Maybe we should stay here. We're fairly well protected, and we don't know what's coming."

What a relief! "I agree." Eli then remembered the mud war they'd had back on the farm. He threw a snowball at Stephanie's back, and the war was on. When Eli finally surrendered, they again sat in the tent and gnawed on alligator strips for dinner. Eli shared his secret, "I have a Christmas present for the three beautiful ladies of my family. It's not much, but I think you'll like it." He drew the peppermint sticks from his pocket.

Happy that Eli had brought some special joy to the day, Sally took her present. "How very wonderful!"

As Ann took her peppermint, tears glittered in her eyes but did not escape. She had liked Eli since he'd ridden to the farm in the wagon with her sisters. The candy was a small thing, but Ann hadn't thought about a Christmas present. She realized how very thoughtful and loving Eli was.

Stephanie threw her arms around Eli and kissed him. "Darling, you're a wonderful man. I'm very blessed to have you as my husband and friend."

"I'm happy that you like your presents." Eli thought it felt good to do something nice for his family.

Ann decided she was not going to eat all of hers but would share it with Noah when she found him. She broke her peppermint into pieces then wrapped them all in a handkerchief, except one, which she popped into her mouth. Ann lay on her back in the tent and enjoyed the delicious mint. Sally saw Ann lying with her hands laced together under her head and did the same as she sucked on her candy. After enjoying their Christmas presents, they went out and played in the softly falling snow until sunset then stood together on the mountain and marveled at the red, orange, pink, and lavender sky reflecting off the snow-covered pines. Sally had never seen anything so glorious. "I think God gave us a million Christmas trees."

Eli stood with his arm around Stephanie's waist and looked into the valley. "It's very beautiful."

Ann shouted out, "Happy Birthday, Jesus!" The other three echoed the birthday wish then they watched the sun sink behind the snow-covered pines.

FORTY TWO

That same Christmas Day, Noah arrived at the top of a dangerously steep trail down the rock wall into the large box canyon of Pine Bluff. He dismounted and carefully led Eyanosa down the path that was barely more than a fissure in the cliff that rain and melting snow had used to wash the land above into the land below. The only ways in were the trail he struggled to descend and an opening from top to bottom almost directly across the canyon that had been partially filled by a landslide. That barrier rose only a fifth of the height of the surrounding cliffs. On the right side, close to the cliff wall, he saw a trail going up then over the pile of rubble. All the way around, except where the trail he was navigating entered, talc piled at the base of the cliffs.

In the flat valley below, he saw a large barn and a fenced area holding two dozen or so donkeys and mules, and some goats. The large building that he assumed was the actual trading post was slightly to the right and back from the center. The land had been cultivated for hay and close beside the trading post he saw the remains of a vegetable garden and several leafless trees.

Noah made it safely to the bottom and put Eyanosa

into the corral with the donkeys and mules. Then, much to the surprise of the proprietor, walked into the trading post. A thin man with short gray hair and a slightly wrinkled face walked into the room when Noah entered. Hazel eyes that said 'welcome' and a pleasant smile greeted Noah. "Welcome to Bacon's Trading Post. I'm Roscoe Bacon."

"You've got quite a place here." Noah made a mental note of what he saw.

Bacon's Trading Post was not a small compound. The central area where he'd entered contained tables with chairs, a large open fireplace, and a dusty bar that looked well stocked but seldom used. To the right, nailed over the open doorway to a room loaded full of goods, was a sign that said, "Come to Bacon's for the Bacon." Even though Noah felt surly and miserable, he smiled to himself when he read the sign. Directly behind Roscoe was an open door, through which Noah saw a large stone structure, constructed to be a stove, an oven, and a heat source. To Noah's left were two doors. Closest to the entry, the doorway opened into what looked like a chapel. The other door stood closed.

"What can I do for you?" Roscoe asked.

Noah thought for a second or two. "I don't know. I just ended up here."

"Then why don't you have a meal? Maybe it'll come to you as to why you're here." Roscoe pointed across the room. "Hang your coat over there."

"I don't have any money to pay for a meal." Now that he was there, and Roscoe had asked, Noah realized he didn't have any idea what he'd expected to happen once he got to the trading post.

"I'll consider your company my pay. Come into the kitchen where it's warmer while I fix us something to eat." Noah followed Roscoe. Several small storerooms surrounded the large kitchen in which there was a water pump and the big stone fireplace with a cistern that held water to keep it warm. Dried vegetables, herbs, and powders covered long butcher tables.

"What are you making?"

"I'm making meal packets that are lightweight and have everything a body needs."

Noah wondered about that. "What does a body need?"

"I don't know what it is, but people have problems when they don't eat enough oranges, lemons, or limes. That's why I grow them. The problem is that you can't easily take them traveling. Other things go wrong when you don't eat other types of food."

"What happens if you don't eat oranges?"

"First, you get a fever and the runs. You don't even want to eat. Then, you start to breathe fast; you get real irritable, your legs hurt and swell up until you feel like you can't move. Next, your gums start to bleed, and your teeth fall out. Little red dots come up all over your skin before your eyes start bleeding and bulge out of your head. Then, your hair gets curly. Last, you die."

Noah didn't believe anything so drastic and strange was real. "Nothing like that happens."

"I've seen it."

"I'm irritable, I don't want to eat, I hurt all over, and I'm feeling hot. You think I need to eat oranges?"

"I don't think that's what's happening to you, but let's eat some oranges anyway." Roscoe went into one of the storerooms and came back with two oranges, which he tossed to Noah. "Peel those for us."

Noah planned to be sure to eat oranges in the future, just in case. "How are you trying to figure this out?"

"I eat some things and don't eat others. I write down how I feel and any changes in my body. I've been doing it for the last thirty years or so."

"Are you going to be experimenting with this meal? Is it going to be safe?"

"Sure, it's safe. It's just plain food. These things only happen to you over a long time." Roscoe served a delicious meal with lots of spices, rice, dried chicken, and dried vegetables rehydrated into a stew. "You figure out what you're doing here yet?"

"I had to go somewhere, so I came here because it's not where I can't be."

"Where is it that you can't be?"

"With my wife."

"Your wife run you out?"

Noah didn't know why he felt he could tell Roscoe everything, but he did, right down to running away because he was afraid to trust God.

"I guess this is as good a place as any when you're running away. Stay until you figure out what you need to know. I'd like the company. You can take the bedroom if you want. After sixty years, these bones don't take well to the cold anymore, so I sleep in here."

"If you have another cot, I'd like the warmth too. That is, if you're willing to share the kitchen."

"Bring one in from the store."

As Noah lay on the cot in the kitchen and listened to Roscoe snore and wheeze, he felt miserable. He missed all of his family. He knew they were also hurting, and the words of Reverend Pratt wouldn't get out of his head; *give it to God and trust Him for the consequences. God loves Ann more than you do. You can trust Him.*

FORTY THREE

In the morning, Noah went to the chapel and prayed, "God, protect them. If you want me to go to them and trust you, give me a sign." He waited. The room remained silent around him. He sat in the chapel without eating, asking God to show him what to do.

On the mountain, Ann was the first one awake. Lately, she had not prayed because she was mad at God for letting this happen. However, on Christmas Day, when she'd stood with her sisters and Eli on the cold mountain while the snow fell and the sun went down behind the pines, she had seen that the world was still beautiful. She realized she could live in the beauty that God put around her or close her eyes in sorrow and anger and see none of it. She felt Sally's sleeping body warm and safe next to hers. Sally, Stephanie, and Eli were with her, and they were on their way to get Noah. *God, I'm going to try to solve this as hard as I can, and pray to You as hard as I can, and trust You as hard as I can, and be as grateful as I can for all that I have. Thank You, for my sisters and Eli, provisions, friends, and the good, beautiful Earth. Please take care of my husband. Let him know that You, and we love him. In the name of Jesus, Amen.*

The sun rose from behind the mountain. Sally opened her eyes. "Are those sunrays?"

"I think they are." Ann hugged her sister. "I'm very grateful that you're here with me. You mean so much to me, and I love you very much."

Sally affirmed their family love, "I love you too, all the way to the moon and back, and I'm glad to be here with you. There's no place I want to be other than with my family."

Stephanie and Eli stirred. Ann spoke again, "You two should be in a warm bed enjoying being married, not out here on a cold mountain with me, but here we are. I know I've been miserable to be around, and you haven't complained at all. I haven't done anything to deserve such a wonderful family, but I thank God that He put me in this one. God has blessed me beyond anything I deserve."

"I know I'm blessed to be in this family." Eli hugged Stephanie closer.

"We all are." Stephanie got up and opened the tent door. A beautiful blue sky hung over the mountains.

Ann followed her sister out of the tent. "If we can pull the carts through this snow, we should move on."

Eli kicked the snow. It puffed out before rejoining the rest on the ground. "It's light and fluffy. I think we can pull the carts through it."

Stephanie stood in the cold, white fluff that was deeper than the top of her boots. "It's deep, but I guess we could stuff socks around the top of our boots to keep the snow out." They went back into the tent, crammed their boots with every sock they had, took down the tent, and resumed their search for the last member of their family. They trudged through the snow to the mountain's summit, crossed over the top, and then down the other side in even deeper snow. At the end of the day, they stopped east of the mountains in the shallow snow of the valley.

FORTY FOUR

After Noah had sat in the chapel all day praying, waiting, and hoping that God would speak or do something to let him know that He was guiding him, Noah spent the night in the chapel begging God to let him know that He was there.

The following day, as Noah continued to fast and pray in the chapel, Eli and the girls pulled the carts along the road. They crossed several small streams on causeways built so travelers could cross then paid to cross the Maumelle River. They slept in Maumelle in the only place they could find. While they lay asleep in the back corner of the loft in a stable, Noah continued to pray in the chapel.

After two complete days and nights of praying and trying to hear God, the sun rays peeked in through the beautiful stained glass window. Noah decided God was no longer there for him. He got up and walked into the kitchen. "I guess prayer and fasting won't work."

"What were you hoping would happen?"

"I want God to tell me to go get my family because He's going to protect us."

"But He didn't?"

"He didn't, but there's something stuck in my mind."

"What's that?"

"It's what Reverend Pratt said. He asked me what I'd promised to do, and if I love Ann more than God loves her. He told me to do what I had promised to do and to trust God with the consequences."

"Maybe that's what God is saying, and you didn't even need to fast in the chapel."

"Hmm, maybe." Noah contemplated that thought when he put down hay for Eyanosa, the goats, donkeys, and mules. It rattled around in his head as he gathered eggs and when he helped Roscoe measure out various ingredients to add to the food packages. Then, tired from being awake so long, Noah went to his cot early and fell asleep.

FORTY FIVE

Noah's family approached Little Rock at the end of another day of travel on foot. Even though nobody was around, Ann whispered, "I think we should make sure that nobody sees us."

Stephanie had other plans. "But I want to see Reverend Pratt."

Ann rejected the request, "No. If he knows we're going the way that Noah went, it would make him an accomplice."

As much as Eli also would have loved to see Reverend Pratt, he did not take the side of his wife. "Ann is right, Stephanie. I'd also like to see him, but it wouldn't be fair to put that on him."

Unhappily, Stephanie agreed, "You're right."

Sally, however, wanted hot coffee or hot tea. "We could stay at the other inn. They wouldn't know us."

Eli continued to state Ann's case, "Ann can't get caught. You know we can't risk it."

Sally didn't want to spend another night outside. "Maybe we can at least find a barn to sleep in again."

Stephanie thought of something. "Eli, remember when we went to get the tent? There was a shed in that cemetery at the very southeast edge of town."

Eli fleshed out the idea, "If we wait until dark, we

should be able to sneak through town unnoticed. We can sleep in the shed and then go right out of town early in the morning."

Ann had spent all but one day of her time in Little Rock in jail and didn't know much about the streets. It would be disastrous if she was caught in Little Rock trying to get to Noah. "Eli, are you sure you can get us across town without being caught or seen?"

"Zachariah and I walked around town trying to find out everything we could about Judge Hall, sorry to mention him, and the moon will be full tonight, so we'll be able to see well enough to find our way."

They had no other choice. They moved off the road and waited. Shortly after the sun had set, Ann stood up. "Eli, get us through town unseen."

Silently, Eli prayed, *God, help me get us to the shed without anybody seeing us.* Aloud he said, "This way," then led them into town on Prospect Avenue. They turned and went down the first road to the right.

FORTY SIX

Noah sat up suddenly wide-awake. *Pray for your family's safety right now*, screamed in his mind. He dashed into the chapel and fell to his knees in front of the cross. "God, something is wrong. Keep my family safe. Protect them. Help them with whatever they need. Hide them."

FORTY SEVEN

Sally stopped walking. "That's the Insane Asylum."

Stephanie assured her they wouldn't have any problem, "It's safe. They're all inside."

"I don't like it." Sally balked at going down the road.

Ann told her the same thing, "We'll be fine. They have everybody locked in. We'll go by quickly and be safely away before you know it." Trusting Ann, Sally walked on, but she stayed on the other side of the road and kept a very close eye on the object of her fear, which they were right beside when they turned left towards the town's center. When they saw the Deaf-Mute Institute, they took the road to the right that ran along the southwest edge of town.

Eli halted his family. "There are people up ahead by the railroad tracks."

Stephanie whispered back, "Can we turn up this street and go over a few blocks?"

Eli thought about where they were. "If this is Crisp Railroad, then we should be able to cut across West End Park." He led them to the street corner with the most shadows. "Wait here." Making sure his family could continue to see him, he walked up the street a short way. He looked around before he waved them forward.

They slipped up 14th Street to West End Park and started across. Suddenly, seemingly out of nowhere, a group of men walked rapidly up 14th towards the rail yard.

Eli, Ann, Stephanie, and Sally stopped and pretended to be people out enjoying the full moon in the park. Ann and Sally looked up and pointed at the moon. Stephanie hugged her husband. "I would love to stand under the full moon in the park and kiss you, my darling." Eli kissed her sweetly and lovingly not pretending to be, but actually being, lovers in the park. The men glanced at the people in the park, disregarded them as nobody to worry about, and walked past.

Eli did not finish that kiss until the men were far down the road. He whispered into Stephanie's ear, "I would too."

Ann contemplated, "I wonder what's going on."

"Something is happening for sure, but we can't worry about it. Let's get moving." Eli led them down Park Avenue to its end, turned left, and followed the road all the way to Gaines Street. "This is one of the main roads that we have to cross." He looked up the street. Coming in their direction, he saw more men looking up and down each side street before they crossed. Eli recognized one of them. "It's Judge Hall, and he's coming this way. Get around the corner behind the house." They slipped around the corner just as Judge Hall arrived where they had stood the moment before.

The sudden appearance of Eli and the girls stirred

up the dogs in the small yard on the other side of a high wrought iron fence. The approaching group of men heard the animals barking and snapping. Judge Hall carefully peeked around the corner of the house just as Sally pulled a hunk of smoked beef from her cart, ripped it apart, and tossed it into the yard. The dogs stopped barking, ran over, sniffed the meat, and then happily gulped it down.

One of the men wanted to get off the main road. "The dogs aren't barking anymore. I think it's safe."

Another of the men thought they should determine the cause. "Maybe it's Bemis."

Judge Hall started down the side road. "We should look. I'm not letting him out of this town with his slave and their half-breed children."

Eli whispered frantically, "They're coming. Leave the carts. Move quickly."

Sally pleaded, "Don't let there be more dogs."

They fled as fast as they could without making noise. Eli added his prayer, "God, hide us."

The judge closed on the corner. The girls and Eli were far from safety and clearly visible in the bright moonlight.

God answered. The owner of the dogs opened the back door as a dense cloud covered the moon, shrouded the street in darkness, and obscured the shapes of the carts on the other side of the fence. "Shut your traps!"

Judge Hall and his companions stopped short. On this night, they did not want to be seen outside. If they found the subject of the clandestine meeting, there was going to be a lynching, and they did not want anyone to know that they were involved.

"You dogs are going to be the death of me. Get in here!" Hearing the beckon of their master, the dogs stopped sniffing along the fence and ran into the house.

"Since we're already headed this way, let's go down this street." Judge Hall led his companions past the carts hidden in the shadow of the cloud as Ann, Stephanie, Sally, and Eli waited safely out of view.

Sally panted from the sprint. "Something is definitely happening."

"Who's Bemis?" Stephanie asked.

Ann angrily stated what she believed was the answer, "Obviously, Judge Hall's next victim. What difference does it make to him anyway?" Silently she prayed for God to help Bemis and his family to get away and be safe.

Eli wished they weren't in town on that particular night. "With this many men out, we need to be extra careful." They gave the people more than enough time to get well down the street before they went back to their carts. The moon popped out from behind the cloud. Eli looked up and down the empty street. "Cross quickly."

In their hurry, Stephanie's cart tipped on the uneven surface. Ann grabbed the cart before it went over, but two tin cups clattered loudly across the cobblestones. Eli ordered, "Keep going." On the other side of the street, they moved into the shadows between the house and the bushes beside it.

Choose Your Consequences

The dog owner opened the front door, this time with a rifle in his hand. "Who's out there?" He stood at the door and looked for what had disturbed the silence. "If you keep messing around my house, I'm going to sic my dogs on you." He peered up and down the street in both directions, walked to the corner, and looked down the street they had just come up. The girls and Eli stood in the bushes crammed as close to the house as they could get. The man looked in their direction, shrugged his shoulders, and then went back into his house. "Probably more rats or cats."

They waited a long time before the man stopped looking out the window. Eli slipped back across the road and recovered the cups. "I think that's the worst of it." They stole down the street to its end, quietly slipped one block up the street to the left, turned right, and headed out for two blocks. On the eastern edge of town, they stopped beside the cemetery. Beyond the gravestones was the Oakland Cemetery storage shed. Eli put into words what they all saw, "We'll be completely exposed. We could go up to 21st Street and take it around, but it's another main street. As many people as are out tonight that isn't good either."

"I don't want to go up 21st." Stephanie looked at Ann.

"I'd say everybody who's out tonight is already on the other side of town. Plus, we can see who's around better from the cemetery."

Eli expressed what they were all feeling, "This way is shorter. We're almost there, and I'm strung so tight right now, I'm about to pop. I'm ready to get safely hidden away."

More to herself than to the others, Stephanie said, "I agree, but the ground is going to be bumpy, and we'll be weaving around the tombstones, so keep control."

"Let's go." Moving with as much haste as he dared, Eli took them into the land above the dead. They were barely beyond the first row of gravestones when yet another man, with evil intentions and out on the streets of Little Rock in the middle of the night, turned onto Barber Street headed towards the cemetery.

Lost in thought, the unknown man told himself, *we can get shovels from the shed and put them back after this is over. Nobody will know who was involved.* Since he was still far up the road, the man didn't notice the people zigzagging between the markers of those reposing in the ground.

They were almost to the shed when Sally saw the man and pointed up the street that ran directly to the cemetery. "Somebody's coming." They charged recklessly over the uneven ground. The carts bounced dangerously at the edge of control until they made it to the door. In case the hinges squeaked and gave them away to the man rapidly approaching, Eli opened the shed door very slowly. They slipped inside. Eli quietly closed the door as two more men came up 21st Street to meet the other nighttime conspirator. "Should we go to the shed and get shovels?" There was only the one door. Searching for a place to hide in the small structure, Eli and the girls scrambled.

"We're late, and we don't even know if we'll find them. We can come back and get shovels if we need to." That comment sealed the decision to go down 21st straight to the meeting on the other side of town.

In the shed, they breathed a sigh of relief. Ann hugged Eli. "Excellent job. You got us here safely!"

"Thank you, Eli." Stephanie kissed his cheek. "And thank you, God!"

They got out their bedrolls. In case somebody did decide to come to the shed for shovels, they lay hidden in the corner far away from the tools behind slat boards used to cover open graves that would soon hold the deceased. Eli remained awake all night and listened for the approach of any would-be-gravediggers who had found Bemis and his family. He prayed that the family would escape and that they would too.

FORTY EIGHT

In the chapel at Roscoe's Trading Post, just as suddenly as he'd felt that he needed to pray, Noah felt that his family was safe. "God, thank You for protecting my family, for letting me know that You're there watching over them, and that You still talk to me."

FORTY NINE

Eli got the girls up with the sun. They immediately rolled up their bedrolls and slipped away down Old Sweet Home Pike towards Pine Bluff.

Noah bundled up to get the eggs. "The strangest thing happened last night." Roscoe wanted to hear. He put on his coat. "I woke up with an overwhelming feeling that I needed to pray for the safety of my family. I felt panic and fear. I prayed and prayed for God to keep them safe. Suddenly, I didn't have that feeling anymore."

"That was strange. Nothing like that has ever happened to me."

"It was just like somebody woke me up and said, 'Pray for your family's safety, right now!' I think God wanted me to pray because they were in danger, and they needed help. I wish I could be with them to protect them."

"I wish I had a family. If I had one, I wouldn't let them go."

All day, Noah struggled with two thoughts. What kind of a husband just walks away from his family because somebody told him to do it? Secondly, how could he take a chance with Ann's safety, let go of control, and turn it over to God? If he could trust God, how would he go about it?

Weary from the short night, from hurrying away as early as they could, and pulling the carts for hours, when the sun reached its zenith, Eli and the girls stopped. Eli moved them far off the road. Even though their loads were getting lighter as they consumed the food, pulling them was taking a toll on all of them, especially Sally.

While they ate, Eli put the lightest things in Sally's cart and the heaviest in his. They wanted to get as far away from Little Rock and detection as they could, therefore, after a short stop for their mid-day meal, they traveled until the sun went down. Exhausted, they wrapped the tarp around the carts and created a small space. They crawled inside, wrapped the blankets around themselves, cuddled together in the middle, and dropped into sleep.

The next day, Eli again led them along the road. Once again, they only stopped briefly to eat and then went as far as they could before they slept for the night. The third day after they'd stolen through Little Rock, the road turned sharply to the east. At the turn, they stood at the top of the bluffs and looked down a steep path. Eli doubted that anybody could walk down the incline. "It's very steep, and we can't see what's under the snow."

Stephanie voiced everybody's perception of the situation, "We're not going to get these carts down there."

Ann saw the same trail the others saw. "I didn't come this far to be stopped now. We can find a place to hide the carts then carefully make our way down."

Choose Your Consequences

Sally knew they weren't going to change Ann's mind. "Let's look for a place to put them." They found a fallen tree way back in the woods that was larger than the carts were high, went back to the trail, retrieved the carts, and hid them behind the tree.

Eli wanted to be the one to take the biggest risk. "Let me go first and find the best way. As I go, you follow."

Stephanie hugged her husband. "Be careful, Eli, don't get hurt." The snow that had fallen the previous week had made the trail into a snowy, slippery path of mud to certain destruction, but that did not stop them. They started down, slid, got their footing again, backtracked to find a better route, made their way further down, and then repeated in various orders until Eli had found a path all the way to the bottom.

FIFTY

Inside the trading post, Noah could not fight anymore. He walked into the chapel and lay prostrate on the floor. "God, I'm turning this over to You. If You don't want me to have them, I trust that You know what You're doing, and that's the best way for it to be. If You choose to bring us back together, I believe that You'll make it happen. I'm going to let You do whatever You're doing." The crushing weight that had beat him down lifted out of his mind.

FIFTY ONE

Ann, Stephanie, Sally, and Eli walked across the canyon to the large building. Eli opened the door for the women. Ann stepped into the room with Stephanie, Sally, and Eli right behind her. Noah felt the cold air rush into the chapel across the floor where he lay then heard the door click shut. The most beautiful sound he had ever heard flowed into his ears when Ann spoke to the man who appeared to be running the trading post, "Hello, sir, we're looking for somebody."

Noah jumped up and hastened to the chapel door. "Ann?"

One of the four people bundled in coats, hats, scarfs, and gloves turned towards him. Noah beheld the beautiful face of his wife. Ann dashed across the room and threw herself into his arms. "Thank God, we found you!"

Noah could hardly believe that Ann was in his embrace. "I thought I was never going to see you again. I love you so much." He waved Stephanie, Sally, and Eli over. Noah had the arms of his whole family around him. Of all the ways he thought things might end up, he had never imagined that God would bring his family to him at Pine Bluff. Gratitude filled his heart and mind. He acknowledged Grace's victory, "God, thank you for giving me my family."

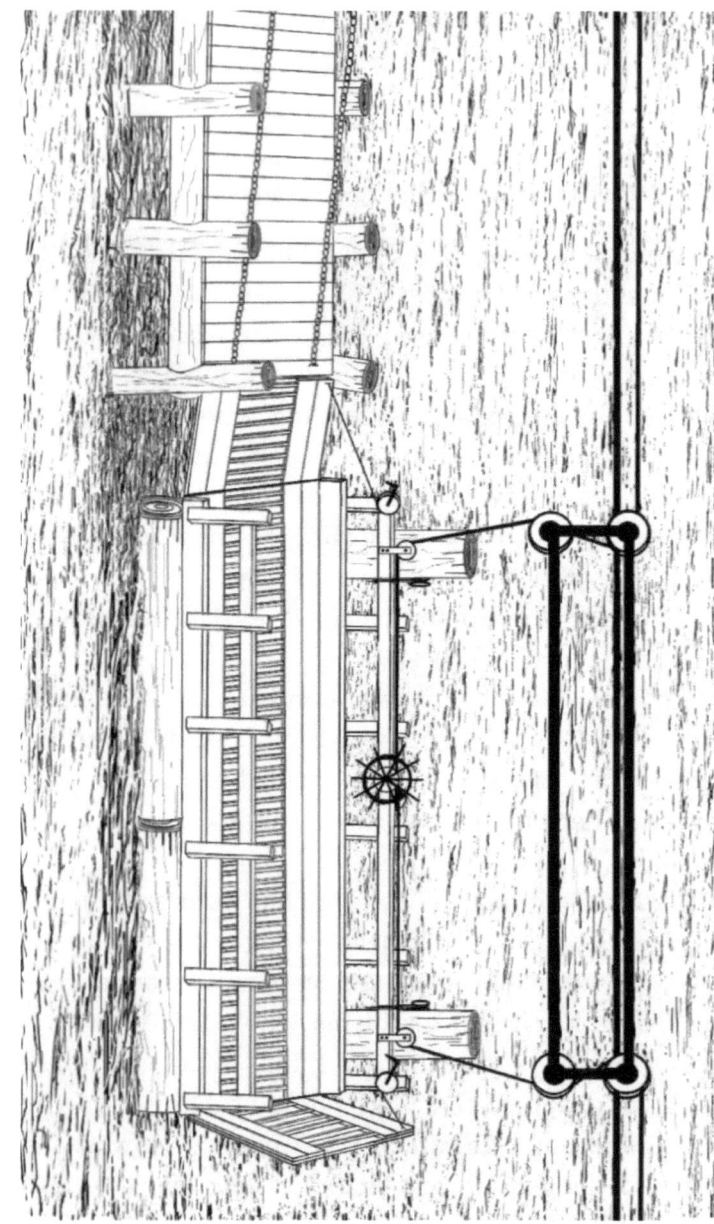

Acknowledgements

Thanks to my husband who has done so much to allow me to have the time to write and to Hristo Argirov Kovatliev for another lovely cover. Chapter heading; *Rusty Old Ball Chain used in 1852 Jail.* Dusty Cline/Shutterstock.com. My most sincere gratitude goes to God who has helped me navigate my own life.

Find Me Online

https://www. ChanceandChoicesAdventures.com

Did you like this story?
Please write a review!

https://www.amazon.com/Choose-your-Consequences-Lisa-Gay/dp/1945858028/

Chance and Choices Adventures
by Lisa Gay

Pray for Justice
Choose Your Consequences
No Remorse
Means of Escape
Torn Hearts
Xida People